ACCLAIM

FOR THE WORKS OF

PEGGY SIMSON CURRY

ON CURRY'S WORK:
Peggy Curry gave voice to the land on which she lived. She gave voice to the people, honestly and without…sentimentality. …Curry's love of landscape was so infectious that even in winter austerity, it revealed its subtle beauty.

CHARLES LEVENDOSKY
CASPER STAR-TRIBUNE

ON NAMING PEGGY CURRY WYOMING'S FIRST POET LAUREATE:
…this renowned author has brought honor to our state being one of only two women in the world to win two Spur awards from Western Writers of America.

THE HONORABLE ED HERSCHLER
GOVERNOR OF WYOMING, 1975-1987

ON *SO FAR FROM SPRING:*
…digs deeply into the raw material of human emotion…One becomes absorbed in these people, so intensely human in their faults and weaknesses, so immensely vital in their passion for life. *NEW YORK TIMES*

Mrs. Curry…packs her novel with vibrant earthiness and psychological tensions that make it a first-rate reading experience. *SATURDAY REVIEW*

LandMarked

Peggy Simson Curry

LandMarked

STORIES OF
PEGGY SIMSON CURRY

COLLECTED & WITH INTRODUCTION BY
MARY ALICE GUNDERSON

HIGH PLAINS PRESS
GLENDO, WYOMING

Copyright © William S. Curry
Introduction Copyright © Mary Alice Gunderson
All Rights Reserved.

Printed in the United States of America.

Cover photograph and artwork by West Magoon.

All of the short stories in this collection are reprinted with permission of
William S. Curry, executor of the estate of Peggy Simson Curry.

The stories were first published in the following publications:
"I Woke Up Last Night," *Gay Love;* © 1944 Columbia Publications, Inc.
"Osage Girl," *Saturday Evening Post;* © 1947 Curtis Publishing Co.
"Night of Champions," *Saturday Evening Post;* © 1950 Curtis Publishing Co.
"The Secret of Bogie Bill," *Saturday Evening Post;* © 1950 Curtis Publishing Co.
"Green Willow Growing," *Collier's;* ©1952.
"The Lady Loved a Jailbird," *Saturday Evening Post;* © 1952 Curtis Publishing Co.
"The Bride Wore Spurs," *American Magazine;* © 1953 Crowell-Collier Publishing.
"A Life Of Our Own," *Collier's;* © 1954.
"Bitter Sunday," *American Magazine;* © 1955 Crowell-Collier Publishing Co.
"The Brushoff," *Saturday Evening Post;* © 1957 Curtis Publishing Co.
"Geranium House," *Frontiers West;* © 1959 Doubleday and Co.
"The Professor is a Beatnik," *Saturday Evening Post;* © 1971 Curtis Publishing Co.
"Gypsy Trainer" *Boys' Life;* © 1974 Boy Scouts of America.
"Heal a Wounded Heart," *Saturday Evening Post;* © 1961 Curtis Publishing Co.
"Bogus Bride," *Saturday Evening Post;* © 1961 Curtis Publishing Co.
"Gooseberry Run," *Boys' Life,* © 1970 Boy Scouts of America.
"Mean Man," *Empire Magazine — Denver Post;* © 1956.
"Invitation To A Wedding," *Good Housekeeping;* © 1963.
"In the Silence," *Boys' Life;* © 1969 Boy Scouts of America.

Library of Congress Cataloging-in-Publication Data

Curry, Peggy Simson.
LandMarked: stories of Peggy Simson Curry /
collected and with introduction by Mary Alice Gunderson.
p.   cm.
ISBN: 0-931271-17-7
1. Western stories. 2. Wyoming — Fiction.
I. Gunderson, Mary Alice. II. Title.
PS3505.U826L36   1992
813'.54 — dc20   91-41306

HIGH PLAINS PRESS
539 CASSA ROAD
GLENDO, WYOMING 82213

"*For myself, the time to start writing is when I know down to my very bones these things: No one who has ever lived can say what I am going to say in the way that I shall say it. It is for this I was born. It is the reason for my living. It is what I am destined to give, freely and gladly, no matter how long it takes or how much work is involved, for the good of my fellow men — to amuse them, intrigue them, enrich their living. I am indeed blessed to be a writer.*"

PEGGY SIMSON CURRY
Creating Fiction From Experience

PEGGY SIMSON CURRY
December 30, 1911—January 20, 1987

Lupine Ridge

Long after we are gone,
Summer will stroke this ridge in blue;
The hawk still fly above the flowers,
Thinking, perhaps, the sky has fallen
And back and forth forever he may trace
His shadow on its azure face.

Long after we are gone,
Evening wind will languish here
Between the lupine and the sage
To die a little death upon the earth,
As though over the sundown prairies fell
A requiem from a bronze-tongued bell.

Long after we are gone,
This ridge will shape the night,
Lifting the wine-streaked west,
Shouldering the stars. And always here
Lovers will walk under the summer skies
Through flowers the color of your eyes.

PEGGY SIMSON CURRY

From *Summer Range*,
used by permission of
Dooryard Press; Story, Wyoming.

For Peg
and for Leah, my mother

ABOUT THE EDITOR

Mary Alice Gunderson is a native Wyomingite who lives in Casper. Since the mid-1970s she has taught writing workshops through the Wyoming Arts Council's Arts-in-Education program. Her articles on a variety of subjects (health and education, Wyoming history, regional personalities, western writers and artists) have appeared in a wide range of commercial and literary publications. Her fiction and poetry have appeared in *Owen Wister Review, Plainswoman, Poet Lore, Voices International;* the anthologies *Poets West: Contemporary Poems from Eleven Western States* and *Point Riders Press Anthology of Great Plains Poetry;* and other publications.

Among her awards are a Wyoming Council for the Humanities writing and research grant, a Literary Fellowship from the Wyoming Council on the Arts, and a residency at the Ucross Foundation.

Her non-fiction book, *Devils Tower: Stories in Stone,* also published by High Plains Press, received commendations from the Wyoming State Historical Society and from the National Federation of Press Women.

She teaches part time at Casper College where she also serves on the Literary Advisory Committee.

EDITOR'S ACKNOWLEDGMENTS

My thanks to Bill and Mike Curry for their encouragement and assistance and for allowing me the privilege of assembling this story collection.

Special appreciation to my good friend Robert Roripaugh, Professor of English at the University of Wyoming, for his fine foreword.

I am indebted, as always, to several librarians for their advice and expertise, among them "Mr. Librarian," Emmet Chisum, Research Historian at the Western History and Research Center, University of Wyoming at Laramie. Also to Casper College Goodstein Foundation Library staff members, particularly the late Nora Van Burgh, Public Service Librarian; Jamie Ring, Head of Special Collections; and Sunny Munns, Cataloging/Reference.

Of particular help were those individuals who granted me interviews or previewed sections of the introduction: Gretchen Wheeler, Theatre and Communications Instructor at Casper College; Casper attorney Hugh M. Duncan; and writer-friends Betty Evenson and Charles Levendosky, currently Wyoming Poet Laureate, as well as editorial and opinion page editor page editor and columnist at the Casper Star-Tribune.

Also thanks to those who assisted in the proofreading process: Patsy Parkin, Edna Langston, and Tracy Eller.

Once again, love and thanks to my husband, Ed, and my son, Jim, and to my editor, Nancy Curtis of High Plains Press.

CONTENTS

FOREWORD

Peggy Simson Curry has long been recognized as one of Wyoming's most accomplished and respected writers. Author of four novels, over two-dozen published short stories, two poetry volumes, many articles, and a textbook on writing fiction, Peggy Curry grew up and lived in this part of the West, absorbing the shapes and shadings of land, the feel of weather and seasons, and the ways of the region's natural and human inhabitants. In her writing, she drew deeply on firsthand experiences with sheep and cattle ranching, putting up hay with horses and machinery, life in the oil fields, teaching at varied levels, observing nature and exploring the outdoors—and used effectively her intimate knowledge of Wyoming and the bordering North Park section of Colorado, where she had been raised by her Scottish-immigrant family on a ranch near Walden.

What Peggy Curry also knew well, about human experience, is evident in her writing's concerns with family life, the difficulties of growth and aging, the ties and strains between generations, the forms and effect of love, and the ways humans are shaped by their pasts and live close to memories, emotions, and experiences that became, for Peggy, the fiction and poetry forming her life's work. "Writing is a way of life," she noted at the beginning of *Creating Fiction From Experience*.

"At best it is a rewarding combination of creative experience and creative expression. One cannot exist without the other. Memorable writing can happen only out of memorable living."

Although Peggy Curry's regional roots and interest are strongly displayed in her work, which she delighted in sharing with people living here, she clearly was writing for readers everywhere. Most of her fiction appeared in national magazines and books published by well-known Eastern firms like Viking Press and McGraw-Hill. Her first novel, *Fire in the Water* (1951), dealt with the lives of herring fishermen in Scotland, her place of birth, and "Osage Girl," the first story she sold to the *Saturday Evening Post* in 1947, was about harness racing in Illinois, where she had lived for a few years. But the three novels to follow—*So Far from Spring* (1956), *The Oil Patch* (1959), and *A Shield of Clover* (1970)—her poetry, and most of her short stories, draw upon Wyoming and the West for background, setting, historical past, characters, attitudes, imagery, and often in the novels and stories, for colorings of plot and theme that are distinctively marked by Peggy Curry's strong sense of place—"her country" both remembered and freshly observed. To be a writer, she commented in *Creating Fiction From Experience*, "is to carry the life force within you, the green-giving water that rises from the heart, that flows freely with its cargo of images, and in the flowing reflects the shapes and shadows of the world around it."

The short stories included in *LandMarked* were published over a span of thirty years, beginning with a romance magazine piece in 1944, "I Woke Up Last Night"—which earned the author her first money from fiction—and ending with a 1974 *Boys' Life* story, "Gypsy Trainer," the last of three harness-racing stories with Illinois settings. Neither is a typical Curry story, but they show the range of her material and readership, as well as the movement in her work from the maturing

professionalism—developed through the "pulp" markets
early in her career—to the sureness of a very experienced
author telling an appealing story for younger readers with
obvious skill and control. In the years between 1944 and 1974
come the other seventeen stories making up this collection,
eight of them published in the *Saturday Evening Post* and
others taken by *Collier's*, *Good Housekeeping*, the *American
Magazine*, and *Boys' Life*. Ten of the nineteen have ranching
backgrounds and characters, and all but seven use Wyoming
or Northern Colorado settings—which contradicts the com-
plaint that national magazines have biases against stories
dealing with life in this region. Other stories in *LandMarked*
use a variety of settings, material, and fictional situations
involving generational conflicts, adjustments to despair and
death, the clash of individualism with academic conformity,
and the difficulties of accepting changes within families. Five
of the stories—"The Brushoff," "The Bride Wore Spurs,"
"Osage Girl," "Geranium House," and "In the Silence"—
have been reprinted in anthologies. Two of these also
received Golden Spur awards from Western Writers of America. Several of the stories in *LandMarked* have been published in foreign countries.

Each reader will have his or her own favorites among
Peggy Curry's stories. Certainly her understanding and emotional commitment to ranch life in Wyoming and North Park,
Colorado—the setting of her fine novel *So Far from Spring*—
mark indelibly six of the pieces in this collection as belonging
among her strongest short fiction: "The Brushoff," "The
Secret of Bogie Bill," "Green Willow Growing," "The Lady
Loved a Jailbird," "Geranium House," and "In the Silence."
Although these are quite differing stories thematically, in all of
them the reader is shown characters in highly individualized
relationship to the land, the ways and hardships of Western

life, and the fashion in which down-to-earth people can make difficult choices which may or may not better their own lives, but offer promise for the younger generation and the West's future. In such stories, a reader can sense the quality that the critic Robert J. Barnes defined in *Twentieth Century Western Writers*: "What is important is that Curry creates memorable reality. Indeed, 'Geranium House' comes near to the work of Willa Cather and Hamlin Garland."

In all the short fiction included in *LandMarked*, there are qualities which add to the pleasure and appreciation readers may receive from Peggy Curry's work. Since she wrote for a wide audience and also held high standards for herself, Peggy's stories had to be honest in her terms and still fit into the requirements for commercial fiction in some of the most competitive markets of the late 1940s to 1970s, such as the *Saturday Evening Post* and *Collier's*. To be successful, she had to develop a high level of professionalism in her writing and a sure knowledge of what made a story publishable in the large-circulation "slick" magazines. Her short fiction presents settings and backgrounds vividly, especially in the Western pieces, but never at the expense of the story being told. The conflict and drama of sharply focused situations are always in the foreground, laid out with immediacy and little wasted writing. Plots unfold almost effortlessly, often with turns and developments which aren't fully expected, but seem, by the ends of the stories, prepared for and right.

The characters in Peggy Curry's stories are ordinary humans with strengths and flaws the reader can relate to, and they are also appealing because of their basic desire, ulti-mately, to bring more good than bad into their lives and those of others around them. In this sense, they fit into a pattern found in much commercial fiction, but also are "Western" in their optimism and hope that through individual effort and growth in understanding, they may work out their problems and make things better. Her people do not give up in despair, though despair is often present, but make changes and compromises without losing their individuality. All this is done with economy, a fine ear for natural dialogue, a controlled yet colorful style of writing, and a commitment to convey to readers the emotional content and human experience, underlying a narrative's creation through the storytelling skill and language she employed. Writing short fiction for magazines like the *Saturday Evening Post* was a demanding art, and Peggy Curry was highly successful at it, while still using the backgrounds, characters, and mixture of real and imaginary experiences that were central to her creativity.

The writing of Peggy Simson Curry—her novels, poetry, and short stories—is of importance to those interested in the literature of Wyoming, that of the West in general, and the accomplishments of women authors from the region. It is quite appropriate that *LandMarked* has been prepared and published in Wyoming shortly after the state's centennial celebration. Readers should be grateful to Mary Alice Gunderson, the editor of *LandMarked* and a writer who knew Peggy Curry well for many years, and to publisher Nancy Curtis, of High Plains Press, for making available this collection of short fiction. The book will provide a much clearer understanding of Peggy's career, an important dimension of her writing skills and concerns, and the relationship between her own work in the short-story form and her teaching of fiction writing in the classroom and through her textbook on *Creating Fiction From Experience*.

Most of all, it is simply good to have these stories brought together for the first time. The publication of *LandMarked* will be welcomed by the many readers who know Peggy Curry's writing and respected her as an author, teacher,

Wyoming's first Poet Laureate, and longstanding supporter of literary arts and writers in the state...and by those who will be reading her work with interest and pleasure in the future.

Robert Roripaugh
University of Wyoming

INTRODUCTION

A MAN SHE HATED TAUGHT her an unforgettable lesson: Jack Patton—commander of the hayfield of her thirteenth summer—thin and sour and bowlegged, climbed down off the hayrake and into her life, repeating, "If you do it, do it right!"

Recalling that long-ago summer sixty years later in an interview, Peggy Simson Curry spoke of a second incident that would also color and redirect her life. "I rode out after supper...at the ranch. Rode out along the edge of the meadow to the head of a place called the Grand Draw, like a canyon. While I was there the whole area illuminated. It was the strangest experience, out of the blue. I thought, *This is part of the creative world.... I love the world of nature.*"

Peg loved the natural colors of Wyoming: fall leaves; the rust and chalk-toned bluffs; the shimmer of a mountain pond with water lilies; purple shadows along an evening road; the pinkish tones of winter willows seen suddenly when crossing a snowy field. To see the Tetons for the first time, she once said, was to be born again.

She spoke often of the animals in her yard at the foot of Casper Mountain—the birds and squirrels and the deer that drifted down to peer in her kitchen windows until someone fed them apples or sunflower seeds.

And she thought of herself as part of it all, as part of the land.

The Colorado ranch country near Walden where she grew up and especially Wyoming, where she lived her adult life, dominate her fiction. But her work spread far beyond state boundaries. Curry's work received widespread recognition and attention from the public, and she became one of Wyoming's best known and most versatile writers.

Curry was the author of four novels (one a Doubleday Book Club selection), a text on creative writing, two books of poetry and numerous articles and short stories. Several stories first presented at the Casper Mountain Lions' Camp for the Visually Handicapped were published in the United States and later in England and Canada. Others were translated for inclusion in Italian, French, African and Scandinavian anthologies. Most were released as recordings for the blind.

Film rights to her first novel, which is set in Scotland — *Fire in the Water* (New York: McGraw Hill, 1951) — were optioned by Marlon Brando, but no film has been produced.

Peg's second novel, *So Far From Spring* (New York: Viking, 1956; London: Muller, 1957) was a turn-of-the-century ranching novel set in Colorado, south of Saratoga, Wyoming. *Kirkus Review* noted that "Mrs. Curry writes with a fine edge for natural beauty and an honest ear" and commented on the novel's "warmth, realness and vigor." The *New York Times Book Review* wrote that "[the book] digs deeply into the raw material of human emotion. One becomes absorbed in these people, so intensely human in their faults and weaknesses, so immensely vital in their passion for life."

In 1983, Pruett Publishing of Boulder, Colorado, reissued the novel. Following an autograph party in Walden that spring, citizens declared April 13 "Peggy Simson Curry Day."

Two of Curry's western short stories also received

national awards. For "doing it right" her peers in Western Writers of America twice presented her Golden Spur awards for most distinguished western short story of the year: in 1957 for "The Brushoff" (set near Laramie, Wyoming) and in 1970 for "In the Silence" (set in the Big Horn Mountains).

Other honors and achievements included: in 1964, Kappa Kappa Gamma National Distinguished Achievement Award; 1968, University of Wyoming Distinguished Alumni Award; in 1975 and again in 1980, Emmy Mygatt awards from Wyoming Writers, Incorporated; 1976, Wyoming Bicentennial Commission Chair. In 1981, Peggy Simson Curry became the first Poet Laureate of the State of Wyoming.

Believing she had been summoned to Cheyenne to receive an award for participation in the Wyoming Arts Council's Poetry-in-the-Schools program, she was surprised when then-Governor Ed Herschler (widely known throughout the state as "Gov. Ed") rose before the assembled Forty-sixth Legislature to read the Executive Order naming her the state's first Poet Laureate. "Oh, thanks, Ed," Peg said as she stood and turned toward the popular governor. "I mean thank you, Governor Herschler."

She, too, was known by her first name to people all around the state. In the 1950s, her first college writing class met on the top floor of Natrona County High School. Her Tuesday afternoon and evening classes, later held on the expanding Casper College campus, became a thirty-year institution, with many writers returning year after year.

In the mid-1960s, Peg toured with the Mobile Arts Symposium. This group of Wyoming writers and painters presented workshops to people in smaller communities in the state such as Kaycee, Tensleep and other towns, in a circuit rider approach. The workshops were funded by National Arts and Humanities monies.

In 1971, Peg and the late Frances Forrister, then Chairman of the Wyoming Council on the Arts, visited virtually every school in the state, laying the groundwork for Poetry-in-the-Schools. Wyoming, Alaska, and Minnesota were the three states selected to introduce the concept of contemporary writers teaching their craft in public schools, in primary through junior college-level classes. The program drew national recognition to Wyoming and continues today across the state. In 1972, poet Charles Levendosky came to the state and, in 1973, assumed the position of Head of Poetry Programs of Wyoming. For a number of years Peg and Charles team-taught poetry sessions. Wyoming-based writers and writers from other states also participated in readings and residencies.

Getting the kids "turned on to writing" was a special thrill for Curry. She entered their classes, printing her name— "PEG"—very large on the chalkboard. Sometimes she included her address so children could mail their poems and stories to her. Although she taught writing from kindergarten through college levels, Peg especially enjoyed small rural schools such as Red Creek and Willow Creek, near Casper.

In addition to her own writing, the statewide traveling, and teaching two sections of college writing classes, Peg managed to participate as panelist or presenter at writing conferences in Missouri, Washington state, Oregon, Kentucky, Montana, the Dakotas, Oklahoma, Nebraska, Nevada, Arizona and other states. She turned to the juvenile writing field, publishing *Shield of Clover* (New York: McKay, 1970), many stories in *Boys' Life*, articles commissioned by *The Writer* and increasing numbers of her own poems.

ೱ ೱ ೱ

But what was she like, Wyoming's first Poet Laureate?

Christened Margaret, for her mother Margaret Munro Anderson Simson, she was born in Dunure, Ayeshire, Scotland to Margaret and William Andrew Simson on December 30, 1911. As a small child she came to Colorado with her parents. Her father—called "Blunt" because he spoke that way—called her "Sister" and sometimes "Betty." When she was seven years old, her brother, William, Jr., was born.

Independence came early to the children on the isolated ranch "Blunt" managed, twenty-six miles from Walden. To attend first grade, Peg boarded with a family of gold miners in Pearl, Colorado, when she was five years old. At home, doted on by the hired men and spoiled by her father, she must have lived a Shirley Temple kind of existence. Her father taught her to play poker and to fly fish. She became expert at both.

When Peg was in her late teens, her grandmother sent passage for her to visit Scotland. There Peg convinced her uncle, a fisherman, to allow her to go sea with him. Though sailing with a woman on board defied tradition and was considered unlucky, that night the crew took a heavy catch of herring. Soon she received invitations to go out on any boat she wanted. Years later, the diary she kept of her thirty nights at sea with the herring fleet provided the background for her novel *Fire in the Water*.

Although her father encouraged and approved of her writing, she was never certain that it pleased her mother.

Peg's mother, Margaret, was known as a "difficult" woman. She came from a well-to-do Scottish family, from a three-story home with servants to an isolated ranch house in Colorado where she often cooked for twenty men on a wood-burning stove. Sometimes she didn't talk with another woman for six months. Margaret had a special love of flowers and in spring and summer cultivated flower beds around the house. Peg always described her mother as "terrific and courageous" and noted "things were done as she wanted them."

In the Simson household, there were only three books:

the Bible, the poetry of Robert Burns—which her father particularly loved— and *Diseases of Cattle*. Reading that one day, young Peg came upon the phrase "Hemorrhagic Septicemia," and, while she probably didn't understand its meaning, the sound and flow of the language intrigued her. Years later she wrote of this in a poem entitled "When Words First Spoke to Me."

Her first poem, written in fourth or fifth grade, when she entered a new school in town, was an "I hate school" poem, and she hoped to be expelled. She wrote of wanting to return to "the ranch, her horse and the red fox in the meadow." The teacher instead had it published in the town newspaper. From rural Jackson County, Colorado, schools, Peg entered East High School in Denver where she continued writing, winning a prize for a short story one year. She then enrolled at the University of Wyoming in Laramie where she graduated in 1936 with a BA in English and Journalism. For several years before graduation she wrote occasionally for the *Laramie Boomerang*.

At college she met the man she would marry, William S. "Bill" Curry, also an English major. Poetry may have brought them together.

As Bill told it in a February 1991 interview, he was dating another girl when he met Peg and soon realized Peg was the one he wanted to marry. The "other girl" was typing Bill's paper on the poet Vachel Lindsey, from his handwritten notes. Learning he and Peg were going out, she came to the boys' dorm, met him on the steps and tore the typed paper into strips. The Laramie wind blew it into the trees. A sympathetic English professor who knew both Peg and Bill gave him credit for the paper based on his rough draft.

For several years after their marriage in 1937, the Currys lived in Illinois, where Bill taught high school and coached baseball and basketball. In 1939, they returned to Wyoming. That same year their only son, Michael Munro Curry, was born. Bill taught at Natrona County High School in Casper five years, and in 1943, the family moved to Midwest, where Bill was both Assistant Superintendent and high school principal. There Peg concentrated on her professional career, writing and selling first to confession and romance magazines and then advancing into the "slick" markets, named for the slick paper used in more expensive magazines. Written some years later, Peg's third novel, *The Oil Patch* (New York: McGraw Hill, 1959) was set in a small oil town similar to Midwest.

In 1946, the Currys returned to Casper, where Bill began a long career as English teacher and, later, Chairman of the English Department at Casper College. He served for a number of years in the Wyoming State Legislature.

Mike followed somewhat in his parents' footsteps, having been a high school teacher, a newspaper reporter, and more recently, Public Relations Director for a large bus transit system in California. Interviewed while visiting at his father's home on Casper Mountain, in February 1991, he spoke candidly and with affection for his mother.

He said she was a concerned parent, but one who also allowed him at the age of fifteen to play trumpet in a local after-hours night spot, the Cozy Club, because he wanted to. "She always did what she wanted," he added.

She never bought anything on credit, but was not stingy. Finding the "different" in the ordinary pleased her, and the particularly unusual she found striking. She had a sense of her own decorum, a standard she applied to herself while accepting other people's widely divergent, terribly unconventional behavior.

Her best friend, Casper writer Betty Evenson, said it this way: "Peg was a disciplined, responsible person...genuine.

Staunch. You knew where she stood. She was real creative, real liberal, without being 'arty.'"

Mike called his mother a gambler. "Everything she did was a gamble. She loved beating the odds, taking a chance, catching a big fish where nobody ever caught one."

As adventurous as she was about traveling and seeking new experiences, Bill and Mike both noted that Peg lived for "about fifteen or twenty" years mostly on hamburgers — because she liked them. She consciously avoided the mundane, disliked housework and grocery shopping.

Raised in the Presbyterian church, Peg was receptive to all religions. Among her missing pieces of writing is a long dramatic reading about the mother of Judas, which she presented at the church one Easter. She had a mystical side and was not closed to the supernatural. Several of her fictional characters studied palmistry, read Tarot cards or gazed into crystal balls. When a great-grandson, Ryan Michael, was born on her birthday, she didn't consider it coincidental. She usually avoided doctors, preferring to try to meditate illness away.

An avid reader of history of the American West, she felt a kinship with earlier people who were here — Indian people, trappers, early settlers. She saw herself as part of a continuum of other lives.

The mystic in her met the gambler to produce a long poem Peg considered one of her most important works. "Red Wind of Wyoming," based on Wyoming's Johnson County War between homesteaders and ranchers, was written in ten days and presented at the Casper Fine Arts Club after she agreed to fill in with an original program for a speaker who canceled. Peg was actually between projects and had been re-reading historical works on the cattle war.

At lunch with a friend several days after accepting the speaking engagement, Peg was suddenly aware of the fall wind roaring, singing a dirge. In an experience she would later describe as "outside of space and time," scenes appeared to her, one after the other, there in the Elbow Room of the old Henning Hotel. She thought she "saw" Nate Champion, the homesteader who was killed in the conflict. ("Peg! That's the bartender!" her surprised friend said.) Later, at the typewriter, Peg wrote the scenes out, adding fictional characters to link past events with the present.

First published by Alan Swallow at Sage Books in 1955, the long dramatic poem went through five hardback editions and one paperback edition and was adapted as a radio play. Some twenty years after it was written, it was reissued: *Red Wind of Wyoming and Other Poems* (Vermillion, South Dakota: Spirit Mound Press, 1977).

Poetry occupied much of Peg's later writing life, and the genre made different demands from fiction. Each of her novels took several years of steady, unrelenting work, and while it was her habit quite often to complete a nearly polished short story draft in a matter of hours, she had likely planned it for six months or more, prior to writing a word. At times, Peg's poetry notebook bulged with forty or fifty poems in various stages of completion, as she waited for months — even several years — to turn a line, to choose the exact tone and texture of a word. Her second poetry collection, *Summer Range* (Story, Wyoming: Dooryard Press, 1981) contained more than forty poems, some new and some published first in literary publications such as the *South Dakota Review,* the *Chicago Tribune, Paintbrush* and numerous anthologies.

She enjoyed giving poetry readings — presenting new poems to an audience, discovering new aspects of an older work. I recall clearly her intense, husky voice as she read in a hushed room.

ᴠ ᴠ ᴠ

It was my privilege to know Peg for more than twenty years, as a co-worker in the Poetry-in-the-Schools program and, also, as my Tuesday night Creative Writing teacher.

"Sharing is what writing is all about," she told her adult students. During class she shared freely of her life and experiences: odd dreams; impulses; interesting people she interviewed such as Olaus Murie, the naturalist; the feeling of driving through the sky, over cloud reflections on a rainy highway; an idea, perhaps someday to be a story, of two lonely teen-aged girls who wore each other's coats; the behavior of the bird who came uncertainly to the feeder in her yard, the bird she believed to be blind.

"Keep notebooks," she said to us. "Relate your inner world to the outer world. Be open to everything that happens."

"Is anybody perishing to read?" she asked us each Tuesday evening, eyes twinkling. Many hands waved in the air. She listened intently, regardless of the writer's level of experience, perched on the edge of the table, wearing slacks, a colorful blouse, perhaps a knit vest. Often a brightly beaded Indian medallion hung around her neck. Peg smoked as if a breeze were blowing, fingers curled around the cigarette she pinched with thumb and forefinger. "Comment?" she always asked, and we discussed the writing.

We learned to give and take criticism knowing none of it would be as damning as that quick, editorial bounce of a manuscript into the "out" pile. Nearly every semester, her students had work accepted for publication. She felt that the prestige of the magazine or the amount of money paid for a piece didn't really matter; what was important was that one had reached the readers.

"Peg could be tough on the ones she thought could write," said Betty Evenson, holder of the longest class attendance record, eighteen years.

There were nights when the ghost of Old Jack Patton must have hovered near the chalkboard muttering, "...do it right!"

Following a frank critique, Peg usually said, "Do as you please, of course, dear. It's your work." She called us by our first names, and often added "honey" or "dear." Occasionally a student withdrew. Others shed private tears, rolled another piece of paper into the typewriter and returned to class with a rewrite. Peg knew the markets well and taught us to stay informed because the path to publication was, she said, a long and lonely road. For those brave enough to submit to local, regional or national markets, Peg sometimes put in a good word with an editor she knew.

Through her classes passed a variety of people, as Casper's economy boomed and busted: young mothers, empty-nest housewives, medical doctors, ranchers, librarians, janitors, lawyers, oil field roughnecks, a minister, retired military personnel, a Catholic nun, teenagers, school teachers, a recovering alcoholic, an airline stewardess, wives of oil company executives, Viet Nam veterans, a dog trainer—those merely curious and with time to fill, and those who had burned, secretly, to write for years. Age barriers melted, and many solid friendships were forged among us.

Perhaps the secret of her success as a teacher was an ability to make each person feel especially valued; she enhanced— and appreciated—the uniqueness of every individual. While many creative writing teachers can write well themselves, not all of them can examine both genesis and technical execution of a particular work. Her popular text—*Creating Fiction From Experience* (Boston: The Writer, 1964, 1967), commissioned by *The Writer* magazine—gave her wide national recognition as an exceptional teacher.

One night in class someone asked, "...but Peg, I want to know why *you* write," and she answered without hesitation.

"I write to find out just who the hell I am."

When a class member placed a poem or article, Peg was as happy as if she, herself, had sold one. I remember that we once closed the classroom door and sipped paper cups of champagne brought by a classmate who had made a first sale.

We laughed with Betty Evenson, a successful author of confession stories and a memoir, *Thirty Years at the Bright Spot*, as she told of papering the interior of the outhouse on her Hiland property with rejection slips.

I remember so much more: that Peg loved anecdotes, those small stories we live and relate daily to each other. For a while during the early 1960s, she jokingly referred to the family Cadillac as "Camelot." She was good company, and, maybe next to writing, she loved to talk. Peg loved theater, performing arts and music—Debussy, especially—and won several prizes for her watercolor painting.

And I won't forget that she stopped her work that day and came to sit with me when my brother was killed. I remember her special story: how circumstance and family objections had put off her young parents' marriage and how her father crossed the ocean alone to work for his cousins in Colorado. How she was born before her parents' marriage and could remember standing there beside them in the town hall in Scotland—three years old—before the whole jubilant town, on her parents' wedding day.

Writing is love: I remember that she told us that.

❦ ❦ ❦

Following the public ceremony to announce her appointment as Poet Laureate, there was a private reception at the Governor's Mansion for legislators and their spouses and special friends of Peggy's. She was to give a reading that night, also. She had planned to read some of her favorite landscape and nature poems, but overcome with the emotion of the day and the honor she had received, she lost her voice. She unexpectedly nudged her friend Charles Levendosky and whispered to him to read, among others, the poem "Jack Patton."

"I had to do it," she said later in an interview with Collections Librarian Jamie Ring at Casper College. It was late, the end of a long day. Levendosky read the final stanzas: "[I] wished him all manner of evil:/ Lord, give him loose bowels squatting in the ditch/ before the President of the United States/ Lord, make him have pimples on his face the size of horse turds/ Lord, let his penis fall off, be eaten by a million flies/ All my life remembering, " 'If you do it, do it right.' "

"All the legislators came alive and clapped their hands and guess what poem they wanted copies of?" Peg said. "Gov. Ed laughed about it."

Three years after her designation as Poet Laureate, in 1984, Peg received the Mountain Plains Library Association Literary Contribution Award for published work which successfully furthers an understanding and appreciation of the Mountain Plains region.

Addressing the graduating class at Casper College in May of that same year, Peg told what Jack Patton had contributed to her life. While she had disliked, even hated him, she came to respect him—his painstaking devotion to his work: hard labor done with pride. Patton appears in her most requested poem, as a character in her juvenile novel, *Shield of Clover*, in stories which appeared in the *Saturday Evening Post* and *Boys' Life,* as well as in four additional school anthologies and a story collection published in London for European distribution.

"I still try to live by the lesson he taught me," she told the audience. " 'If you do it, do it right.' " She was 74 years old.

Peg continued teaching writing in public schools around the state for several years, but limited her working days. Her health had begun to fail. In February 1985, she was honored by the staff at the Goodstein Library at Casper College during Women's History Week where she presented an afternoon reading.

She was still keeping journals and poetry notebooks and had begun to think through an approach to an autobiography—to be called *A Way To Begin*—but she had not yet begun writing it.

In declining health, Peg fell at home, breaking her hip. Following surgery she was confined to a wheelchair and lived for some months at Poplar Living Center, though she remained active, often visiting with other patients in their rooms. Her poetry notebooks went with her, and one of her last poems was written in honor of the hundredth birthday of another resident, Elna Norgard.

She died on January 20, 1987, at age 76, survived by her husband and son, two grandchildren and two great-grandchildren. Following memorial services in Casper, Peg was buried in the family plot at the Walden cemetery.

❧ ❧ ❧

Some four years later, in 1991, I visited Bill Curry in the kitchen of his log home on Casper Mountain on a bright day Peg would have loved. The sun was high and the sky a polished blue. Wind shook the leaves of the gold-tipped cottonwood and aspen trees. It was the first day of autumn. Two deer, a buck and a doe, came warily into the up-sloping yard to nibble grass. I fed them sunflower seeds from their special pan. When I tried to tell Bill how much Peg had meant to me, he nodded. "She meant a great deal to a great many people," he said.

Later that evening I read again a letter I had received from the Currys' son, Mike, which contained these words: "...when I think of my mother, I think of the land. The Place.

Her sense of it and her being a part *in* it were inextricable from the land itself...as I was coming into Casper from the Medicine Bow Cutoff, the shadows, the hues and feelings along the road—especially where the mountain runs down to the Platte—were resonances of her. And she thought of herself as part of the land. Part of the on-going life force. Part of the mystery and reality."

Her spirit has enriched this land of ours, and we are proud to present her stories.

MARY ALICE GUNDERSON

"THE BRUSHOFF" WAS FIRST published in the *Saturday Evening Post* in October 1957 and received a Golden Spur Award from Western Writers of America for most distinguished western story of the year. The story was also included in two Spur Award collections: *14 Spurs*; editor, Will Henry (New York: Bantam, 1968) and *WWA Spurs: The Best of the West;* editor, S. Omar Barker (New York: Bantam, 1977).

About two "tough and tender" characters, it pits an old man, Jack Patton, against The Kid, a boy who had spent time in reform school and carries a chip on his shoulder toward the world.

Not long after publication of "The Brushoff," Peg received an invitation from the director to read a story to residents of the Casper Mountain Camp for the Visually Handicapped. She took her carbon copy of the story from her files and drove up the mountain road.

Peg wrote movingly of the incident in her writing text, *Creating Fiction From Experience:*

"In the bare-floored, drafty, recreation cabin with its dusty smell, I stood before the blind people. My heart went out to them, for I wanted desperately to let them know I cared about them, wanted them to accept me and what I had to say. I trembled, feeling inadequate to the situation, and I began to read about my old man and the tough kid and the haying fields in the summer sun. And as I read, the faces lifted toward me, and the unseeing eyes seemed to search beyond the wall of darkness....

"When I had finished reading, an old man got up and came to stand beside me. He was very brown-skinned and handsome, and I had been told he was eighty years of age. He began to talk of the haying fields he had known, of the men with whom he had shared bunkhouses and haylofts, and of horses he had driven.

"'Your story brought it all back,' he said. 'I knew fellows like the ones in your story. They were just that way. All you say is so true.' And then he spoke with love the names of his horses. The light lay on his face and his face was beautiful with mixed emotions of a lifetime. It seemed all the warmth of the room centered on him, for the others turned toward him and leaned forward as though they rested and were comforted in the shade of his experience.

"I was moved to tears. I could only stand, speechless, and cling to the strong, old hand that touched mine. This is the thing I shall remember long after the money for the story is spent. This was the ultimate reward my tough and tender people brought me."

THE BRUSHOFF

I T WAS A SUMMER when ranchers in the valley wrote to relatives they didn't give a darn about and asked them to
come for a visit. The ranchers mentioned how good fishing was and how many young sage chickens had hatched out
and would be of eating size by haying season. The idea was
that some of these shirttail relations might be persuaded to
hook up a team and help put up hay, for hired men were hard
to find.

The boss didn't write any letters. He said all his relatives
were women and scared of horses. Instead, we went to Denver when we got ready to put up the hay. We had some men at
the ranch, but not enough. We had the old steadies — the
Madson brothers from Steamboat Springs, Slim the stacker,
the Swede sickle grinder, and old Jack Patton, who drove a
lead rake. And we had our share of drifters who'd happened
along at the right time.

The boss and I went down on the street in Denver where
the newspaper had said men would be waiting for hire, and
there they were, standing around in the sun. It was a seedy-
looking outfit, I can tell you—some sobering up from the night
before, some too old and frail for any kind of work, and some
who looked as if they'd walked out of the hoboes' jungle.

The boss gave them the eye and was about to go on past

when this kid came walking up the street and stood off by himself near the other men. He was a big, mean-looking kid with thick blond hair that was greased flat to his head and eyes that were as clear and cold as our mountain lakes. He took out the makings and built himself a cigarette and let it hang in the corner of his mouth while he sized us up. His overalls were clean and faded, and I judged him to be around seventeen. He didn't have any fuzz on his cheeks yet.

"Well," the boss said in a low tone, "it's husky and alive. Wadda you think, Jeff?"

"Y'know that wild steer that was always bustin' outta the pasture? That's what it is, only two legged. You finally had to butcher that steer, boss."

"Yeah," the boss muttered, "and even the meat was tough." He gave a tired sigh and started to move away.

Just then a little girl came running up the street, with her mother yelling behind her. The little girl was carrying a small doll, and when she got in front of the kid she dropped it. The doll broke and the little girl began to cry. The kid got down on his knees and tried to put the doll's head together, but it kept falling apart. The little girl kept watching him and whimpering, and the little girl's mother said, "Oh, shut up, Lindy! I'll buy you another doll."

The kid got up and looked at the broken pieces on the sidewalk. "It don't stay together no more," he said. Then he reached in his pocket and brought out a tiny figure of an Indian doll. It looked old and dirty and he handed it to the little girl and said, "Here, you keep this."

The little girl smiled, and her mother yelled, "Put that filthy rag down!" But the little girl went skipping on up the street with the Indian doll in her hands, and the mother ran after her.

The kid looked at us and his lips drew tight and thin. "It

didn't cost me nothin'," he said coldly. "I swiped it at a carnival."

The boss walked over to him and said casually, "Ever make any hay, stranger?"

"Yep." The tight lips barely moved.

"You know how to handle horses?"

"Yep."

"You want a job working in the hayfield up at my ranch?" the boss asked.

The kid shrugged. "Why not? I got nowhere else to go."

"Well," the boss said, "we'll pick up your stuff then."

"You're lookin' at it," the kid said, and something glared at us from the green eyes, a light that dared us to ask if he didn't have a coat or a jacket or a suitcase or something.

"Let's get moving," the boss said, and the three of us walked up the hot, bright street where we'd parked our car. The kid got in and he never said a word all the way to Laramie, Wyoming. We picked up three men in Laramie; they were talkative, smelled like whiskey and had battered suitcases. They spoke to the kid, but he just gave them a nod and acted as if they weren't around.

We went to a café to eat, and the boss said the meal was on him. The kid looked at the menu a long time, and finally the boss said, "Order anything you want, boy."

The kid finally said to the waitress, "Just a hamburger. I don't care how it's cooked."

He tried to eat it without hurrying and his face got red. He didn't order any pie, and when the pie was in front of the other men, the kid got up and walked out to the car.

"He's been in reform school," one of the new men said. "I can spot 'em a mile off."

"That so?" the boss asked politely.

"Why sure. And if you don't mind, mister, I ain't bunking in the same place with that kid."

It turned out that nobody had to sleep near the kid. When we got to the ranch, he took a shine to the old sheep wagon the boss had parked by the river. "Anybody livin' in that wagon?" the kid asked.

"No, it's not much of a wagon anymore," the boss replied.

"I'd like to be by myself," the kid said.

"Help yourself," the boss answered. "I'll rustle you up some bedding."

The next morning at the corral, the boss said to the kid, "You know how to harness a team, boy?"

The kid nodded, but when he got in the barn he put the first collar on upside down, and the men began to snicker and make talk. Old Jack Patton straightened the kid out. He came walking through the barn, thin and sour and bowlegged. A scowl settled over his lined face, and his gray hair stuck out in uncombed tufts above his ears.

"Well," he said dryly, "at least you got it on the right end of the horse, and that's more than some dumb city kids know." Old Jack Patton set the collar right and said, "You and me are going to be lead rakin' in the hayfield. I give the orders. You take 'em, see?"

Nobody in a hay crew ever got along with Old Jack Patton, but he was the best hayraker in the country. When a man worked with him Old Jack set the pace; if he drove slowly, he wanted the man following him to go at the same pace; if he speeded up, he expected the man with him to speed up. Old Jack Patton said when it was time to start and when to quit.

That first day the kid raked he was as mad as a hornet when we stopped for the noon meal that was always sent out hot in the lunch wagon. "What's goin' on around here?" the kid said angrily. "Everybody else gets to quit and gets their teams unhooked and we make two or three more passes at that grass."

"Old Jack Patton believes in outworkin' the rest of the crew," I said. "He wants to keep a lot of hay raked up so the stackers can be busy."

"Bossy old devil," the kid muttered.

We didn't see Old Jack Patton come up beside us until he spoke.

"Listen, you city punk," he said harshly to the kid, "if you don't like the way I do it, you can quit—see? I don't need you. I don't need anybody. I can handle any job and handle it myself—see? Don't get the idea I want you around."

"And I don't want to be around you," the kid shouted back at him.

Old Jack Patton's strange yellow eyes glinted. "Good! Suits me. Run and cry to the boss, then. You tough reform school kids gotta cry about the world."

The kid stiffened and his fists came up. His face was mean and ugly. "You call me that again and I'll beat your head in!"

Old Jack Patton spat at the kid's feet. Then he turned with slow deliberation and sauntered toward the lunch wagon.

The kid stood clenching and unclenching his fists."I could break that old man in two," he said.

"Wouldn't change him none," I said. "He'd be the same in two pieces or one."

That night the kid was late for supper. As usual, Old Jack Patton made a couple of rounds with his rake after the other men had unhooked their teams and started for the house. When the kid came into the cookshack, the crew began to ride him about playing nursemaid to Old Jack Patton. Lola, the peroxide-blond cook, said, "You guys shut up. Lay off." And she let her big blue eyes get soft as she looked at the kid.

Everybody knew what was happening; wasn't that she felt sorry for the kid or anything like that. She just had him marked for a sucker, and Lola always had suckers in every hay crew. I figured since the kid was so tough and had been in reform school, he wouldn't fall for the line. But he looked up at her as if she might be some kind of angel.

Old Jack Patton leaned close to me and muttered, "Reform school didn't teach him nothing. He's so soft inside it's pitiful."

It seemed to me that, after that, Old Jack Patton set out to make life hell for the kid. He worked the tail off him and bawled him out in front of the men. The kid didn't say a word, but his eyes got hotter and brighter, and sometimes the look in them scared me. Every night at the supper table Lola gave the kid the soft soap plus an extra-big piece of pie. And the first chance he had to go to town, he spent all his wages buying her candy and perfume and a red silk handkerchief.

"I'm gonna ask her to go to the haymaker's ball next week," he told me one night when I stopped by the sheep wagon. He was sprawled out on the bunk. In the light from the kerosene lamp, he didn't look mean and hard. He only looked young and lonely.

"Look, kid," I said, "there's some women do a man good because they want good to come to a man. And there's other women who don't care a hang for anything but the money that's spent on 'em."

"Lola's not what you think," he said in a low tone. "She's had a hard time, like me. And nobody understands her, just like nobody understands how I am inside. She stands for something; she's not fulla lies, like most people. She stands for being good to me."

"I guess if a man's thirsty enough he'll drink poison and think it's good," I muttered. I sat quiet and still and heard the river murmuring by, and the river said that some people were born to trouble and had it always because they never got things straightened out. I looked at the kid again and I knew he was thinking of Lola and how, to him, her greedy eyes looked kind. I said, "Ain't you got no folks, kid?"

He made a choked-off sound, and for a while there was silence. Then he said, keeping his voice low and steady, "If I still got 'em, I wouldn't know where they are. Both of 'em run off with other people. That's when I got drunk, and I don't mind tellin' you I broke in a liquor store to find the whiskey. After I had enough of it, I stole all the cash I could find. That's why I got sent to reform school." Again he was quiet. Then he said in a small tone, "Yeah, and when Christmas come, neither one of 'em even sent me a card. Every other kid there — no matter what bad thing he had done — got something from someone who remembered him, a card or a present or something." He began to laugh. "I made myself a card, but it didn't fool nobody."

Old Jack Patton stuck his head in the doorway then and said in his usual hard tone, "You didn't bathe the horses' shoulders. You drive a team with me and you take some care of your horses or I'm askin' the boss to tie a can on you."

I heard Old Jack Patton's footsteps echo away. The kid said, "I hate the old buzzard! If he wasn't so sure he could make me quit, I'd have gone long ago."

"Better men than you have quit because of him," I said. "But I want to tell you something, kid. Old Jack's not hard inside. He's only lean and tough and honest. He wants to make a man out of you."

"Yeah?" The kid laughed. "Don't give me that stuff. He's like all the rest of 'em around here. I smell reform school and no matter what I do, it won't make any difference. But I can be as mean as he can." The kid rolled off the bunk. "I'll see to those horses, but I swear there ain't a mark on their shoulders. They don't need their shoulders bathed any more than I do."

The next week was the haymaker's ball in town, and the kid asked a couple days in advance to borrow my car. "Lola said she'd go with me," he said, "and I'll be real careful with your car."

We were standing by the barn, and the evening light was creeping in over the meadows. "Sure," I said, "sure, kid." He walked away toward the sheep wagon, and Old Jack Patton came out of the barn and stood beside me.

"I wonder where he'll get a suit," Old Jack Patton said. "He can't take her in them thin overalls he's been washing out at night and putting on half wet in the mornin'."

"I've got no suit," I said.

The next night I stopped by the sheep wagon, and the kid was whistling and polishing his old work shoes. "I'm gonna clean your car early in the mornin' so it'll look nice," he said.

"That's good," I said.

"Hey, kid!" It was Old Jack Patton calling from the outside.

"Yeah? What do you want?"

"Just wanted to be sure you're here." And Old Jack tossed a big box into the sheep wagon. I heard him walking away.

"What's that?" the kid asked suspiciously.

"You can look," I said.

It was what I had figured. It was a fancy suit and it was the right size. The kid kept turning it over and over and staring at it. Finally he said, "Where'd he get it, anyhow?"

"I figure he had the boss's wife buy it for him in town," I said. "Lord, kid, Old Jack Patton hasn't put a suit on in forty or fifty years."

The kid's head went down and he said in a low voice, "I guess he wanted me to look right, didn't he?"

"I guess he did."

"A fella's father wouldn't do more," the kid said wonderingly.

The next morning at the corral the kid tried to thank Old Jack Patton, and Old Jack glared at him and said, "It's mothy. Only time I ever wore it was to a funeral. It's ready to fall apart. I'd given it to the trash barrel before now if I'd thought about it." And he turned and led his team from the corral, shouting back at the kid, "Get the lead out! We got hay to rake."

When we came in from work that night, all the younger men started cleaning up for the haymaker's ball. They shaved and scrubbed themselves in the creek and took their good pants or suits out of their suitcases. Slim, the pusher driver, was the handsomest man in the outfit, and that night he spent a lot of time sizing himself up in the mirror. "A big night comin'," he said. "I'm takin' cooky."

"You mean our cooky?" I asked.

"Only one around here, ain't she?" Slim asked innocently.

"Don't, Slim. Don't take her."

His mouth came open and he stared at me. "Why? You got a shine for her, Jeff?"

"She promised the kid," I said.

"Y' mean the reform bird? I'm not steppin' aside for that stuff."

"I'm asking you to, Slim."

Slim put down the comb. "You want me to tell you something, Jeff? You're a softhearted old fool. You been kiddin' yourself all along, telling yourself he isn't so bad. Well, you're wrong. That kind don't change."

"Who don't change?" The words came cold and hard from the doorway of the bunkhouse, and there stood the kid in his fine suit and his hair all slicked down and his eyes ablaze like July lightning.

Slim told him and told him hard and fast. The kid went after Slim then. We got them separated, but not before the kid's eye was black and his lip cut, spattering blood onto the white shirt that had come with the suit. The kid started for the cookhouse, and I ran after him, shouting, "Wait a minute, kid!" He went up the steps in two long strides and me right after him.

Lola was frying the supper potatoes. She turned and looked at us, and the kid blurted out, "You're goin' with me to the dance. You promised!"

Lola yawned and stretched and she looked like a sleek, happy cat. "That was a while ago, honey," she said. "I got a right to change my mind."

The kid turned and walked out. He went to the sheep wagon and he didn't come in for supper. I told Lola off in words a gentleman don't use on a lady, but as the boss sometimes says, "A man can't spit enough to water dry ground."

I waited around the bunkhouse that night until they'd all gone, and in the quiet there was only the smell of hair tonic and shoe polish and whiskey. I waited until Lola had gone with Slim, and the darkness lay deep on the meadows that smelled of the cut hay. Then I walked down by the river to the sheep wagon. There wasn't any light, but I knew he was there. I said, "Kid?" There was no answer, and I stepped inside and sat in the dark and I could hear him breathing there on the bunk.

After a while I said, "You may not think it, but you're better off. You're a lot better off she turned you down. She never was anything but a—"

"Shut up!" It was a snarl of sound. "I get it, see? I get the picture like I got it before. Nobody tells the truth; nobody stands for what they pretend to stand for. Nobody's anything real and steady; they all change into something lyin' or mean or ugly. They told me in reform—the big guy said, 'The world will treat you right. Nobody'll hold a mistake against you.' He lied and he knew it, see? First I believed him, and then I believed Lola, and it was the same. Nobody's what they pretend. It's all pretend."

"Wait a minute, kid. Not all of us. The boss and I and Old Jack—some people stand for things they believe. Some people—"

"Get out! Get out and leave me alone!"

I went back to the bunkhouse, and there sat Old Jack Patton reading a story about cowboys and rustlers. He looked up and said, "Well, she did give him the runaround, didn't she?"

"He didn't have it coming," I said.

"A man's got to have enough inside him to take anything that's coming—trouble, death and lyin' women. Until he's got that inside, he don't amount to nothing."

"But he's only a kid," I said.

"The hand of cards life dealt him, he better grow up fast," Old Jack Patton said and went back to his reading.

The next morning the kid got some whiskey from the men and got drunk. He was already sick when we reached the hay-field. He hooked up his team and then he leaned against the wheel of the rake and looked terrible.

Old Jack Patton walked up to him and grabbed him by the shoulders and shook him hard. He said, "Get on that rake and rake hay. If you got a job to do, you do it, see? You do it whether you're sick in the belly or the head. And you do it right. Straighten up, you weak punk! Straighten up, damn you!"

The kid called him names, and Old Jack Patton laughed in his face and said, "Get on that rake and get to work." The kid dragged himself onto the rake and began to make the windrows.

We had only a few days of work left, and the kid and Old Jack Patton were just as they had been in the beginning—the man driving the boy as hard as he could, and the boy hating him. The kid looked more mean and sullen than when he'd first come to the ranch, and even the boss thought Old Jack was going too far.

"Lay off the kid, Jack," he said. "He can only take so much."

"He's got to take everything," Old Jack Patton said grimly.

That was the day that Lola quit, and the boss sent the kid to the house to help get supper for the men. "My wife needs you," he told the kid. "You give her a hand. Old Jack can finish up that piece of meadow he's laid off to work."

The kid nodded and said, "Well, this is one day I'll get to leave the field ahead of time, and it's killin' that old buzzard's soul."

"He won't have nobody to chew on the rest of the afternoon," I said.

"Tough, huh?" And the kid suddenly grinned at me.

Old Jack Patton was still raking, as usual, when we left the field. The kid helped the boss's wife dish up supper, and we finished eating, but Old Jack hadn't come. The men went back to the bunkhouse, and the boss and I stood by the cookstove while the kid washed dishes.

"I better have a look," the boss said. "Old Jack didn't have much raking left to do. It's taken too long."

The kid swung around from the dishpan. There was something I had never seen before in his green eyes. "Nothing's wrong with him, is there?"

"I couldn't say, kid," the boss answered.... "You want to come with me, Jeff?" he said, turning to me.

Before I could answer, the kid had yanked off the dish towel he had tied around his middle. "I'm a-goin' with you," he said.

"I reckon that's all right," the boss replied.

There was moonlight, the kind of moonlight that makes the world almost as bright as in daytime. We rode up the meadow in the wagon and none of us said anything. Then we saw the team standing dark and still, and we saw the little piece of meadow where the cut grass was flat and silvery between the shining waves of the windrows. There wasn't much left to rake there, maybe half a dozen trips back and forth with the rake.

The boss stopped the wagon and wound the lines around the wheel so the team wouldn't walk off. We went across the little space between us and the rake, our feet swishing through the grass. It was so still I could hear my heart beating loud. Or maybe I was just scared.

Old Jack Patton lay by the rake wheel, and the lines were there in his hand. His face was toward the sky, and it was so peaceful that I knew before the boss knelt beside him that he'd never cuss the kid out again.

The boss didn't speak for quite a while, and when he did his voice was husky. "He was a good man, one of the best I ever had. And he was old — older than he ever let on to any of us. It came to him where he would have wanted it, and it came easy and natural." And the boss gently took the lines from Old Jack Patton's quiet hand, and he lifted Old Jack Patton in his arms and carried him to the wagon.

The kid stooped and picked up the lines. He climbed on the seat of the rake and just sat there. After a while he said, "I'll finish up what he started." And then I saw the shine on the kid's cheeks, and I heard the sound he was trying so hard to hold in. "He was a man stood for something," the kid said. "Like you — and the boss."

As the boss and I drove down the meadow toward the ranch, I could hear the silvery clanging of the rake. It rose clean and sure in the still night. That was when I knew the tough kid was going to turn out all right.

THEY WERE THE REAL McCoys: Bogie Bill, Little Shorty, Kansas Slim, Rosicrucian Martin, Copper Bracelet Lee, Drunken Swede and Gabby, who never spoke a word if he could help it. Some of them preferred nicknames and, for various reasons, never revealed their real names. They followed the harvest from state to state and arrived with the birds, returning year after year to work in the Boettcher Ranch hayfields which Peg's father, "Blunt" Simson, managed for nineteen years

Peg borrowed some of their names for stories. She admitted in a *Casper Star Tribune* interview (October 23, 1970) with then-editor Phil McAuley to "considerably cleaning up their language."

The real Bogie Bill was a gambler, one-eighth Indian, who in winter worked the Nevada casinos. Bill Curry, who also knew him, described him as an expert hay hand, wonderful with horses and good at anything he wanted to do.

"I may be idle part of the time, and I may be broke, but I'm not going to work and be broke," Bogie Bill often said. He never gambled while on the ranch.

"The Secret of Bogie Bill" appeared in the *Saturday Evening Post* in July 1950 and featured as secondary characters Gabby and the Drunken Swede, among others.

Some time after the story's publication — back in pre-zip code days — Peg received a postcard from Las Vegas addressed to "Peggy Curry, Casper Mountain, Casper, Wyoming." Bogie Bill wrote his thanks for "putting me in a story."

THE SECRET OF BOGIE BILL

W E DRIFTED INTO the valley late in July. Gabby came from Iowa, the drunken Swede from cutting timber in Washington, and Bogie Bill from dealing cards in Reno. It was the third summer we'd worked for the boss and he said we were the best hay shakers in Colorado.

Things started off like any other haying season — getting up at daylight, harnessing teams and being in the field before the dew was off the grass, and working hard till sundown. We didn't mind the work. We got paid well, with a bonus if we stayed to top off the last stack. It wasn't money, anyhow, that brought us back every summer like the birds. It was the big country, the mountains, our friends, and having a square-shooting man like the boss to work for.

There wasn't any sign of trouble until the rain started. It hit us early one afternoon and when we got to the barn, water was running everywhere. We went up into the hayloft where we slept, put on dry clothes and started drinking. That was when the drunken Swede began telling the story about cutting down a tree and how it fell on this friend and killed him. Then he began to sob. "I'm a no good son-of-a-gun," he said, tears running down his face. "I work and work, and when I quit workin', I yust want to get drunk."

Gabby blinked and shook his head, as though he were

trying to think of something to say. Gabby never said much. Most of the time he just listened, his brown eyes turning from one face to another. He was little and had a lonesome look about him, like an orphan calf you see in the meadow with its tail turned to the wind. Gabby's shoulders sloped down instead of being straight and square like Bogie Bill's. He always wore faded yellow corduroys, way too big for him, and a worn jumper with sleeves that hung over his hands, and a greasy cap with a cement ad printed across the front of it. He claimed the cap kept his head cool when he was raking hay. "It ventilates me real good," he said.

Now he kept looking at the Swede and shaking his head. Then he thumped his fist awkwardly on the Swede's bent shoulders. "Carl," he said, "take it easy, Carl."

The Swede started to cry and tell the story again. We sat drinking and listening, and after a while the Swede stopped sobbing and raised his head. He pushed his thick blond hair back from his face and looked at me. His eyes were very blue and they had a strange, wild light in them.

"I'm no good," he said, his voice shaking, "plumb no good."

"Man," Bogie Bill said, "you got the blues. Get on your best duds and we'll go in and paint up the town. Comin', Gabby?"

"Nope," Gabby said. Gabby never went to town.

Bogie Bill and I went down the loft ladder and waited in the barn doorway for the drunken Swede. It was quiet and just turning dark.

"Something's happened to the Swede," Bogie Bill said.

"Just drunk," I said. "You know how he is. Always takes too much and drinks it too fast."

"He's had a bad time," Bogie Bill said. "Could tell it when I first saw him this summer. Don't sing any more when he's stacking hay, like he used to. Don't talk loud about his women and his poker bets. And last year he didn't tell any stories about trees."

After a while the Swede came down, dressed in his good suit, and we headed for town. We hit the Wagon Wheel Café about midnight. The Swede was taking a wide swath down the sidewalk and Bogie Bill said we better get some coffee in him. It wasn't much of a café, the Wagon Wheel. Just like any other eating joint where poor people spend their money.

First thing we knew a little guy in a neat, dark suit came up to us and said, "Where do you fellows work?"

"Bar X for Hank McGowan," I said, "and what's it to you?"

He took a picture out of his pocket and laid it on the table. "Ever see this fellow before?"

We squinted at the snapshot and then Bogie Bill said, "Hell, no."

The man went away and we saw him go to another booth, flash the picture and start asking questions. "Damned nosey," Bogie Bill said.

Then all of a sudden the drunken Swede hunched down in the booth like he wanted to slide clear out of sight. We looked up and saw the blond waitress standing beside us, her eyes getting that moist look that means trouble. She was painted up plenty, but it didn't hide the hardness underneath. She leaned toward the Swede.

"Carl," she said in one of those husky voices, "why did you run away? Didn't you know I'd find you?"

The Swede turned red and then white. "Listen," he said, his face beginning to twist up like he was going to cry, "yust leave me alone. All I want is to be left alone."

There was a silence. Then she said, "You want me to talk up here in front of your friends — or will you step out back?"

The Swede got up and followed her toward the kitchen. Another waitress came and took our order. Bogie Bill said he wanted some fried chicken. When the chicken came, he started chewing up bones and all. He had strong, very white teeth and when he was drinking, he had this hankering to chew up bones. The waitress stared at him, her eyes wide and her mouth hanging open. It made an awful racket when Bogie Bill chewed up bones.

Bogie Bill was part Indian and you could tell it by his dark skin, high cheekbones, his black eyes and the way his black hair fit sleek against his head. He wasn't such a tall man, but built the way most of us would like to be built — with wide, powerful shoulders that tapered down to narrow hips. He had soft, long-fingered hands and always wore gloves to protect them, for he dealt cards all winter.

The boss thought a lot of Bogie Bill. He said Bogie Bill was the finest horseman he ever knew. And it was a fact. Horses would do most anything for him when he talked to them.

We sat around the Wagon Wheel until they closed up the joint, but the Swede didn't come. We stood on the sidewalk until daylight and then Bogie Bill said the Swede had really fallen overboard and we might as well go home.

I lay awake in the barn loft, listening to the mice moving in the hay and watching the eastern sky turn red.

Bogie Bill said quietly, "You asleep, Pete?"

"Yeah," I said disgustedly, "you hear me snorin', don't you?"

"That picture," he said, "did it remind you of someone?"

I thought a minute before answering and then I said, "I reckon it did."

"You think we ought to tell him?"

"What for? It probably don't mean anything."

The weather cleared off in a couple of days, but the drunken Swede hadn't come back. The boss was mad. He told me and Bogie Bill to get the pickup truck and go to town.

"Bring that fathead home. If he pulls a stunt like this again, I'll fire him."

The boss said that every summer, and every summer the Swede got drunk and we had to haul him home.

We looked all over town — in the back end of the pool halls, in the hotel down by the railroad tracks, and in all the cars that weren't locked up. We didn't find the Swede.

"Let's talk to the blond doll," Bogie Bill said, so we went over to the Wagon Wheel and there she was, dishing out pie for a couple of fishermen.

Bogie Bill walked up to her and said, "Where is he?"

Her mouth began to tremble and she didn't look so hard then. "I got him locked up. He's not fit to be turned loose — drinkin' and swearin' and bawlin' about a tree killin' that friend of his."

"We can take care of him," Bogie Bill said. "Where is he?"

She gave us a key and told us where to go. It was a room above the drugstore, and we climbed a flight of dirty stairs and went into the place, where the Swede lay on the floor. He was out cold, but he'd torn up the joint before he got quiet. There were broken dishes and chairs and a shade ripped half off the window.

He was a big man and it was all we could do to lift him and carry him down the stairs. We laid him out in the back of the pickup. When we got to the ranch we hid him out in the barn loft so the boss's wife wouldn't see him. She was touchy about drinking.

The Swede came out of it late in the afternoon and started crying and saying he wanted to die. Bogie Bill stuck the Swede's blond head in a pail of water and said, "Don't be talkin' thataway, you ornery cuss. You know you're too mean to die. Why did you tear up that joint and have the doll all worried about you?"

Then the drunken Swede began to talk again about his friend and the tree. "You don't know the truth and I gotta tell you. I yust gotta."

"Now, Carl," Bogie Bill said quietly, "don't take on so. Ain't one of us but got something inside of us we wish we could forget. Ain't that right, Gabby?"

"Yep," Gabby said.

"My friend Jim," the Swede said, "I saw him standin' there, and the tree was bound to hit him. I yust kept cuttin' and cuttin' and never shout, 'Look out, Jim! She's fallin'!' He was a good man, Jim. Yust like you fellows. A good man and I killed him." He pressed his fist against his eyes and sobbed. "Ask that woman in town, ask her how I come to kill Jim. We both wanted her. She act like she wants both of us. And I watch the tree fall on Jim and never shout to him to get safe."

He rolled over on his face and whimpered like a little kid.

Then he sat up, and he put a big hand out and took hold of Bogie Bill's arm. "Bogie," he said, "you're the squarest guy I ever met. And you yust can't help thinkin' I'm a skunk — can you?"

"Reckon I'm not judgin' you, fella," Bogie Bill said. "We been friends, the four of us here, and we've had lots of fun up in this old hayloft. Think about that for a while."

The Swede was quiet. He stared through the open loft window toward the river that ran red with sundown. And I knew he was thinking about what Bogie Bill meant, about this fine thing that's between men who come back each summer to work the hay together. And I felt it deep inside of me, and warm — like a lighted window shining through a snowstorm.

The Swede said, "Sometimes I want to kill that woman — but I can't. Not now. Bogie, I gotta talk to you. I gotta talk to you alone."

I touched Gabby's shoulder. We went down the loft ladder

and walked over to the corral fence. We stood there, listening
to the river sound and watching the color fade out of the sky.
After a while Bogie Bill came down and stood with us,
rolling a cigarette. He stuck it in the corner of his mouth,
lighted it, and said, "Wind's shifted to the north. We'll hay
tomorrow." And that's as close as he ever came to telling us
what the Swede said up there in the hayloft.

In a few days the Swede was back on the stack and moving more hay than any three men, but he wasn't the same.
His blue eyes kept looking past us instead of at us. Sometimes the blond waitress would drive out from town and park
near the bunkhouse. The Swede would sit in the car with her
and the men could hear them arguing and her pleading and
him swearing.

Bogie Bill said the whole thing made him sick at his stomach. "I come here to get away from women," he said, "and now
we get the same old fat chewed up there in the front yard."

The boss asked us what was the matter with the Swede
and why the waitress kept hanging around. We told him we
didn't know. The boss was a square guy and we didn't want to
tell him the truth.

We moved into the upper meadow the middle of August
when the nights were getting cold in the high country, and
that's when the little guy with the picture came out to the field
on the lunch wagon.

It was one of those still days. The mountains had moved
up close and looked troublesome, the way they always do
when a storm's brewing. I could hear every sound — the jin-
gle of harness, the jangle of rake teeth, the men swearing, the
creaking of the pusher as it rammed a load of hay and sent it
up over the slide.

Bogie Bill was riding the slick sweep tail in his high-
heeled cowboy boots, and Gabby was driving back and forth

full speed behind him, picking up the scatterings with his rake. The drunken Swede was stacking hay to beat the band, his shirt dark with sweat and his face gray with hay dust.

When we saw the lunch wagon coming, we stopped work, unhooked the teams and put out grain for them. As I started toward the lunch wagon, I noticed the little guy. Just then Bogie Bill took hold of my arm and said, "I figured we'd see that bird again. Pete, we should have talked up."

Gabby lifted a box of food from the wagon box. He set it down carefully and started fishing in another box for his tin plate. Then he looked up and I saw the fear leap in his brown eyes and he began to back off slowly, his hands spread out in front of him like he wanted to push something away. The little guy moved toward him, and I saw the gun glint in his hand.

"Take it easy," the little guy said, "and we won't have any trouble."

The Swede came around the wagon and saw the whole thing. Gabby started to run and the Swede stepped in between him and the little guy, spreading out his big arms as though he wanted to protect Gabby. The gun went off then, just as the Swede moved, and I saw the surprise on his face and how his mouth came open. He fell loose and quiet, like a sheet blowing down in the wind. Gabby turned and came running back. He fell on his knees beside the Swede. His lips moved, but no words came out. His hands kept rubbing the Swede's limp fingers.

The little guy came up and put handcuffs on Gabby, but Gabby didn't seem to notice. He was staring at the big red stain spreading on the front of the Swede's blue work shirt.

I heard the little guy tell the boss how much money Gabby had stolen. The boss had a strange look on his face. I guess it was as hard for him as it was for me to believe that Gabby had stuck up a bank.

Bogie Bill and the boss put the Swede in the back of the pickup. Bogie Bill wiped the Swede's dusty face with his red handkerchief and put a slicker over him and weighted the edges down with sickles.

Gabby got in the front of the pickup between the boss and the little guy in the neat dark suit. Gabby didn't look at any of us. He kept his brown eyes fixed on the mountains. I guess he knew it would be a long, long time before he saw them again.

The boss drove the pickup away, and Bogie Bill turned and saw the lunch boxes standing open and none of the men making a move to eat. He walked slowly to the boxes, filled a tin plate, and poured himself a cup of coffee. Then he went over to the sweep and sat down on the tailboard. A little later I saw the plate of food sitting in the stubble and the boss's dog eating from it. The coffee cup was overturned in the meadow. Bogie Bill was hooking up his team.

We buried the drunken Swede in the graveyard in town. It's a lonesome place to lie, with nothing but sagebrush growing between the graves and only a few wilted flowers in Mason jars in front of the headstones. Bogie Bill said the Swede wouldn't mind. "It ain't far from the valley," Bogie Bill said, rolling a cigarette, "and the smell of the hayfield comes around on the wind. I reckon it suits him as well as any place."

A week after the Swede was buried, Bogie Bill started driving to town alone, never saying a word to me about whether I wanted to go with him.

Then one day he told me he was moving out of the hayloft and into the old sheep wagon the boss kept for his irrigating men to live in when they worked the big ditch in spring. He pulled his suitcase from under his bunk and started throwing stuff into it.

"What's eatin' you?" I asked. "Don't my company suit you?"

"Don't seem right up here without the drunken Swede and Gabby around," he said. "I got a hankerin' to be off by myself."

A few nights later he went to town again, and the next morning on the way to the hayfield, I saw a woman sitting on the tongue of the sheep wagon. I didn't have any trouble placing her — not many women have that kind of blond hair.

The boss was sitting beside me on the hayrack — we always rode out to work on the hayrack with our teams tied behind — and I could feel him bristle up like a porcupine. Then he shoved his false teeth out against his upper lip, the way he always did when something made him sore.

That night the boss called me to his office. "Pete," he said, "what's going on down by the creek?"

"Reckon I couldn't say, boss."

He began to pace back and forth. "Never was a man I liked better than Bogie Bill," he said. "I even figured on offering him a steady job with me and maybe an interest in the place if he'd quit drifting and dealing. He ought to settle down and do something with his life — something worthwhile." The boss paused and looked at me and I could tell by his eyes that he was hurt. "Then he pulls this dirty trick on me. It's not right, Pete."

Men don't look at some things about other men as being bad — things like having a taste for whiskey or women — not if a man does those things where they won't hurt anyone but himself and keeps his mouth shut about them. Bogie Bill never had much luck with women. We got to asking him questions once — just kidding him — and he told us he'd been married three times. "Never did get along with a wife," he said, grinning, "but the mother-in-laws always liked me."

This business down by the creek wasn't what you'd expect of Bogie Bill. It was low-down and an insult to the boss. And it made me feel ashamed of Bogie Bill.

"He claimed he come here to get away from women," I said, "and he never had a woman on the string in hayin' season till now. It don't make sense."

The boss put on his hat and said, "Let's go down and talk to him."

We got in the pickup and drove past the cook shack, the bunkhouse, and the barn, and took the river road. The boss never had any respect for a vehicle, so when the road ended he put the truck through sagebrush and around willows till we stopped by the sheep wagon.

Bogie Bill came out and stood leaning against one of the wagon wheels, his black hat pulled low over his eyes. He just looked at us in a cool, strange way and didn't act like he was going to say anything.

The boss said, "You got a woman in there?"

"Reckon so," Bogie Bill replied.

"Are you married to her?" The boss's voice came out like a bark.

"Figurin' on gettin' around to that," Bogie Bill said quietly.

"We had one man all mixed up over her," the boss said, "and you know a woman like that doesn't do any man any good. I can't have her on the ranch."

Bogie Bill carefully rolled a cigarette. "I'm keepin' her," he said.

The boss got red in the face. "Then get the hell off the place," he shouted, "and take her with you!"

When we got up for breakfast the next morning, Bogie Bill was gone. And the boss was still mad. "Never even came for his paycheck," he fumed. "And how do I know where to send it? A drifting man never has any home."

"Well," I said, "Bogie didn't care about the money. He liked the country and workin' horses."

"It's an awful thing," the boss said, "when a good horseman makes a fool of himself over a chippy."

"It is," I said. "And it just don't seem like Bogie Bill. I never figured he was such a fool. But sometimes you can live around men and not know much about them. Reckon we learned that this summer."

"This summer's been a jinx," the boss muttered.

Even the weather went against us before haying was over. In late August it rained and in September it snowed. We finished up the first of October with a third of a crew left and nobody in a good humor.

When I left the valley, I said I'd never go back, for I knew it wouldn't seem the same. I didn't like to think about Gabby and the drunken Swede and Bogie Bill.

For five years I rolled hay in Utah, Montana, and up in Jackson Hole. I tried to stop thinking about the ranch and the boss and the fun I had drinking and talking in the hayloft. Then it was like a hunger I had inside of me and nothing I did would ease it, so I went back.

The boss was glad to see me. He held onto my hand for a long time and said, "Pete, we don't have any hay hands like you and Gabby and the drunken Swede and Bogie Bill. I got a bunch of punks that don't know how to put a collar on a horse."

It was good to hear him say that and I was happy as I carried my bedroll to the hayloft. But something was missing. There wasn't anyone to talk with about the summers that had gone by. I went up to the bunkhouse and there wasn't a familiar face around the poker table. Right then I wished I could turn back time and start over, the way it was the first year I hayed for the boss — with Bogie Bill getting a drink under his belt and chewing up bones at the supper table, and Gabby just sitting and listening, his soft brown eyes watching us, and the drunken Swede singing as he stacked hay.

Five years hadn't changed the mountains or the meadows or the way the mist hung over the river before sunrise. Five years had only changed me and made the boss's hair white around the edges.

We'd been haying two weeks when the boss came to the barn one morning and climbed the loft ladder to sit on the edge of my bunk. We were laying off for green hay, and only the mowing machines were working.

"Know what I heard in town last night, Pete?"

"What?" I said.

"Bogie Bill's back. He's grinding sickles at the Wolver Ranch."

I sat up and threw the dime magazine toward the ceiling. "The old son-of-a-gun! The old crap-shooter!" I felt warm and happy inside, like I had the world by the tail and everything was down-grade and shady.

"Can't figure a man that's so good with horses spending his time grinding sickles," the boss said. Then he took out his pocket knife and worked on his fingernails. "I never got over that dirty trick he pulled here," he said, "but I figure I ought to give him the money he left behind. He earned it and it doesn't belong to me."

I couldn't help smiling. The boss could have mailed that check. And I knew he didn't want to admit how much he cared about seeing Bogie Bill again. The boss was a proud man and he never forgot a dirty trick that was pulled on him.

"Well," I said, "I sure would like to see him."

"You haven't got a car," the boss said, closing his pocket knife. "Why don't we drive over in the pickup?"

We took off in a cloud of dust and made fast time around the mountains to the Wolver Ranch, which is stuck in between two hogbacks and is a long way from nowhere.

We drove up before the scattered log buildings and got out.

The cook told us the sickle grinder was in the blacksmith shop.

We started to walk to the shop, but before we got there the door swung open and Bogie Bill stepped out, holding a sickle in his hands. He saw us and a quick grin lighted his lean, dark-skinned face. He rested the sickle against the side of the shop and came to meet us.

He looked just the same. I gripped his hand tight and couldn't say a word. The boss didn't offer to shake hands. He shifted from one foot to the other and said, "I got a check for you, Bogie Bill."

"No hurry about that," Bogie Bill said. "I ain't broke yet."

The boss cleared his throat. "Your wife — with you?" he asked.

Bogie Bill looked at him a minute and then said, "Nope. She took off with some guy from Texas — 'bout three years ago." He smiled and added, "Never did get along with my wives."

The door of the blacksmith shop swung open again and a little boy came running across the yard and put both arms around one of Bogie Bill's legs. He peeked at us, sort of shy and wild and then hid his face.

The boss said, "Hi, sonny. Turn around and let me have a look at you."

But the blond head pressed closer to the gambler. Bogie Bill smiled. "He calls me Bogie Bill," he said, "and we take a dip in the creek every night. Pretty good boy, boss."

"Well," the boss said, "I can't say till I get a chance to size him up. All I can see is the back of his neck."

"Go on," Bogie Bill said, pushing gently at the kid, "turn around. The boss don't aim to bite you."

He pulled the kid around in front of him and I saw the clean overalls, and the clean, wrinkled white shirt and the little comb in the pocket. And I saw the blond hair turning in the wind and the eyes that were so blue I couldn't look away.

The boss spoke and his voice was rough in his throat. "You're a long way from home, aren't you, sonny?"

"Reckon he's as close to home as he'll ever be," Bogie Bill said quietly and a light glinted in his black eyes.

We knew then why Bogie Bill wasn't out in the field working horses. And we knew why he had brought the woman out to the sheep wagon that summer, for the blue eyes looking up at us, shy and wild, were the eyes of the drunken Swede.

"I call him Carl," Bogie Bill said, and his arm pressed the kid close against him.

My throat felt tight and it wasn't from working in the hay dust. The boss put his big, rough hand on the kid's blond head and said, "The missus wouldn't mind having a boy like this around, to carry wood and feed the chickens." Then he looked at Bogie Bill. "I could use a steady man — make the job worthwhile for him. Got lots of horses waiting for the right hand to gentle them down."

Bogie Bill squinted at the hills that were getting deep and dark with afternoon. "Reckon that's nice of you," he said gently, "but a drifting man don't stay put and settle down. We'll make out. Maybe he won't grow up like some kids — but he won't be too far wrong, either."

"Well," the boss said, "look at it this way. Most kids like to be on ranches in the summer. Might be nice if he could come back and summer with us."

"I reckon we could try that," Bogie Bill said. "And I reckon when the time comes, he'll settle down — if he has a mind to."

The boss put the check in the kid's pocket, ruffled his hair, and we walked away. We drove toward home and the boss didn't say a word, but I could see he was smiling to himself — like he was real pleased about something.

I knew just how he felt. I felt the same way myself.

"MEAN MAN," A LITTLE known short-short story was published in *Empire Magazine* of the *Denver Post* in 1956. The story is set in the North Park area of Colorado. One of four great, natural valleys in Colorado, North Park borders Wyoming and is about sixty miles long and forty miles wide.

Though the action in the story takes place indoors, the background of "Mean Man," like a number of Peg Curry's other stories, is the old-time hayfield in the days before machines took over, when harvesters used horses.

A full hay crew was usually twenty-one men and sixty head of horses. Seven men drove mowing machines, six operated rakes and four worked sweeps—sometimes called bull rakes. Four men made up the stacking crew, building up the loose hay into rectangular stacks with rounded tops.

The pusher driver drove the pusher, handling four horses to send the sweep loads of hay up the high, slick-poled stacker to drop the green hay to the stacking crew.

Sickles for the mowing machine were ground at a grindstone powered by a waterwheel in the river. The sickle grinder's second job was to bring the full-course, noon meal out to the meadow. Men took an hour off to eat and rest. Sweep drivers changed teams then, and the horses were grained twice a day.

The Boettcher Ranch, where the Simsons lived for a number of years, was one of the major hay-producing ranches for the area. The hay crop in a good year was about 3,300 tons.

MEAN MAN

MONTE DANIELS STOOD by the kitchen stove, rolling a cigarette. "Lunch ready for the field?" he asked. He didn't look at Ruth Ann as he spoke and she felt an emptiness in her heart — an emptiness that had been there ever since the day Old Dad returned to the ranch a month ago.

Monte had seen him walking down the dusty hill road that led toward town. "Didn't think he'd come back this year," Monte muttered. "Must be past seventy. Dangerous for a man his age to work horses."

"He can drive the stacker team," Ruth Ann said. "The stacker team's gentle. A child could handle them."

"Don't need him," Monte said briefly.

Ruth Ann felt her face turn hot. "This place is home to him. He's a lonely old man. You can't turn him away."

Monte's jaw tightened. "I've got a full crew."

"That's not true!" Ruth Ann cried. "You don't want him. Your heart's hard — like these mountain meadows that sprout rocks between timothy and clover."

She saw Monte wince, almost as though she had struck him. Then his eyes hardened to a cold silver-gray. "Old Dad can stay," he said coolly, "but the first mistake he makes I'll write his time. I'm running a ranch, not a pension place."

Well, Monte was watching for that mistake, Ruth Ann

thought now as she filled the lunch boxes. He was watching every day, standing over Old Dad just as though Old Dad hadn't driven a team for years and didn't know all about it.

Monte loaded the lunch boxes in the truck. Ruth Ann took a candy bar from the cupboard and slipped it into the pocket of her gingham dress. Old Dad needed extra energy to keep up with the other men who were young and strong.

Sultry wind fanned Ruth Ann's cheeks as the truck headed across the meadow toward the stacking crew. She stole a glance at Monte's square-jawed impassive face. A mean man, that's what he was and she'd quit tomorrow if it wasn't for Old Dad.

The crew had their teams unhitched and were waiting. Monte lifted kettles of food from the truck and placed them on overturned boxes. Men crowded around, noisy and hungry, the tin plates glistening in their hands.

"Hello, honey," Old Dad said to Ruth Ann. She thought he looked frailer and thinner than usual. His faded blue eyes watered, his white hair was damp with sweat, and his twisted hands shook as he filled his plate with food.

When they had finished eating, Ruth Ann usually drove the truck back to the ranch house but today she lingered, watching them put up hay. The mountains seemed big and close and she felt as though they were looking down the back of her neck. That meant a storm was brewing in the high country.

She noticed with anger that Monte was standing beside Old Dad. There was something pitiful about the way Old Dad held the reins in his twisted hands and guided horses and pusher toward the slide. After each load of hay had gone up and over he would turn to Monte and say eagerly, "How's that, Monte?" And Monte would merely nod and look more taciturn than before. Finally, he went to help the men stack hay.

Ruth Ann walked over to Old Dad and handed him the candy bar. "Extra dessert," she said.

Old Dad smiled. "You're awful good to me, honey." His faded eyes were intent upon her face. Then he added gently, "Why don't you and Monte make up? Shucks, honey. I know you been in love with him for three years, ever since that first summer you come to cook for us. And I reckon Monte ain't much with fancy words but he's got deep feelings. Right now he's eatin' his heart out over you."

Ruth Ann tossed her brown head and looked the other way so he couldn't see the tears in her eyes. "You're wrong," she said in a tight voice, "Monte hasn't got a heart."

When the men came in for supper that night it was raining. The dining room had a dim, dreary appearance. Should have lighted the lamps, Ruth Ann thought, as she glanced around, looking for Old Dad. He came in late and stumbled to his accustomed place beside Monte.

Ruth Ann hurried to pour his coffee and move the plate of spice cookies close to his elbow. She hoped the other men wouldn't eat them all before Old Dad got ready for dessert.

Old Dad smiled at her and forked three cookies onto his plate. "Ketchup," he said and one of the men shoved the bottle toward him. Old Dad scattered ketchup over the cookies.

Rough laughter began around the table. The men leaned forward, watching the old man. Then Monte Daniels spoke sharply, "Ketchup." And while the men stared, Monte pushed two cookies onto his plate and covered them with ketchup. The men looked away, suddenly quiet.

Ruth Ann looked at Old Dad. He bit into a cookie. Shocked surprise spread over his wrinkled face and then he glanced fearfully at the men but they weren't watching him.

Ruth Ann felt a sudden ache in her throat; she understood now why Monte had stood beside Old Dad in the hayfield.

Old Dad couldn't tell cookies from brown meat because he was going blind.

She fled to the kitchen and leaned trembling against the sink. Tears began to run down her face. Then she felt a strong hand on her arm. "Don't fret, Ruth Ann. We'll find something for him to do when he can't drive the stacker team."

"Oh, Monte...," her voice broke as she put her arms around his neck and pressed her face against his shoulder.

He cleared his throat. "Ruth Ann," he said awkwardly, "you've got the softest hair."

It was as close as he'd ever come to telling her he loved her, but for Ruth Ann it was close enough.

RIDING ON A BUS ONE DAY, Peg overheard a snippet of conversation. A woman ahead of her confided to her seat partner, "I hate Sunday. *His* mother comes to dinner *every* Sunday." She knew a story was there, although it was several years before she wrote of a proud old man and his unhappy daughter-in-law.

Mike Curry, Peg's son, suggested that this incident forced her to consider, with piercing insight, both interpersonal as well as inter-generational relationships so much a part of all our lives.

One of the most moving letters Peg received from a reader about this short-short story came from an old man who wrote that the truth in it helped him "accept the dignity of living alone."

"Bitter Sunday" appeared in the *American Magazine* in April 1955.

BITTER SUNDAY

MARY ANN TOLD herself she was cruel and selfish. How could she feel so hateful toward a nice old man like Joe's father?

She punched her bed pillow and then raised on her elbow to look at Joe. He opened his eyes and looked at her. They were sleepy brown eyes, but they brightened as he reached for her, pulled her down against him, and kissed the tip of her nose. Once that would have been the wonderful beginning of a wonderful day, the only day in the week they had to spend together. Now it was a nagging reminder that there was a big one-o'clock dinner to cook, that a tottery old man would sit at the head of her table and serve the plates with unsteady hands, dripping gravy on her clean tablecloth.

Asking his father to serve had been Joe's idea. It had started that Sunday when Joe said, "Mother always expected him to fix the plates, and it'll fill some of the emptiness now that she's gone. It'll make him feel he's still part of a family."

Mary Ann hadn't know then that the Sunday dinner would become a pattern that pleased everyone in the family but her. Now, even the six-year-old twins spoke of Sunday as "Grandpa Pete's day."

"S'matter?" Joe asked, tugging at her tousled blond hair.

"Nothing." She turned her face away from him.

"Mary Ann!" Joe's voice was anxious. "What's wrong, honey?"

She sat up in bed. "I'm just sick of it!" she said firmly. "Sick of having your father here every Sunday—cooking all morning—" She paused and saw Joe's shocked face.

"I'd think," Joe said softly, "you could give up one day a week to be kind to a lonely old man. You have all the rest of the time to do as you please."

"Do as I please!" She was furious. "I'm stuck with children, cooking, washing.... I want Sundays like they used to be!"

"All right," Joe said sharply. "I'll tell him he's not welcome here any longer."

She pressed her hands to her head. "No! It's not that...."
Then she saw the twins standing in the doorway; Billy with his thick, blond hair tufted into peaks that caught the spring sunlight, and Johnny scowling at her from under his black crew cut.

"You're mean," Billy said. "You don't like Grandpa Pete."

Johnny said, "It's Grandpa Pete's day and your tryin' to spoil it!"

Joe got out of bed, saying sharply, "You kids clear out of here. Get ready for Sunday School."

Mary Ann put on her housecoat and went to the kitchen. She set the table with the breakfast dishes Grandpa Pete had given her. They were such pretty dishes. He had said, "Take 'em, girl. They're too fancy for me." He'd given her lots of things—silver, tablecloths, a string of beautiful old-fashioned beads. "But," she thought bitterly, "*I don't want him around on Sunday. Heel that I am....*"

At twenty minutes to one that afternoon Mary Ann put the rolls in the oven. The twins sprinted past her, slamming against the table on their way to the dining room. "I sit on this side of Grandpa Pete," Billy cried. "No," Johnny's voice rose.

"That's my place!" There was a sound of scuffling, and then the crash of breaking glass.

"Boys!" Mary Ann rushed to the dining room. She stooped to pick up the broken goblet. "Oh!" A little cry of pain burst from her lips. Blood trickled from her finger. Then, Joe was beside her, folding his handkerchief over the cut, urging her toward the bathroom.

She stood close to him, feeling the sting of the disinfectant. She wanted to press closer, to put her face against his broad chest and say, "Forgive me. It's only because I love you so much I want this one day for just us."

"There," he said. His hand moved, unsteadily, to straighten the collar of her dress. "Mary Ann—"

She trembled. In a moment she'd be in his arms and somehow they'd make right this day that started so wrong. Then she heard the twins shouting, "Here comes Grandpa Pete!"

They hurried to the living room. Through the picture window Mary Ann could see Grandpa Pete coming slowly up the walk, his lined face impassive, his knotted fingers gripping the cane as he limped toward the front door. Once Joe had offered to go after him in the car, but Grandpa Pete had replied, "A man should walk while he can."

Joe's voice was full of false heartiness as he opened the door: "Well, Dad, glad to see you looking so sharp. Been following the Yanks? They're getting warmed up!"

Grandpa Pete took off his hat and passed his hand over his thin white hair. The twins rushed at him, grabbed a leg apiece and swung against him, shouting, "We're gonna play games! Right after we eat!"

Grandpa Pete's mild blue eyes moved to Mary Ann. "Hello, girl. How've you been?"

There was an ache in her throat. His eyes were so kind.

"Just fine," she said. "Come along. Everything's ready."

Grandpa Pete went to the head of the table. Mary Ann sat down and unfolded her napkin. "Your turn to say grace, Billy."

As they bowed their heads, Mary Ann saw Johnny reach for a roll. She struck his hand a resounding whack. Johnny let out a bellow of protest. "You're mean!" he shouted. "You've been mean all day — pickin', on me — just because you don't want Grandpa Pete around!"

There was a shocked silence. Mary Ann stared down at the floor. Carefully, Grandpa Pete rose from the table.

"Dad —" Joe's voice was strained. "Wait a minute, Dad. Where are you going?"

"Home," the old man said, and he left the room.

The twins began to cry. Joe sat silent. Mary Ann went into the bedroom and closed the door. She shut her eyes tight to hold back the tears, and all she could see in her mind was the tall, bent figure walking away — walking out of her life. She'd have her Sundays now, but she didn't want them like this, not with the twins upset and Joe hurt and Grandpa Pete no longer her friend. This was terrible; this was worse than one-o'clock dinner every Sunday.

She heard Joe trying to quiet the children: "Eat your dinner and I'll take you to the park."

When they had gone Mary Ann bathed her hot face, put on fresh powder, and went down to Grandpa Pete's house. She walked to the back door and hesitated. She heard a strange sound inside the house. Someone was humming.

She stepped into the house and stopped. Grandpa Pete, wearing a pair of faded dungarees and a T-shirt, was eating a peanut-butter sandwich at the kitchen table.

"Grandpa Pete — I —" Her lips felt stiff. What could you say after you'd hurt someone you loved? How could you ever again bring back the warmth and the closeness?

"Sit down," the old man said softly. "Have some coffee."

Mary Ann drew a deep breath. "It's not that I don't love you," she began. "It's just—"

Grandpa Pete nodded. "Mighty glad things came up the way they did today. You know, Mary Ann, I don't mind playin' games with your kids once in a while, but it got mighty tedious every Sunday. Just like it got tiresome listenin' to Joe talk baseball, hashin' over all that stuff in the newspapers. I can still read, you know."

Mary Ann stared at him. Then a slow warmth began deep inside her. She smiled. "You should have told me, Grandpa Pete. You shouldn't have put up with it."

He shrugged. "Well, that first Sunday I figured it was a thing I wouldn't have to go on with, exceptin' when I felt like it. Then every time you called I didn't want to hurt your feelings when you'd gone to all that fuss. The longer it went on, the harder it was to speak up. I tell you, girl, I just naturally don't like big Sunday dinners. Never did. My wife, she was all for 'em, and I humored her. But I always did like the idea of Sunday being a day of rest and not like every other fussed-up day in the week. A person doesn't get new ideas for what's ahead of him if he's all tied up in knots on Sunday. And let me tell you something else: If there's one thing my wife and I *did* fight about it was me puttin' a dab of this and that on somebody else's plate!"

Mary Ann couldn't help herself—she burst into laughter. "Why," she thought wonderingly, "we're two of a kind." And her hand went out impulsively to grasp the thin, sandpapery fingers of Grandpa Pete.

"Trouble is," Grandpa Pete went on, "most young people don't know how to treat older folks. They either pass us up completely—like we was a potted plant or something—or they fix up everything so we don't have a life of our own."

He grinned at Mary Ann. "Have some coffee, girl? I like it strong. Yours is too weak."

For a moment she didn't answer. She was dreaming about the good times that were ahead for both of them—waffles for Friday-night supper, picnics, coffee together on mornings when they were in the mood for it. No more worrying and planning. Fun — that's what they were going to have.

Mary Ann put her elbows on the table. "I'd like some coffee and a peanut-butter sandwich, too, please." And, with a happy sigh, she settled herself to enjoy Sunday dinner with Grandpa Pete.

GRANNY SHIELA IN "Bogus Bride" knows how to spread the word to people in the valley.

"She waddled to the phone and cranked the old-fashioned handle. 'That you, Mrs. Green? Although it's your custom to listen in every time there's a ring on the party line, I feared you'd missed our good news. Bruce got married. What? Of course it was sudden. And why should a man of red blood put up with a long engagement? ...Oh, she comes from a fine old family indeed. Sheep people and Scotch, like us. Now dearie, I trust you'll pass the fine news to all our neighbors.' Granny hung up and sighed. 'And all the receivers clicking up and down while I talked to her.'"

"Bogus Bride" appeared in the *Saturday Evening Post* in March 1961.

Bogus Bride

I T CAME AS A TERRIBLE shock to us. My brother Bruce went to Cheyenne to hire a few hay hands and was gone a week instead of a day. Then he phoned us from town, which is twenty miles from our ranch. He told my mother he was married and would be home with his wife as soon as they'd eaten some supper.

My mother started crying. My father swore. And in a few minutes Granny Sheila, who'd been listening in on her telephone down at the old house, came waddling across the slope to the new house, a black shawl over her shoulders and her white hair streaming in the July wind.

"Boil the kettle, Annie," she said to my mother. "I need a cup of tea."

"Tea, hell!" My father opened the kitchen cupboard and brought out a jug and poured a cup half-full of whiskey. "You know it wasn't love," he said. "Bruce has always been a backward lad. She got around him."

"He's no lad," Granny Sheila replied tartly. "He's thirty years old, and it takes two to get around. I'll not blame her a bit more than him. I told you long ago you'd got too fussy about the woman he should marry. Fanny Hankins didn't suit you because she put tint on her hair. You'd have none of Mary Duncan because she stayed up all night at the dances. You

83

said she'd never rise from her bed to cook a rancher's breakfast. And the Widow Williams —" Granny's bright blue eyes rolled.

"He loved none of them, or he'd have ignored us!" my mother cried.

"Well, love's a delicate thing," Granny said, "and not meant to be picked to pieces. I just came up here to tell you that now it's happened, fair or foul, we're going to make the best of it. You hear me?"

"The best would be finding us a lawyer," my father muttered.

"There's none in the county except old drunken Tom McCloud," Granny said. "And by the time you could find one, there's like to be a grandchild on the way. Do you want your flesh and blood growing up in a broken home? And who's to have the kid, huh, Bruce or the girl he married?"

My father straightened, a tall, dark-eyed man with a stern mouth. "Once a McKenzie, always a McKenzie. I'll do right by the wee lad."

"Humph!" Granny spat on the big kitchen stove that was still hot from cooking supper. "He's that smart, my son, that he decides the sex of the bairn before it's certain it's begun. Well, let me tell you this, John McKenzie: You'll never hold a candle to a woman when she stands up in court and asks a judge to give her care of her offspring. Motherhood will melt hearts of iron."

"There's no doubt the hussy married my son for our money," my father said, scowling. "I told him to watch out for that. I told him —"

"And what are you to do with all your money?" Granny demanded. "Pay the devil to fan you with a palm leaf?" She waddled to the telephone and cranked the old-fashioned handle. "That you, Mrs. Green? Although it's your custom to listen in every time there's a ring on the party line, I feared you'd missed our good news. Bruce got married. What? Of course it was sudden. And why should a man of red blood put up with a long engagement? Don't believe in 'em myself.... What? Oh, she comes from a fine old family indeed. Sheep people and Scotch, like us. Now, dearie, I trust you'll pass the fine news to all our neighbors." Granny hung up and sighed. "And all the receivers clicking up and down while I talked to her."

"A fine cock-and-bull story you put out," my father said, looking glum.

"Oh, my!" my mother went on, wringing her hands.

"Where will they sleep?" I asked. "Should I put fresh sheets in the spare bedroom, Father?"

"Let them stay at the old house," my father muttered. "Your granny's already arranged the hussy's past. She may as well take care of her future."

"That I will," Granny said stoutly. "Come on, lassie." She took hold of my arm. "We've work to do, and you're good at it for a sweet thing of fifteen summers."

"You've made some fine botches of things in your day," my father said, glaring at Granny, "and see this isn't another."

She stuck out her tongue at him, and the two of us set off for the old house on the slope above the river bend. "Y'know, lassie," Granny said, "your father's just as your grandfather was. A dull time of it I'd have had if I hadn't taken the bit in my teeth from the day we met. Both of them so careful and tight-fisted they'd squeeze the very juice from life." Then she chuckled. "It's my blood showing up in your brother Bruce that brought this on."

The meadowlarks rose singing out of the fields, and the wind smelled of wild mint and clover. The last golden light was fading off into dusk. "Aye," Granny murmured, "it's the hour the heart fills up for what it's had — and for what it's missed."

The old house was high-ceilinged and built of logs. The night's coolness lingered in it, even on hot summer days. It had a feeling of space and peace, and there wasn't one new thing in it — only the furniture, pictures and dishes Granny had lived with for fifty years.

"Modern living," Granny would sometimes say, "what is it? Chairs and sofas so soft they won't support a body's bottom. And the worst is most folks parting with their stuff before they get to know it or shape it to fit their lives. Like clothes, Jeannie, things a body lives with have to be old to feel right."

Granny lighted the kerosene lamp in the old house and said, "Now you look in the bottom kitchen drawer, honey, and get what's left of the Christmas candles. There ought to be a dozen. Don't matter they're red and green instead of white. Put them in candlesticks and set them in every room, even the kitchen."

"Granny, where are you going to stay if the bride's to be here?"

She smiled. "I'm going to move into the sheep wagon close to the river. It'll be fun to sleep in a wagon again. Lived in one two years when I first came to this country with your grandpa."

While I fixed the candles, she got out all her patchwork quilts she'd worked through many winters. She selected the prettiest one and put it on the old four-poster bed in her bedroom. Then she said to me, "You run out in the willows and pick some flowers. Take the flashlight. The blue gentians are in bloom. Blue's a lonely color, but most brides feel lonely, for it's like saying good-bye to yourself when you love a man. You're never the same again."

When my brother's car came over the hill, Granny had the lantern lighted and went out holding it high so they'd see her.

I stayed close beside her, and I felt important, for I'd changed into my best clothes, and Granny had on the dress she wore only to funerals and charivaris. It was a red dress and, once when my mother said there were occasions it didn't fit, Granny had answered, "Red's the color of living. I like to feel alive whether I'm at a wedding celebration or a funeral."

Bruce's car came to a stop. I saw right away that he hadn't hired any hay hands. There was only this girl beside him, and all I could tell about was her hair. It looked awful bright — like pale gold — in the lantern shine. Granny nudged me. "Tint on it," she said, and sounded as though she'd found something special, like a first wild rose or a bird's nest.

Bruce got out and then the girl. She wasn't very big, not coming to his shoulder, and the first thing I noticed was that she didn't have on stockings. She was wearing tight pants that came just below the knee and from there on her legs were bare. Her feet were almost bare, too. Only a piece of rope went between two of her toes. And her toenails were as red as Granny's dress.

Granny went right up and kissed her, but the girl looked funny and drew back. Bruce cleared his throat. "We'll be going back to town," he said. "No trouble for anybody."

"You'll be coming in and making yourselves at home," Granny said, and she took hold of the girl's shoulder, just as she did mine when I wouldn't study my arithmetic, and marched her to the house.

"And what's your name, dearie?" Granny asked when we were inside the old house and sitting in the candlelighted living room where the air had the faint warm smell of sheets brought in from the sunlight.

It was Bruce who answered. "Nancy," he said. He looked very moody with his dark hair not combed and his black eyes staring past us.

"And tell me about your kinfolk," Granny said to Nancy.

Nancy sat up stiffer and straighter, her little thin hands doubled up tight in her lap. "I've got none," she said coldly.

The living room was full of quiet. Then Granny made a clucking sound with her tongue. "You got some now," she said.

Nancy's eyes were gray and big and a look came into them I'd once seen in the eyes of a trapped coyote. She turned from Granny toward Bruce, and I saw his jaw get stubborn, but he didn't say a word.

"You want to go to the new house and meet the rest of us?" Granny said.

Nancy shook her head. Granny stood and looked around and nodded to herself. Then she said, "Jeannie, you come with me. You can walk me to my wagon.... Nancy, you and me will have some tea down in the wagon tomorrow afternoon — just the two of us."

There, by the river, with half a hill between us and the old house, we could hear their angry voices. "There's nothing worse than honeymoons," Granny said. "When you go on one, see to it you stay where there's lots of people and things to do. It's awful hard at first; men and women know so little about each other when they get married. For that matter, sometimes it takes most of a life to find out whether you married the right person."

There was a loud banging of doors, and a few minutes later I saw a lantern had been lighted in the bunkhouse that stood off to the side of the old house. Sometimes Bruce went there and slept when he'd had a tiff with my father. My father spent a night in it the winter of the bad blizzard when he lost so many sheep. And mother stayed down there for half a day the time she came home from losing a baby in the hospital. Granny was in the bunkhouse several days after grandpa died, and last year, when I lost the county spelling contest, I sat in the old log room for quite a while.

Granny shut the door of the sheep wagon and told me to quit fidgeting and rest a spell. She got very quiet after that, and I could hear the river and the wind coming up in the willows. It was the kind of wind that meant a storm. And after a while the door was flung open, and my mother and father came in.

"He's locked himself in the bunkhouse and won't come out," my father said. "Just as I told you, she got around him. A waitress, that's what she was, in a cheap café. And as soon as she got him to marry her, then she'd have none of him but asked for money to get out of his life. Little tramp!"

"Lots of people marry for money, but won't admit it," Granny answered. "And you leave Bruce alone."

"He's drinking," my mother said, and got out her hanky, blowing her nose loudly. "And now we know the terrible truth, I don't know what we'll do about the charivari that's planned for tomorrow night. Everybody's called me and planned to come. It's so embarrassing."

Granny bit her lip. Then she said firmly, "Well, let the valley people have the charivari. We'll go through with it and make the best of it."

"But they're not even really married," my mother protested. "All they've done is fight."

"Lots of people aren't married," Granny said calmly. "All they do is share the same quarters." She got up from the narrow bench on the side of the sheep wagon and said, "I'm going in and see Nancy.... You come with me, Jeannie. And if I sound anything but pleasant, you pinch me."

Nancy was sitting where we'd left her. She looked so pretty and tired that I wanted to run right to her and put my arms around her. Granny patted the girl's thin shoulder and said gently, "Come on and I'll show you to bed, honey."

Nancy moved as though she were walking in a dream and followed Granny to the big bedroom. She went over and put her hand on the patchwork quilt and said, "It's real nice. I always thought I'd like—" Then her hand drew back as if she'd touched a hot stove. She glared at us, saying fiercely, "It's all true. I married him to get the money!"

"You must have had a good reason to do such a thing," Granny said. "There's a pitcher of fresh milk in the kitchen and cookies in the jar beside it, Nancy. If you get hungry, help yourself."

"I'm not much," Nancy's head sank lower. "He's better off without me."

"Don't think you can decide what's best for another person," Granny said. "Good night, Nancy."

We closed the outside door of the old house and went over to the bunkhouse. Through the window we could see my brother. He had a big bottle on the table, and he lifted it up and yelled, "Champagne for the bride!" Then he flung the bottle across the room, and it shattered against the old logs.

"My!" Granny said wonderingly. "Didn't know he had that much spark in 'im. He never acted this way about any of the other women in his life. Why, when he broke off with the widow, he came to my house, and I cooked him a chicken dinner. He ate it all and went to sleep on the couch. Never budged when I took off his shoes, either."

The next morning it was cloudy and sultry. I could smell rain on the wind. The telephone kept ringing and ringing. Everybody in the valley was coming to the charivari. My father sat glumly by the stove and said it was the worst hoax since somebody stuffed the ballot box at the schoolboard election. My mother said it was a scandal as bad as when my father's younger brother ran off with the fortune-teller from the circus.

"I don't know why you take delight in bringing that up about my brother," my father complained.

Granny was the only one who seemed cheerful. She asked us down for a late breakfast at the old house. "To get acquainted with Nancy," she said.

Nancy was polite but quiet. She had on a dress with no sleeves, just thin straps over her shoulders, and she was barelegged. Bruce didn't come in to eat; he was still asleep in the bunkhouse. Granny did all the talking. While mother and father sat as stiff as could be and looked worried, Granny told Nancy about the old country and growing up by the sea. "Ah, the glens on a summer night!" Granny said. "Once I took up with a tramp who came along the shore to watch us dancing in the moonlight. Real fancy manners he had and not a tuppence to his name. 'Never blame folks for what they do on a summer night when the moon's out,' he said. 'They've no more control than a seed in the ground when the rain and sun start making love to it.'"

"You've never told us that one before," my father said, looking at Granny with something like suspicion on his face.

"I never had Nancy here before. She reminds me of myself. Of course, I was thinner then. But what's there to do but eat when a body gets too old to be falling in love? Dear me, it's boring at times." She gave a great loud yawn.

A small sound came from Nancy, and I saw she was smiling. It was wonderful when she smiled, like the sun coming out on the meadows. And suddenly my father laughed and my mother laughed, and for that moment it was as though my brother had brought home a real bride who would be one of us. Then it began to rain and the room turned dark.

"It's going to last all day and all night," my father said. And he got up and put on his hat and walked out, his breakfast half finished.

"It's a weak-minded soul who lets the weather warp his appetite," Granny said, looking disgusted.

"He ate earlier," my mother explained, turning to Nancy. And she added with pride in her tone, "We got up early, four o'clock."

"I go to work at two," Nancy said squaring her shoulders and looking prouder than my mother. "I work the early shift at the café."

My brother Bruce came stumbling in, his hair on end and his clothes rumpled. He didn't notice any of us but Nancy. "I've had enough," he said. "You win. You don't have to stay another minute."

Nancy jumped up. I could see she was shaking. "You bought me, that's why I won't stay! It was only a bet with those silly cattlemen who ate supper with you at the café. I said I'd go ahead with the ceremony because I could use the money, but I never promised to come here so you could show me off—like a cow you traded for!"

My brother was very angry. He dug in his pocket and brought out some bills and laid them on the table. "There! Bail your no-good brother out of jail, then!"

"He's not no-good. He only got in with the wrong people. But you wouldn't understand,"—her mouth quivered—"not with your fine family background and your money and this— this beautiful place to live. You never grew up poor in a city— a dozen people in two rooms and no place to go to be alone. You're nothing but a spoiled, selfish—" Her hands fastened like claws on the bills and she began to count the money. "One hundred, two hundred, three hundred, five hundred—is this what your clever friends bet you couldn't marry me?"

"That's it," he said.

"Thanks," Nancy said coldly and thrust the money in her pocket.

Granny said, "Oh, I wouldn't feel too huffed about it, Nancy. One of the best citizens of this county won his wife in a poker game. He was off to Laramie shipping cattle. She turned out to be a wonderful wife and one of my best friends. A person's always gambling on a marriage, Nancy. I'd say Bruce made a shrewd bet, but he's too damn stubborn to admit it."

Nancy moved toward the bedroom door. "I'd appreciate a ride to town," she said, "but I'll walk if I have to."

"Just a minute," Bruce caught her arm. "If you stay through tonight, I'll double the money."

"You will? Why?"

"A lot of people want to charivari us the way they do every newly-married couple. I'd like everybody to meet you."

Nancy laughed harshly. "That's pride for you! Well, why shouldn't I stay until morning? I'm making money faster than slinging hash. Now, if you'll please take your big paws off my arm—" She brushed past him with a swish of her skirt and closed the bedroom door behind her.

"Bruce," Granny said, "wash your face and comb your hair. You'll find aspirin in the medicine chest. The rest of you clear out. I don't want anybody around here until charivari time. Nancy needs the quiet." Granny gave a wicked little grin. "She can count her money in peace."

"It's terrible," my mother said. "A thousand dollars! What will John McKenzie say?"

"He'll suffer," Granny replied and chuckled.

All day it rained and the river rose to bankful, but nobody paid much attention, for the telephone kept on ringing and the very air seemed to crackle with the excitement of the coming party. My mother said when a McKenzie got married it was a real special day in the valley. Then she sighed and added, "It's a shame it isn't a right marriage. I don't know how we'll hold our heads up afterward."

"We're going through with it for Bruce's sake," my father answered. "We couldn't call the charivari off now. We've waited too long. I wish I'd kept my mouth shut about the widow and Fanny Hankins and Mary Duncan. They'd never have got us in a mess like this."

It was dark when we went down to the old house. The river's swollen angry murmuring filled the night. Bruce met us at the door. "Come in," he said. "Join the cozy family scene."

Granny was knitting, and Nancy was reading a book. Nancy's hair looked brighter than ever, and it was combed more plain. I wondered if she'd washed it and added the tint Granny spoke of. She was wearing stockings and a pretty blue dress. "No one in the valley is as beautiful as Nancy," I said. She held out her hand to me then, and I ran to stand beside her.

It wasn't long until I heard the roar of cars and the cracking of pistols. Nancy's eyes got round, and she looked scared. There was more shooting, wild yelling and the rattling of tin cans. Then people came rushing into the house. The men kissed Nancy, and the women kissed Bruce. Then the men shouted, "Off to the water trough with the groom! Dip him!" And two big ranchers lifted Bruce and carried him toward the door while he shouted and swore and struggled.

"Stop them!" Nancy cried, hurrying to Granny. "He's got a cold and they might—"

"Won't hurt that McKenzie temper to be cooled off a little," Granny said soothingly. Then she shouted to the men in the far end of the room. "Get the fiddles going, boys. I'm in a dancing mood."

Oh, how the fiddles sang! With a whoop and a holler the caller began. "Birdie hop out and crow hop in; all join hands and circle again! Square up! Square up! I come for fun."

And the furniture was all pushed back, and couples began to bob and sway, prance and curtsy. The skirts of the women flew wide like big flowers in a high wind, and Granny got right out in her red dress and danced with the rest of them even if she did look a little tired. A big cowboy grabbed Nancy, and another grabbed me and I held onto his belt to keep from flying off the floor.

The men came back with Bruce, who was soaking wet and grinning. And while he went to change to dry clothes, the dancing went on until the old house shook and red dust trickled from the mud chinked between the logs.

Bruce never got to dance with Nancy, for she was the most popular woman there. She kept whirling from one partner to another until her cheeks were red and her eyes sparkled. Her shiny hair fell over her forehead, and the blue dress swung high, wide and handsome and showed her pretty legs.

After a while the fiddlers went outside to rest, and I could smell coffee cooking in the kitchen. I pushed through the women to get a drink of water, and there was Nancy, staring at all the cakes and pies, salads and fried chicken. "And homemade pickles," she said touching a jar. "Gee!"

One of the women took a pickle from a jar and said to Nancy, "Open your mouth, honey. These are special — the best for the bride of Bruce McKenzie."

But Nancy moved back and said with a funny little choke in her voice, "I guess I don't want any."

It was raining harder at midnight. A cloudburst, somebody said, but the people didn't pay any attention, for the mock wedding was about to begin. Big Bill Barnes was the bride and wore one of Granny's old dresses. A little bow-legged puncher from the Bar C was the bridegroom, and the head of the women's club read a poem about his pants being cut with a circular saw. The doctor was the preacher and read the ceremony from the mail-order catalogue. And funniest were two hired hands from the neighboring ranch who were dressed as flower girls and skipped through the living room tossing sagebrush from two old slop jars.

Everybody was laughing so hard we didn't notice Granny was missing until Bruce looked around and said, "Where's Granny?" Then one of the women spoke. "She said she was tired and going to take a little rest in the wagon."

"Wagon?" My father's voice was strained. "What wagon?"

"The sheep wagon," I said. "By the river."

Maybe it was then I heard the terrible rush and roar of the water outside, or maybe I only heard Nancy scream and saw her running like a deer and gone from the house before anyone else could move. Then my father was running, too, and everyone crowded out into the wet, dark night, some carrying flashlights and the men shouting, "Light the lanterns!"

Down the slippery hill slope we went to the river, the lanterns bobbing. And I couldn't see much except that the sheep wagon wasn't where it was supposed to be. There was only water, black and ugly and swirling along logs and pieces of wood and torn-up willows. I couldn't tell where the bank of the river began. And across the dark, rising above the sound of the water, came Nancy's voice, thin and high, "Granny! Granny!"

We ran toward that sound, and then the people came to a stop. In the glare from the flashlights and lanterns, I saw the sheep wagon turned on its side and half under water. Then I saw something else—Nancy in water to her waist and holding Granny's head against her breast. Her back was braced to a bunch of logs that were jammed against a willow. Her face was pale and her mouth hanging open like she'd been running too far or too fast, and Granny's white hair hung over her arms and trailed in the water.

There was a sudden roaring in the night. My father shouted. "Grab them! More water's coming! Run for the house, all of you!"

I wanted to stay as Bruce and my father plunged toward Nancy and Granny, but people pushed me along, back up the hill toward the old house.

They brought Granny and Nancy in and put both of them in the bedrooms, and river water ran from their clothes and soaked into the pretty patchwork quilt. Bruce was kneeling by Nancy and wiping her face with a towel, and my father was bending over Granny. It was Granny who spoke first. She half raised herself and said, "Damn it, pull down my skirt! You think I want my legs showing the shape they're in?"

Then my father hurried to Nancy and started stroking the wet tinted hair. "Poor wee thing," he murmured, "risking her life to save one of us."

"Nancy," Bruce said, lifting her till he held her against his chest, "when I made the bet, I didn't know I'd fall in love with you."

Nancy sneezed, and Bruce fumbled for a hanky to wipe her nose. He made a terrible job of it, but she didn't seem to mind. "I don't have a brother in jail," she said, coughing. "But the rest of it about no family and growing up poor is true. I had to think of a reason for letting you marry me, and I thought — I thought —" She sneezed again and muttered, "I know it was terrible to marry a man I didn't even know — but I couldn't help myself."

Granny heaved herself off the bed. "Like the grass when the sun and rain make love to it," she said, smiling. Then she waddled toward the door, shooing the people before her like flies. "Scat! Out of here, all of you!"

She sat down, shivering, at the worn table in the living room. My mother hurried to her with a cup of tea. Granny looked at it, sniffed and pushed the cup aside. "I'll have stronger stuff than this," she said sternly, "but in the same amount." Then she put her arm around me and pulled me close to her.

ONE NEW YEAR'S DAY, Peg went next door to borrow a cup of flour. There she met a man named Robert Brady and his wife. Brady began telling stories about his father, an old time saddlemaker who had once made a "Mother Hubbard" saddle for an outlaw. Brady's description of the saddle intrigued her. Made from one large piece of leather, the "Mother Hubbard" has no jockey skirts — just one big skirt on either side — and fenders coming out underneath.

Peg became so interested in the conversation that the dinner simmering on her stove at home burned. A story had begun in her mind, about a saddlemaker named Big Lee

"The Bride Wore Spurs" was published in the *American Magazine* in October 1953. When Peg was invited to edit an anthology for Western Writers of America, of which she was a member for many years, she included this story (*Western Romances*; Greenwich, Connecticut: Fawcett, 1973).

THE BRIDE WORE SPURS

IF YOU'RE UP IN THE valley, you might still find a Big Lee saddle hanging in one of the barns. There are a few left, but folks won't part with them, for Big Lee's become a legend. Of course, saddles have changed, and now all the cowpokes ride the ones with bull-moose trees that became so popular along with rodeos, but old-timers will tell you that no one can make a saddle the way Big Lee did, shaping it exactly right for a man and putting it together with good leather that would stand up to all kinds of wear and weather.

Big Lee suited his name. He was six feet three in his stocking feet and had powerful shoulders and narrow hips. Maybe it was his size that impressed folks to elect him sheriff, although he didn't want the job and hung the shiny star on the wall of his saddle tent and paid no heed to it at all. Or maybe they elected him because he was so quiet and never looked for trouble and wouldn't bother the men who slapped their brands on other men's calves.

The valley was wild then and the range open, and some big cattlemen were willing to dicker with the outlaws who rode in the North Fork country. If a sheriff went out of town to enforce the law, he didn't come back, and there wasn't a married man in the country who would take the job.

Ace McLean, who ran the outlaw bunch, said they were

lucky when Big Lee was elected sheriff. "We won't have to waste no lead on him," he said.

And it looked like Ace had it figured right, for Big Lee kept right on making and repairing saddles, and when Ace and his gang came in and shot up the town, Big Lee acted like he didn't hear the commotion.

This made some folks mad, and a group of men who owned the store, the livery stable, and the town's three saloons went to see Big Lee and told him off properly.

Big Lee took a piece of leather out of the soaking tank and put it on a marble slab on his work table. He found a big darning needle and began drawing the head of a Texas longhorn steer on the wet leather and let on like he didn't hear the ranting of the men.

After a while he looked up and said, "It's a raw country, and it's got to grow up slow. You can't wipe out rustlers overnight. Besides, Ace hasn't bothered me none." Then he looked at the men and added, "Could be you'd find a man who's set on getting himself shot. There's the badge. Take it. I don't want it."

But they left the shiny star hanging on the side of the tent, for they couldn't figure out anyone else to pin it on and had no hankering to get shot themselves.

After they'd gone, Big Lee cooked himself a pot of coffee on the coal range in one corner. Then he stood in the tent doorway, drinking coffee and looking up Main Street, which was a dozen rough, slab buildings with the sagebrush growing around them and the prairie stretching toward the mountain on all sides.

It's a funny thing, he thought, *that a man can't be left alone to do what he wants without folks trying to force other jobs on him—like going after Ace McLean.*

Big Lee shifted his weight from one side to the other and

smoothed the front of his leather apron. All he cared about was making saddles. Let somebody else worry over bringing law and order to the valley. A man ought to content himself with what he was cut out to do.

He saw three riders coming down the deserted street, the hoofs of the horses sending up little spurts of dust in the still air. They came on toward him and pulled up before his tent.

They were poor folks. He could tell that right off. Not so much by their worn saddles, lean-flanked horses, and shabby boots as by their faces, which had the look of wanting things and not being sure they'd ever get them. He took the girl for a boy until she dismounted and pulled off the dusty hat and shook out her hair.

It was the kind of hair that even a solitary man like Big Lee looked at twice, for it was brighter than a gold-colored aspen leaf in the fall, and it didn't go with her sun-browned face, her man's pants, and the determined thrust of her chin.

"You Big Lee Dunnigen?" the older man asked. He had a thin, dried-up face, all wrinkles around the eyes.

A face too old for his years, Big Lee thought.

"That's me," Big Lee replied.

"Name's Hank Davis," the stranger said. "Need some rope, and they told me you had a saddle shop. We're new here — just come in from Kansas last month. We're out on the North Fork."

North Fork River country, Big Lee thought. *Good grass and plenty of water. Fine land for a poor man to make a start with a few head of cows — if Ace McLean didn't have his hangout there.*

"You ought to try the east side of the valley instead of North Fork country," Big Lee said. "East side's got good range, too."

"North Fork suits us mighty fine," Hank Davis said.

"This is my daughter, Sara, and my son, Charlie."

Big Lee nodded. The boy was young and thin, with big red hands—not more than fourteen years old, Big Lee figured. The girl looked tired and dusty.

Not much of a saddle, Big Lee thought. *About to fall apart.* She lifted her hair back from her neck with her hand, holding it up so the air could move next to her skin.

Big Lee said, "Come inside. It's cooler in there."

The tent was large and boarded halfway up the sides, and the air smelled sharply of good leather. There was heavy leather cut from the backs of hides and ready to be used for saddle skirts and seats, thin leather from belly and flank for reins and saddle strings, and fine calfskin for making latigos.

Pushing the stitching horse out of the way, Big Lee said, "Sit there on the bunk and I'll rustle you up some rope."

It was the girl who went to the assembly horse and stood looking at the saddle that Lee had been carving. The assembly horse was made of wood and shaped like a horse's withers.

Her small browned hand went out and stroked the leather skirt of the saddle, stroked it the way some women would finger a piece of fine silk.

He thought then that anyone so tall and slim and with such a brave, open face ought to ride a better saddle than the old rig she had there on the gaunt cow pony. He felt something he'd never before felt for a woman—a desire to see her have what she wanted.

Big Lee looked her over carefully. "Let's see," he said. "What inch tree would you take?"

Then her face changed, and he saw the hard pride on it. "Reckon my saddle suits me fine," she said coolly.

"Just wondered about your size," he replied. "I figure a twenty-inch tree'd be about right. Leave room for you to fill out. You're mighty thin, Miss Sara."

"Built like her mother," Hank Davis said, a sadness drifting across his wrinkled face. "Her mother was a high-strung filly and never carried an extra ounce of flesh. We planned to bring her out to this country, but she didn't live that long."

There was a silence. Then Big Lee said to Sara, "You ought to have a double rigging on your saddle. It would stay settled better when you got a calf on the end of a rope."

"Sara's right handy with a rope," the boy Charlie said. "Handier than I am."

"A rawhide-covered horn is what she needs," Big Lee continued, "and stirrups with rawhide laced in the leather covers. What inch stirrups you ridin', Miss Sara?"

She picked up the coil of rope he'd laid out for them and started toward the door. "Pay him, Pa," she said. "We've got to drift."

Prouder than all get out, Big Lee thought. *Proud and poor.*

"Two-inch stirrups would be right for her," he said to Hank Davis. "You know, I been dreaming up a special saddle for a long time. Don't know if I thought of it first or heard someone talk about it somewhere, but I've got this notion to make a saddle with one piece of leather — skirts, seat, and everything in one piece, see? Then slide the leather over the cantle and the pommel. No jockey skirts, just the one big skirt on either side and the fenders coming out underneath. Everything covered up — the way it is with a Mother Hubbard apron."

"Pa!" The girl's voice was sharp.

Hank Davis and Charlie stood up.

Big Lee picked up a tack hammer and pounded softly against the palm of his hand. "A Mother Hubbard saddle," he said dreamily. "Now, that would be something to see!"

Hank Davis paid for the rope and they left. Big Lee stood in the doorway and watched them ride away, Sara's hair glinting where it fell from under the old shabby hat.

Good folks, he thought. *Hard-working and hopeful, and too bad they settled on the North Fork near Ace McLean.* He remembered Sara's big eyes and the look in them when she had touched the saddle.

He went back into the tent and rolled out a hide on the floor. It wasn't big enough to make a saddle in one piece. Then he thought about seaming two pieces together. That wouldn't spoil a thing, for he made a neat, smooth seam. He set the hide back in its corner and found the scrap of leather he'd drawn the steer's head on.

"How'd that suit you, Sara?" he murmured. "A fancied-up saddle with a steer's head in each corner of the skirts."

Shucks, he thought, *I must be gettin' soft in the head, for she couldn't pay for that kind of saddle — not now or later. They won't have a herd of cows long — not with Ace runnin' around out there with a hot iron in his hand and a long rope ready.*

Still, he thought, *a man has to do some things just for the pleasure of doing them.* And it wasn't like he was letting himself fall in love with her. No, for a man traveled farther and faster if he made up his mind to go it alone. There wasn't any harm in making her a saddle, though, just as a present that would tell her she was welcome in the valley....

It was along toward dusk when Ace McLean rode up with his two top men. Ace came into the saddle shop wearing his guns — the way he always did — and said to Big Lee, "Got any good cinches?"

"Right from Cheyenne," Big Lee said. "Take a look at 'em." And he spread the cinches out on his workbench.

"Gimme four," Ace said, dragging a roll of bills from his pocket. He was broad and thick-shouldered, with a round, flushed face and small blue eyes.

"Met your neighbors," Big Lee said.

"Neighbors?" Ace's crooked teeth hung out in a grin. "You mean that Kansan with a few cows who thinks he's goin' to ranch on the North Fork?"

"Seemed like a nice fella," Big Lee said. "Ought to be room enough for both of you, Ace."

Ace looked sharply at Big Lee, "Meanin' what?"

Big Lee shrugged. "Meanin' he's just a poor Kansan trying to get a start in the cow business. If you've got to use the long rope and the hot irons, Ace, use 'em on the big men who can stand the loss."

"I don't have troubles with the big ones," Ace said. "They go along with me." He picked up the cinches and left.

Big Lee stood quietly, listening to the sound of hoofbeats fading away in the evening stillness. The men who ran big herds on the open range tried to deal peacefully with McLean. Some even bought his protection against the drifters who came into the valley and hoped to pick up a few strays and start their own herds. No one wanted trouble with Ace McLean.

Big Lee looked at the pistol and cartridge belt hanging at the end of his bunk. He picked them up, buckled on the belt, and walked out across the prairie a short distance from his saddle shop. He drew the gun and took a few shots at a jack rabbit and missed.

Shucks, he thought, *I never was a man to handle a gun.*

With a little sigh, he went back into the tent and hung the belt and gun in the usual place. The only thing to do was to persuade Hank Davis to move away from the North Fork range.

Early the next morning, Big Lee went to the livery stable, got his horse, and rode out toward the North Fork country. It was a fine day, with a breeze blowing out of the north. The antelope were gathered at the water holes drinking. When they saw him, they wheeled and scampered away, their white rumps flashing in the sunlight.

The North Fork River stretched back into a green valley with aspen-covered slopes rising on either side. He found the tents just where he had expected to find them, at the head of the valley, set up next to a thick fringe of aspen with the grassy bottomland sprawling before them.

At first he thought there wasn't anyone around, and then Sara came out of the largest tent. She was wearing men's pants and run over boots and a buckskin shirt that was laced up the front. Her hair was brighter than he remembered.

"Where's your pa?" Big Lee said.

"He's out with the cattle," and she nodded toward the aspen grove behind the tent. "The flies drive them to shade when the sun starts getting hot."

He dismounted and began rolling a cigarette. "Miss Sara," he said, "I wish you and your folks would move to the east side of the valley. You're not wanted here."

Her chin lifted stubbornly. "Who doesn't want us?"

He licked the cigarette paper and lighted up before answering. "Ace McLean."

"He doesn't own this whole country," she said. "And he's not running us off. We've heard about him and we're prepared. We're not the kind of people to be bluffed, Mr. Dunnigen."

"I know," he said. "That's why I came out this morning. There's been a lot of blood shed over cattle in this country. All you have to do is move to the east side. He won't bother you there."

Angry lights glinted in her eyes. "You're the sheriff," she said tartly. "Why don't you do something about McLean?"

"I'm a saddlemaker," he replied, a flush spreading over his cheeks. "I never wanted the sheriff's job. I told 'em so. I took off the star — and when they wouldn't take it back, I hung it on my tent wall. I told 'em to find somebody else."

She looked him over carefully, as though examining every

part of him. He began to feel uncomfortable. Then she said, "We may be from Kansas, Mr. Dunnigen, and we may not have much to start on, but we're not cowards!" She turned and went into the tent.

Big Lee headed back toward town. "Some folks just won't listen to reason," he muttered. Halfway across the flats, he yanked out his gun and shot at some prairie dogs. They kept on barking right in his face. Swearing, Big Lee stuck the gun back in the holster. *I'll find somebody to buy their cattle,* he thought. *Maybe if they had some money, they wouldn't mind movin' off the North Fork.*

When he hit town he met a few ranchers and talked with them, but they weren't interested in Hank Davis or his little bunch of cows.

"We're sellin', not buyin'," they said.

That night Big Lee worked late and hard on the special saddle, putting his heart into the job, trying to shut away the sound of Sara's voice, trying to forget the scorn in her gray eyes.

Two days later, young Charlie rode up to the saddle shop. "I tore off a stirrup chasing cows," he said. "It don't stay fixed."

Big Lee put on new stirrups and a new cinch. "No charge," he told Charlie. "I been wantin' to get rid of that cinch and the stirrups. They're used ones, but I guess they'll last you a little while."

Charlie looked down at the floor. "We don't take somethin' for nothin'," he said.

"Take it!" Big Lee shouted impatiently. "I was throwin' this stuff away anyhow."

Charlie didn't say anything. Big Lee watched him ride toward the North Fork with a sense of helplessness. "They're all alike," he said to himself. "They're the kind of people that'll squat out there like settin' hens until Ace McLean kills 'em."

He didn't see Sara for three weeks after that, and by then

he had the saddle almost finished. It was the night of the dance in the log schoolhouse, which had just been completed. When he came in and heard the fiddles and saw her standing by her father, his heart beat loudly in his big chest, and he felt a strange aching need to go to her.

She was wearing a bright new dress, and it made her look different from the way she looked wearing the old pants and boots. It made her a woman whose mouth was soft and whose eyes made talk all of their own. He asked her to dance and heard the singing fiddles saying what was in his heart.

At first she just looked at him as though she intended to say no to his invitation. Then Hank Davis gave her a little shove and winked at Big Lee. They began to dance, and all the thoughts Big Lee had held about traveling far and fast and alone were forgotten. The skirt of the dress belled out and swept back to wrap against him, binding him to her, making it seem they were meant never to be separated again.

When the dance was over, he took her hand and drew her outside, where the sky was bright with stars.

"I got something to show you," he said. "Come on."

They walked across the prairie to his saddle shop, and he took her in and lighted the lantern. When she saw the saddle on the assembly horse, her hand went up to her throat. Her breath caught with a little broken sound, and she just stared at it.

"It's for you," he said, his words rushing out. "It's a present — not quite finished yet, but I — I couldn't wait to have you see it. There ain't another saddle in the world like it, Sara. Far as I'm concerned, there never will be. It was made special — for you."

She turned to him then, the light welling up in her eyes as she started to speak. Might have been she was only going to say thank you — or maybe going to say a lot more — but Big

Lee didn't find out, for just then Hank Davis came running into the tent.

"We gotta get home, Sara!" he cried, and Big Lee noticed the white face and shaking hands. "We gotta get home quick. Ace McLean run off part of our cattle and shot Charlie."

"Charlie!" Sara's face crumpled. "Oh, Pa — is he —"

"No, it's his leg. He rode clear to town. I've got the doc working on him now. Looks like it's up to you and me, honey."

She swept past Big Lee as though she had forgotten him.

When they had gone, he stood there staring into the night. *I told her,* he thought. *I tried to get them to move. I did what I could and she wouldn't listen.* He looked at the sheriff's badge hanging on the side of the tent. It glistened in the yellow lantern light. *I'm not the law,* he thought. *I wasn't born to handle a gun. I can't keep a fool Kansan from losing his cattle — and maybe his life.*

He tried to sleep and couldn't. He went back to working on the saddle, working feverishly to still the rising clamor of his conscience. After a while he sensed rather than heard the movement outside the tent. The door came open slowly, and he saw Ace McLean and beyond him the two top men standing back toward the shadows.

Ace spoke first. "Up late, ain't you, Big Lee?"

"Late enough," Big Lee said. He straightened, his back aching from being so long in one position. "Ace," he said, "you're gettin' pretty low when you shoot a kid."

"He was takin' a man's place and packin' a man's gun."

"He's still just a kid — not more than fourteen."

"He's old enough to shoot a gun. He shot at me."

"You were botherin' their cattle, Ace. Why can't you leave them alone?" Big Lee heard his voice go rough and angry.

But Ace wasn't paying any heed to him. Ace was looking at the Mother Hubbard saddle. He made a whistling sound and walked up to it and ran his hands over the leather. "Some rig. How much, Big Lee?"

"Not for sale," Big Lee said shortly.

"Name your price. I'll pay it." Ace McLean's small eyes grew bright as he bent to examine the steer's head stamped on a corner of the skirt.

"Get your big paws off her saddle!" Big Lee shouted, his fists clenched, his legs trembling. "And get out!"

He saw the gun glint in Ace McLean's hand, heard Ace's voice, cold and thin, saying, "What I hanker for, I take, Big Lee—one way or another. Get him, boys!"

Big Lee lunged at Ace. He caught the hand holding the gun and twisted it back. They went down hard, rolling over and over on the floor, upsetting the stitching horse, overturning the soaking tank. Big Lee felt the pain in his head as something struck him again and again, but he fought like a wildcat—fought and swore, and felt the darkness closing in on him....

When he came to, thin daylight streamed into the littered tent. Slowly and painfully he got to his feet and saw around him the hacked leather, the broken assembly horse, the ripped canvas of the walls. The Mother Hubbard saddle was gone. A cold, hard anger stirred in him. Settling his hat on his blood-matted hair, he reached for his gun belt that still hung on the foot of his bunk. He started for the livery stable, staggering from side to side as he walked through the dew-wet sagebrush.

It was past sunrise when he rode his lathered horse to the Davis tents on the North Fork. As he was going past, Sara came out. Big Lee kept on riding, only half hearing her as she cried, "Lee! Lee! Your face—it's all bloody! Lee—wait!"

Nothing to wait for, Sara, he thought. *I'm not coming*

back, but he'll never live to ride that saddle!

The night's coolness still lingered in the timber, and the wild pea vines rose tall, dragging against his stirrups. He followed the river, knowing he'd come to Ace McLean's cabin before long. He found it before he expected to, coming suddenly out of the aspen to a grassy park that lay at the foot of a ridge. Across the clearing he saw the dirt-roofed cabin, the corrals and horses close by. There was no smoke curling from the chimney, and he knew they still slept, having no need to rise early like poor folks who tried to live the honest way.

He went first to the corral where saddles hung over the top poles, but the Mother Hubbard wasn't there. He knew then that Ace McLean had taken it inside the cabin. Lightheaded, with a strange sense of detachment, Big Lee walked slowly to the cabin. He drew his gun, kicked open the door, and walked in. He saw the saddle there in the middle of the floor, and beyond it, as though in some distorted dream, Ace McLean rising and coming toward him, the gun leaping in his hand.

Big Lee felt the burn along his shoulder, as though lightning had struck him. He moved forward, firing and firing until the empty click told him the gun was empty. Then he buckled forward, falling across the saddle, his big hands clutching at the familiar leather.

That was where they found him later that morning. He lay across the Mother Hubbard, and he was smiling. Near him Ace McLean lay also, his face drawn in death. It was Sara who knelt by Big Lee and cut away his bloody clothes and packed his wounds with moss and leaves. And it was Sara who kissed him when he opened his eyes along about sundown....

Folks in the valley will tell you that Big Lee killed ten men that morning, but Sara knows the truth. Sara's ninety-two years old, and you'll find her at the home place on the North Fork.

"Ten?" she'll say, rubbing a hand across her eyes as though to clear her mind. "No, there were only three. Ace and his two top men. The others had gone somewhere, and they never did come back." Then she'll smile and tell you Big Lee didn't kill anybody. "It was my father and I who shot them. We followed Lee that morning."

The rocker will creak on the hard floor of the big living room, and then the creaking will stop. "Yes," Sara will say, "Lee was sheriff for forty years in the valley, and a fine sheriff he was. He was feared and respected. But he never would wear that star."

Some folks will tell you Big Lee carried nine bullets in him until the day he died.

"No," Sara will say carefully. "It was only five, but they didn't slow him up. He was a big man — a lot like my grandson. No, Lee didn't ever kill anybody. He wasn't any hand with guns. Worst shot in the country. Saddles were his specialty."

Then she'll look at the Mother Hubbard hanging there on the living room wall, and such a softness comes in her eyes that you forget she's an old woman with a lifetime behind her.

BEFORE ITS PUBLICATION in a major market, "Green Willow Growing" was rejected by seven magazines. Several editors wrote letters, commenting on the fine and beautifully told story. One editor suggested that Peg rewrite it and "stir up a gun fight." Peg declined, replying in a letter to him that it was "not the kind of story where men face each other with blazing guns. As a matter of fact...I have no desire to stir up anything; all I wish to say was in the story." She considered it among her best work.

"Green Willow Growing" eventually appeared in *Collier's* — a top-paying market — in March 1952 and was later sold to six foreign markets. For some years after it was written, when Peg traveled to workshops and conferences, she met people who remembered the story of the willow shoot and the three people who wanted to plant it.

Writing about this story in *Wyoming — the Feature and Discussion Magazine of the Equality State* in the April-May 1957 issue, Peg noted that she "felt great respect and sympathy for many hired men, many drifting men with their own clear concepts of principle and into ["Green Willow Growing"] I tried to put a part of the reality of their characters."

It is an emotional story, and one which contains large pieces of Wyoming landscape.

GREEN WILLOW GROWING

TOM HARRISON WANTED to put his arms around his wife and hold her close to him, for he no longer felt sure of himself, no longer was certain a job was waiting beyond the next hill or the next valley. He had come to the end of his road, and this knowledge lay like a sickness inside him.

He turned toward her, but the child slept between them, her face small and lovely in the moonlight. He looked away from the child and toward the old lard pail which glinted there in the clearing by the river. He could see the dark outline of the willow rising out of the lard pail, a young branch of willow the child had kept in water until the roots were long and tangled. Now the willow was ready for the earth, but they had no place to call their own, no place where a little girl could plant her willow and watch it grow.

He closed his eyes and hoped for sleep to blot out the sense of frustration and failure that clouded all his thinking. There was only one thing left now — a job in town; and he disliked town, for he was a ranch-born man and he had known only ranches, and a few days in any town left him feeling depleted and like a caged animal wanting to be free.

Still, he would have tried for a town job before now if Judith, his wife, hadn't protested. "Tom," she had said again yesterday, "you'd never be happy at anything but ranching. There might be a chance —"

They had been driving down the highway, away from a ranch house, and he had said, "That was the last chance," not telling her he had practically offered to work for his room and board, not confessing the shame he had felt as he'd stood before the sun-wrinkled rancher and said, "I'm not particular. I'll do anything if you can use me."

The rancher's eyes had taken him apart, and then the man had looked away as though he were embarrassed. "Full up," he'd said gruffly. "No time of year to be looking for a job, young fella."

The rancher had been right, Tom thought. *It wasn't the time of year to be looking for a job — not in the ranch country.* There was a lot of talk about labor shortage but he knew only too well that this didn't apply to steady men who stayed with ranching year in and year out. It was true there was a shortage of migratory workers — the drifting men who put up hay, picked cherries, harvested beets or dug potatoes. Once, these men had returned yearly, like the birds; now city jobs had absorbed many of them.

But Tom wasn't a drifting man; he was a steady man who wanted to stay put. And now nobody would hire him, for ranchers had their old year-round hands or had hired new ones early in spring. No rancher, he thought with bitter honesty, was going to wait until the end of June to find a steady man. There was too much work that needed doing. And no rancher was going to hire a man with a wife and kid and let them cool their heels until haying time in August.

He sighed and shifted wearily in the hard bed; they had come in the evening to this Wyoming valley bordered by peaks that thrust against the sky like giant blue teeth. And tomorrow — tomorrow there wouldn't be anything left but a job in town.

Wind played among the cottonwood trees towering above his head, and his hard brown fingers dragged the tarpaulin closer. *Like gypsies*, he thought bitterly, *sleeping along creek banks, begging to live. I never meant to bring her to this.* Again his hand groped toward his wife. He heard her move, and then her fingers touched his across the sleeping child and her touch was warm and gentle, as though she were saying, "It doesn't matter, Tom." And this hurt him more than ever.

He knew she wasn't sleeping, and he said softly, so as not to wake Penny, their child, "I haven't taken very good care of you, Judith."

"I wouldn't say that, Tom. We've had"—she paused— "extra expense."

He knew she was referring to his mother and the years they'd kept her in the sanitarium. It cost a lot to live, but sometimes it seemed to cost more to die. He'd had no choice, and Judith had complained only once. She'd watched him write a check, his fingers holding hard to the scratching pen, and she'd suddenly cried out, "It's not fair! There's Penny and our whole life together and your mother's old and doesn't even know us and —" Then her hand had come up and pressed against her mouth and her eyes had looked stricken.

"Oh, Tom, I'm sorry!"

He hadn't blamed her, for he'd thought the same thing so many times but never said it.

Now her fingers tightened over his, and she added, "And you know, Tom, we haven't had any breaks."

No, he thought, staring at the clean, sharp shapes of the mountains, *they hadn't had any breaks*. There was that job managing Burk Flannerty's cattle outfit. They'd been there three years and managed to start a very small bank account. Then Burk had sold out and the new owner had brought his foreman with him.

"Sorry, Tom," Burk had said, "but you'll find something."

There was the job he'd got as foreman of the old Simkins place down in Colorado. He'd been trying hard to get on his feet there, for his mother's expenses were draining him dry. Simkins had decided to retire and Simkins' son had taken over.

"Sorry, Tom," the son had said, "but I'll be running the ranch now. You wouldn't be happy being my hired man, not after you've been foreman. But you'll find something. You're a good man."

Then, this spring, his mother had died. He was ashamed of the relief he had felt at knowing he no longer had those bills to meet. After all, he told himself, she'd lain helpless for six years, helpless and not knowing who he was when he touched her hand or spoke her name. But still he felt guilty. *A man ought not to be so pushed for money,* he thought.

They'd thought everything would work out, until last month when Pete Evans called him into the office and said, "Tom, you've been a good man, but my daughter's getting tired of town life. She wants to bring her husband back here and run the ranch." Pete had looked past him toward the sage-brush-flecked prairie that ran between the ranch and town. "I don't figure he'll make much of a rancher, Tom, but she's my daughter and I've got to look out for her. You can understand how it is. You better find something else, Tom."

They were practically broke after they'd paid for his mother's funeral and cleaned up the few bills that were left, and it was the wrong time of year to find work. Most ranchers had already hired their steady men. He'd spent what little money he had running all over the country and trying desperately to find a job.

First he'd looked for a place to lease, for that had always been his dream. Then he'd tried to get a foreman's job. Finally, he offered himself as a hired man at ninety dollars a month, never daring to think how he'd send Penny to school, never letting himself wonder when he'd be able to buy Judith that new dress she'd been waiting for.

Penny turned, murmuring in her sleep, and snuggled against him. His big arm caught her and held her close with sudden, fierce love. "We'll find a place to plant that willow," he'd promised. Her big blue eyes had shone with adoration and her slim brown hands had held up the willow. "Look, Daddy, it's got long hair of its own."

She had a passion for the outdoors and for all living things. Some people had told him he loved her too much, as though such a thing could ever be possible. And it was the same way with him and Judith. His wife, his child—he felt the pain tight in his throat.

He'd failed them and failed himself and he didn't know why. Certainly he had tried—maybe too hard; maybe men saw the naked desperation in his eyes and it made them uneasy. Maybe it would have been better if he'd stooped to ask Judith to go back to her parents, who thought she'd married beneath her, being a college graduate and taking up with him when he was jingling horses on a dude ranch. He hadn't felt beaten then; he'd been bold and sure of himself, for he'd had a little money saved and he'd figured someday he'd have his own ranch. And he'd known then he couldn't live without Judith.

He'd tried to read more after they were married, tried because she had the college degree and he didn't, but he wasn't much for books. It seemed they were only a pale shadow of the real things he knew, and it was his way to read the land and all that was a part of it and to draw his simple knowledge from this. And finally Judith had said, pressing her face against him and holding him tightly, "Tom, don't try to make yourself over. Reading isn't everything; a college degree isn't everything."

"I want Penny to have it," he said. "Four years at the best college we can find."

And now, now he had ten dollars in his pocket and no job, and they slept on the ground like gypsies.

He was still awake when the light began to thin in the east and the shapes of the mountains moved closer, the mists trailing out of the canyons. Then, at last, his burning eyelids closed.

When he woke up, they were up and starting breakfast. Penny's blond hair hung in two neat braids and her blue jeans were clean and she wore a sweater the same rich, brown color as Judith's hair.

They didn't know he was awake, and he watched them, loving them and seeing in his tall, dark-eyed wife, with her fine rounded hips and high breasts, the symbol of all that man has lived and died for, and seeing in his child the promise of the future. It was a good thought and he held on to it, remembering other mornings, mornings when he'd got up in the winter dark to milk cows and Penny had come softly into the kitchen that held yellow-gold light from the kerosene lamp. She was always up early and, while he built the fire for Judith, Penny would put on the heavy coat and old Scotch cap with ear flaps and find her mittens. Together they would go through the snow to the barn, her thin, reedlike voice reminding him of the birds that would come back when the ridges bared off with spring.

"I gave the old cow extra hay last night, Daddy. She needs it so she'll have milk for us. Look at her, Daddy. She's glad to see us this morning." And then Penny would put her arms around the old cow's neck and murmur in her ear.

And when they came back to the house and the good smells of breakfast, Judith would say to Penny, "Honey, you ought to sleep more." Then she would kiss them, and he would forget winter and the long days ahead with the cold wind nagging him while he fed the cattle.

He stretched under the tarpaulin-covered blankets, and the warm thoughts passed away and the harshness of reality came at him and struck him hard in the pit of his stomach.

Then Penny saw him and came running, a tall child for her age, tall and thin and high-strung. Like a well-bred horse, he thought. She fell upon him, pressing her cheek to his and whispering, "Guess what's for breakfast."

He grinned, rubbing the stubble on his chin. "Mmm, let's see. Barbecued hens' teeth."

She giggled. "Try again."

"Scrambled frogs' tails."

"Oh, you silly!" And she began pounding him with her fists.

It was an old game and one they'd played many times and always enjoyed.

He got up then and struggled into his clothes. He found his shaving kit in the car and went down to the creek and washed and shaved. Then he came to his wife and put his arms around her and held her.

Over her shoulder, he saw she had a card table set up in the dew-wet grass and a clean cloth spread over the table. There was a tin cup in the center of the cloth and from the cup a spray of blue gentians nodded in the small morning wind.

She always makes something out of nothing, he thought. And he felt the clean, hard strength of his wife resting there in his arms, and for a moment he forgot his daughter. He was kissing Judith when he felt the tugging at his leg and looked down. Penny was laughing up at him.

"You women," he said, making his voice light, "sure beat me to the draw this mornin'."

Judith broke away from him and started the coffee. Penny made toast over the fire. It was burned but Tom ate it and told his daughter it was good and saw her pride.

They took a long time to straighten up the camp and pack their bedding in the two-wheeled trailer back of the old car. It was as though they prolonged the moment when they must drive away.

At last, Penny brought the willow to the car. "You promised today we'd plant it," she said.

"That's right, honey." Tom looked away from the trusting eyes and the tilted nose with the splash of freckles trailing across it.

"Drive on up this valley," Judith said. "We might as well see all of it."

Tom headed the car west, and the valley flowed past them. There were lush hay meadows on either side of the road, and farther back, toward the foothills, he could see ranch buildings — big buildings with red roofs and white sides. It was no poor man's country, but he looked with longing and tried to pretend this valley — or a part of it — might be his. But pretending didn't work, and his mouth felt drier as the miles passed.

"I figure I can pick up some kind of work in town," he said casually.

"But my willow!" Penny's voice was sharp. "You said we'd find a ranch and plant it."

He nodded and said, "This valley's as good a place as any to leave your willow, honey. Wild willow don't belong in town, sitting in a tin basin in an apartment. We'll fix it so you can come and see the willow."

Her expression was doubtful, and he saw her fingers stroke the small green leaves and her face bend toward them.

"We'll go to the end of the valley," Judith said, her face turned away from him.

"Daddy"—the child's voice was uncertain—"what about my horse? I want my horse."

"We'll get him—later," he said, and remembered he hadn't been able to tell her he'd had to sell their horses. It was pitiful the way she loved horses and cattle.

He saw they were coming to the end of the valley, and a cluster of ranch buildings squatted at the bottom of a hill. Behind the hill, the mountains were big and topped with snow. They crossed a cattle guard and were driving through what was obviously a pasture.

His eyes squinted at the yearling calves grazing along the road. Good calves, the best, and pasturing on thick grass. He felt a hunger to own them. *No use wishing,* he thought; *no use acting like a kid with a penny in his pocket who wants a nickel candy bar.*

The car slowed down before a big red gate. Penny jumped out and opened the gate, shouting, "I see a place for my willow!"

Yes, he thought. *The end of the road. End of my road, too.*

"There!" Penny squeezed into the car and pointed, her eyes big and very bright. And he saw the low, log building and the small creek trickling past it, a building that stood apart from the corrals and barns and bunkhouses, a house that looked down the valley and would hold the sunrise and the sunset in its windows. Farther on, set on the slope of the hill, he saw another house, a two-story house, also built of logs, a big house that had an air of security about it. A broad lawn and flower gardens lay before it.

He pulled up before the smaller log house and stopped. "Nobody living in this one," he said, staring at the uncurtained windows. Still, it was a warm and friendly-looking house, close to the earth, with a tangle of hop vines climbing over the narrow porch.

"Ask up at the big house," Judith said. "They surely won't mind — about the willow, I mean. You stay with me, honey." She put a quieting hand on Penny's eager, restless body, and they sat there in the car while he began to walk slowly up the hill, breathing in the good and familiar fragrance of the grass and water and cattle.

He was a big man, over six feet, with hair the same bright gold color as his daughter's long braids, and he carried himself tall and straight, even though the sickness of defeat was heavy inside him.

As he went up the flagstone walk that had wild roses blooming on either side of it, he saw a woman sitting in a rocking chair on a square terrace that was built in front of the main door.

She was an old woman, with white hair flattened under a net, and the shoes she wore were big and broad, as though her feet troubled her. She had on a thin, black dress with a high, white collar, and there was an air of neatness and finality about her as she sat there quietly, waiting for him to speak.

"I came to ask a favor," he said, clearing his throat.

"Yes?" Her eyes were small and very black and bright, like those of a bird.

"My little girl, Penny — she's six — wants to plant a willow down there by the creek, the one that runs past the empty house."

The rocker creaked and then was still. "Plenty of willows round here, young fella. Grow like weeds."

"None there, though, by the house," he said, wondering if he was to be defeated again, even on this.

She got up slowly and fumbled for a cane and came out to stand beside him in the sun. He saw then that she wasn't a tall woman and that her face was brown and weather-lined. *Been outdoors a lot,* he thought.

"Well," she said with a thin smile, "lots of people want to take things away from here, but you're the first who wanted to leave something. Mostly they're interested in the fish or in hunting — if it's hunting season."

"It's not my idea," he said, keeping his tone level and indifferent. "Penny's sentimental about the willow. We — she got it the last place we worked, and when we had to leave she brought it with her. I'm on my way to town — some town — and she wants to plant her willow."

"You don't look like a town man," she said, her black eyes studying him. "Lose your job?"

"In a way. We've had to move four times in the last six years."

"Doesn't go good with a man's reputation — having to move so often," she said.

He wanted to defend himself, to tell her the truth. But he set his jaw and kept quiet.

"Campbell's my name," she said, "Sara Campbell. There's a shovel there by the side of the house. I'll go down with you."

He got the shovel and walked slowly so that she could keep up with him. "You've got good meadows," he said, nodding toward the waving grass.

"The best," she agreed. "My husband settled here a long time ago. He's been gone almost as many years as you've lived. Died young. I carry on."

"Noticed your calves as I drove through the pasture," Tom said. "Mighty fine cattle you have, Mrs. Campbell."

"They ought to be," she said. "I pay enough for the bulls."

"It takes good bulls," he said.

They came to the car, and Penny ran to meet them. Sara Campbell put her old, wrinkled hand on Penny's bright head. "So you got a willow rooted in that pail?"

Gravely, Penny showed her the roots, and the brown impassive face lighted. "Good roots. It'll grow here, all right."

"Come on, let's hurry," Tom said impatiently, anxious to get the thing done and be turning back down the road.

Judith waited in the car, not looking at them, while he dug a hole in the creek bank. "Now fill the can with water," he told Penny. "We've got to plant it wet."

He put the willow down carefully and sorted out the tangled roots and held the willow while Penny poured water around it. Then he began to fill in the soil, working slowly and methodically.

"It won't be lonesome," Penny said quickly, "and I'll come back and see it, won't I?"

"That's right," he said. He stood up, brushing dirt from his knees, and looked at the old woman. "Thanks," he said. Then he wet his lips and added, "Need any hired men this time of year?"

She leaned on the cane, her eyes suddenly as sharp as those of a hawk. "Got more than I need. No future for a man with a woman and child working for wages. You know that."

Yes, he knew. And he'd known better than to ask her for work, he told himself bitterly. He'd known better than to let her know the shape he was in. A clever man would have acted big and choosy and would have asked for something big. Still, he couldn't keep from blurting out, his face red, "A foreman—don't suppose you'd need a foreman, would you?"

He had to look at her then and he knew the bleakness was in his eyes and hated himself for not being able to hide it.

Her smile was thin. "I've got a foreman," she said.

He was glad Judith was in the car where she couldn't hear what they were saying. "Penny," he said, tugging at his daughter's shining braids. "You go to your mama, honey. I'll be right along."

She went to the willow and knelt beside it to stroke the thin, waving length of it and put her cheek against it. Then she got up and walked slowly to the car.

"We never had any children, Jim and I," Sara Campbell said. "Wonderful things, children."

"Yes." Tom's voice was tight. "If you can take care of them." He picked up the shovel. "Do you want this at the house?"

"Just leave it here for now. I'll have someone pick it up," she said.

"Thanks," he said, and turned toward the car.

"Just a minute, young fella."

He turned to face her, and he felt old and tired and beaten and didn't care any longer what she read in his face.

"You asked about being my hired man or foreman," she said, her black eyes watching him. "You didn't ask if I wanted to lease the place — to the right man."

He sucked in his breath and set his heels hard against the ground to keep his legs from shaking. He couldn't look at her now, but turned his head and stared at the buildings which blurred and ran together in the bright sunlight.

"I've been waiting a long time," she said slowly, "for the right man to come along, one who cares about the land and the things that grow on the land — like a young willow shoot. There's a bus takes kids from this valley to school in winter, so it wouldn't be hard to take care of the little girl. A lease I'd offer would be for ten years with an option to buy when anything happens to me. The pay would be half the calf crop beginning this fall. That way the right man could start his own herd and have something to keep him rooted. How about it?"

He nodded, unable to find any words that would express what he felt.

"Tell Penny to bring the shovel to the house," she said.

"I've got some fresh cookies. And you can start moving into the house there by the creek — if you're ready."

Again he nodded. She made a little grunting sound of satisfaction and began to walk slowly up the slope, bent over her cane.

"Penny!" he shouted. "Take the shovel up to the house for Mrs. Campbell."

When she had gone, her young colt's legs flying and the shovel in her hands, he turned at last to the car where Judith sat.

He could see the outline of his wife's face, the beautiful and proud profile that held so much strength and so much love. He looked at her and then had to look away, for his desire to take her in his arms came up in him like a blinding tide.

He said, still not looking at her, keeping his voice casual. "We'll get our stuff unpacked, Jude. This is where we stay."

There was a long silence and then she answered, matching her tone to his, "All right, Tom."

PEG CURRY OFTEN VISITED the Duncan ranch, ten miles southeast of Glenrock, and had a particularly warm friendship with Hugh Duncan, father of Casper attorney Hugh M. Duncan. One day she and the old rancher rode out in the pickup to check some sheep in a hilly pasture. It was sundown, and the animals were moving down to the bed ground with their backs to the low evening sun. As they parked to watch, Duncan recalled a remark he had heard years ago from another sheepman: "Lad, sheep never like to look into the bright glare of sunset. They go east with the evening."

Startled by the beauty of the poetic phrase, Peg sat in silence, knowing that in her imagination a story had begun. A few days later she wrote a short-short story, adding some additional details that—according to Hugh M. Duncan— closely paralleled events that happened in his family.

"Dad probably visited more with Peg about his life than he did with members of the family," said Attorney Duncan, interviewed at his law office in Casper in June 1991. The "crying porcupine" mentioned in the story is a true anecdote, he added.

"A Life Of Our Own" presents the age-old problem of the young wanting to leave home and the parents wanting to cling to them.

After the story's publication in *Collier's* in February 1954, Peg received a letter from an old man in the east whose circumstances were very different, but who felt the story helped him to better face conflicts in his own life.

His letter was one she kept in her files, often bringing it out to remind herself of the writer's responsibility to her work, "of the privilege and necessity of sharing any experience that may help others to understand life and its problems."

Discussing the letter in an autobiographical sketch in a magazine article, she added: "I also read the letter to strengthen me in the ability to say 'No' to the ever-present and crowding demands that may completely sap a writer's ability and take away her time for creating."

A LIFE OF OUR OWN

JIM JAMISON DIDN'T see the porcupine until he'd almost run over it. He slammed on the brakes and got out, carrying the .22 rifle. It was a young porcupine, and as he drew a bead it turned and looked at him.

"Why are you cryin' at me?" he asked impatiently. "I've got trouble enough now." But he lowered the rifle, for the look in the little eyes reminded him of the hopelessness in Mary's eyes when he'd told her about Sue-Ellen. "Get on with you, Spike," he said, and turned back to the truck.

He drove on down the dirt road. In a few minutes the buildings of the lower ranch came into view, the red roofs bright in the amber sun, the big barren cottonwood trees towering above them. It was here that he had brought Mary as his bride so many years ago, and it was here that their daughter, Sue-Ellen, had come only six months ago with the shiny new wedding ring on her finger.

He and Mary had never had either the money or the time to fix up the ranch house for themselves. They'd talked about it a lot, pretending they had money to spend, and they'd planned every room in detail. But the years had gone by, and the house had stayed the same.

Then Sue-Ellen wrote that she and Roy, her husband, would be coming to stay, and Jim and Mary had moved up to

133

the old house, the original homestead on the property, which was too far gone to permit any daydreaming about it. Jim had hardly noticed the moving; all the available hours had been spent getting the lower ranch house ready for the day Sue-Ellen and her husband would move in. He'd felt a great sense of pleasure and accomplishment when that day finally came: his and Mary's dream had finally come true — for their daughter.

He got out of the car now and walked slowly toward the house, remembering sharply the money he had spent on it. He'd had it remodeled and had put in a gas stove and electric lights. He'd even started a lawn.

His daughter was in the kitchen, packing the last of her cooking utensils. "Sue-Ellen..." he began and then paused, not knowing how to go on. Instead of a young woman of twenty he seemed to see the grave face of a little girl with dark pigtails. For a moment he wished with all his heart and soul to return to that time.

"I'm sorry, Pa," she said. There was a stiff set to her lips, and she did not look at him.

She was prettier than Mary, he thought. Mary had been a sturdy little bride with strong capable hands and a way of walking that set the dishes jiggling in the kitchen cupboard. But Sue-Ellen was like a willow growing along the ditchbank in spring, tall and slender and beautiful.

Jim looked down at his big hands and his heavy wrists. How had he fathered a wonder like Sue-Ellen? And then the pain of losing her came up in him and he blurted out, "Your mother and I...the hard years with nothin' fancy...and then fixin' all this up for you and —"

"I know," she said softly. "But Roy doesn't like the ranch. And I — I get lonesome for town, Pa."

"And so you're pullin' out and leavin' me to run this

place and the homestead too." He couldn't keep the bitterness from his voice.

"The boys," Sue-Ellen said. "They'll help you."

"A fat chance of that," Jim said sourly. "They get home from that high school in town and what do they do? Mike has to practice the violin. All Joey wants to do is ride the calves." He glanced around, seeing the open, empty cupboards. "You're not leavin' this afternoon?"

There was a long silence. "Yes," Sue-Ellen said finally. "Roy's gone to borrow his father's truck. I've got to finish packing." Then she began to cry. "Don't try to keep us, Pa," she said. "Just leave us alone. We only want to live where we like —"

"And where's that?" Jim shouted. "What's he got to offer you? Where's he gonna work?"

"In a filling station."

"A filling station!" he muttered. He yanked his dust-stained hat lower on his forehead and walked blindly out of the house.

Outside, he stood looking at the land. He'd paid for every acre in sweat and backbreaking labor. And Mary — Mary had worked just as hard. For what? For a daughter who didn't care about the land or the sheep and cattle that grazed on it.

He drove home, remembering how afraid he'd been that he couldn't keep Sue-Ellen here; that was why he'd spent so much money fixing up the house, while he and Mary went on doing without. The old homestead looked shabby in the afternoon light; the log walls were bleached silvery gray by time and weather. When he stopped outside the kitchen door, he heard young Mike's violin. *...Like a yowling she-cat*, he thought.

He walked across the back porch and into the kitchen. "Mary," he called. "Where are you?"

Mary was in the front room. She sat with her hands folded, a soft smile on her face as she watched Mike practice the violin. She looked up at Jim, her clear gray eyes shining, and motioned to him not to interrupt. Jim clapped his big hands over his ears and walked out.

He was part way to the corral when he stopped and stared, for his older son was riding the milk cow. "Joey!" Jim cried, running toward the fence. "Get off that cow! You want sour milk for supper?"

"Okay, Pa," the boy said and slid off the cow's back. He was short and stockily built, with a fine fuzz showing on his cheeks.

"If you've a mind for exercise you can begin shovelin' out this corral!" Jim leaned against the fence, breathing heavily. Then he looked at his son and added, "Didn't mean to yell at you, Joey. It's just —"

"That's okay," Joey said. "Listen, Pa, can I have a rodeo out here Sunday and invite the class?"

"No!" Jim shouted. "Think I spent my life learnin' to raise steers so a bunch of kids can ride 'em thin?"

Joey frowned. "I already asked the kids, Pa," he said.

"Then tell 'em I won't have it!" Jim said, and turned back to the house.

Inside, the violin was still being worked over by his younger son, but Mary was in the kitchen starting supper. She paused beside him and put her hand on his shoulder. "Jim —" she began, and then stopped. The question in her mind showed in her eyes.

"Sue-Ellen's leavin'," he said. "She'll be finished packin' and gone by now."

Mary's mouth quivered and he wanted to hold her in his arms, to feel her softness against him. In the living room the sounds from the violin stopped. Mary turned and shouted, "Mike, get on with that practicing."

Mike appeared in the kitchen doorway, fair-skinned and blondheaded as Jim had been as a boy. "This stinky deal!" he said, glaring at the violin.

"Music lessons cost money," Mary said. "You practice."

Mike looked over his shoulder at his father. "Is Sue-Ellen pullin' out, Pa?"

"Yes," Jim said shortly. "You better go check the sheep before supper."

"I can't, Pa. I gotta get started on a theme for Miss Murphy. I gotta have it in the mornin'. Ain't that a deal?"

"Isn't," Mary corrected. "Your grammar, Mike." She paused and then said, "Play the waltz for me, honey. I always wanted to be a violinist." Her eyes became soft and dreamy. "There's nothing like music."

"Lord," Jim said when the boy had left, "you don't call *that* music."

"Hush, Jim!" Mary cried. "Let me think of something besides Sue-Ellen."

"I can't," he said dully. He picked up his hat. "I better check the sheep."

He knew Sue-Ellen and Roy were gone when he drove out the gate to the lower ranch. The curtainless windows reflected the red fire of sunset. He drove past, making a mental note to stop and milk the cow on his way back.

As he drove up the long slope toward the fenced pasture he saw the sheep there above him — three hundred purebreds with black faces, drifting slowly toward the flatter land with the blazing sunset behind them. He recalled suddenly the words of an old sheepman he had worked for as a boy: "Sheep don't like to look into the sunset, lad. It's too bright for their eyes. They'll go east with the evening."

He stopped the truck and sat quietly, the words ringing as clear in his mind as the tinkle of the sheep's bells. Beyond the flock, in the higher pastures, he saw his cattle standing dark against the crimson skyline.

Mary had supper waiting when he got home. "It took you a long time," she said.

"Yes," Jim replied. It had taken him years, he thought, but he didn't tell Mary that. Nor was there any need to tell her now that Mike wouldn't ever be a musician or that Joey might never want to carry on the ranches.

When supper was over, he asked the boys to do the dishes. "Mary, we're goin' for a little ride," he said. "I've got something to tell you."

She put on the torn sweater she wore outdoors to feed the chickens, and they got into the truck and drove down the narrow dirt road. When they came to the lower ranch, Jim turned in. "Get out," he said. "Come inside." And he held her small, strong hand tightly as he led her into the kitchen. He turned on the electric light.

"Mary —" he said, and drew a deep breath, "we're movin' back here. I'll sell the other place or hire a man to run it. This is ours and always will be — if it suits you."

She touched the shining gas stove and the new sink. He saw a gleam of tears in her eyes. "It's fine, Jim," she said, "only — I wish it could have been for Sue-Ellen. She's young. We're not, not any more."

For a moment a terrible ache was in Jim's throat and then he smiled. "We're still young, Mary," he said. "We just forgot it for a while."

He looked at Mary and realized that it was true. She was still young — and even the torn sweater couldn't take away any of the beauty that was there. He reached out and brushed her hair back gently. "The way I figure it, Mary," he said, "a man can't live his kids' lives. It's hard to learn that, but it's true. And there's something else I want you to think about: A strong man shouldn't be afraid to look into the sunset—by himself, without his kids to lean on."

Then he put his arms around her, holding her hard. "It's only sheep," he said, "that go east with the evening."

LIKE MOST WRITERS, Peg was often asked, "Where do you get story ideas, anyway?" Her answer (in a 1957 article in *Wyoming — The Feature and Discussion Magazine of the Equality State*) was "From Life, of course. I am constantly finding an exciting scrap of experience that produces an idea; and impressions, emotions, bits of conversation, a thousand small yet memorable aspects of living are always finding me and sticking to me like burrs.

"It is impossible for anyone desiring to write to be otherwise and have anything to say.... Every time I step outside my front door, I come across material.... The challenge is not in being aware of the beginning of a story, but in being able to make a story from the initial impulses. How, for example, to take something about Wyoming and set it in a series of incidents tied together with a basic idea or theme that makes for memorable reading."

An anecdote told her by an acquaintance, about a woman who fell in love with a man in jail, prompted "The Lady Loved a Jailbird," published in the *Saturday Evening Post* in October 1952. The story is set in Riverton, among people of Dutch descent. Like so many of her short stories, "The Lady Loved a Jailbird" was read to residents of the Casper Mountain Camp for the Visually Handicapped.

THE LADY LOVED A JAILBIRD

J UDITH STARED THROUGH the kitchen window of the farmhouse, her long hands idle in the dishwater. She could
see the stretch of field, green in the green evening, the
brown patch of plowed earth next to it, and, farther on, the
shapes of the Wind River Mountains. A sweet-sad aching
began in her heart. *I am so big,* she thought, *and so plain.
Only when Tommy was here I felt different; Tommy made me
feel the magic.*

It was always this time of year, when the river ran open
after the long winter, that she thought of Tommy, and the
queer tingling stirred deep inside her. It was like listening to
the symphony that gave concerts in town, listening and
aching and wishing she were small.

With Tommy she had felt like a queen, for he treated her
that way; opening the car door when he brought her home
from high school, sending her flowers the time she was sick,
giving her the silk scarf once at Christmas. People said
Tommy was wild and bad. They said they always knew he
would end up as he did — in reform school for stealing.

But he had plenty of money, Judith thought now, as she
had many times in the past five years. *He did not need to
steal. He did not mean to be wicked. Because he drove the car
so fast and was always playing tricks, people thought he was*

141

wild and bad. But he was kind, kind and gentle, and she loved him — even when she was a little girl she loved him.

"Yudith," her father said, "the water gets cold. Maybe you forget you wash dishes."

Her hands moved automatically in the soapy water. From the corner of her eye she could see Papa sitting by the kitchen table — so big, so tall, so Dutch. And Mama — Mama was big, too, and strong. The men in the Riverton valley talked about Mama's strength. "That Gina Udema," they said, shaking their heads and laughing, "she is a horse. She can lift the end of a wagon easy as a man."

There was no magic on the outside when one was big, Judith thought sadly, and how could she help it when she was part of Mama and Papa? People could eat things to make them grow bigger, but nothing would cause her to turn small.

"Yudith," Jake Udema said, "you going to the dance tonight? Saturday is time for a girl to go out."

"Yes," Gina answered for her daughter, "Yudith goes to dance. Hilder asks her. Hilder is good boy. Hilder is our kind, not Dutch, but almost; Swedes are almost like us."

No magic, Judith thought, *but yes, he is like us. He is big and blond and has a red face. I hear no symphony when he puts his arms around me. He holds me too tight when we dance and makes my arm go up and down like a pump handle.*

"Yudith has a new dress," Gina said, her round red face shining. "Blue is good color for Yudith.... Honey, why you wash dishes? You want nice hands for the dance. Now you make them redder with hot water."

They were so afraid Hilder wouldn't ask her to marry him, Judith thought. They were so anxious because she had not been popular with boys — only with Hilder and Tommy. Tommy — she swallowed the lump in her throat. After five years one should be rid of a lump. After five years and never a letter, one should cross his name away, like a word scratch-ed off a sheet of paper.

She carefully cleaned the sink and turned to face her parents, a tall straight girl with a fully developed figure, fine blond hair and blue eyes.

"Come here, Yudith," Jake said gently. "I have a little talk with you."

"Not tonight, Papa." She tried to say it lightly, but she sounded desperate.

"Come," he coaxed and patted his knee. She went to him then and sat awkwardly, her spine stiff, her eyes guarded.

"You work hard on this farm all winter," he said, his voice gentle. "We send you to college and you come back to help us. We need you and we are glad you come, but you are not happy, Yudith. We see the sick heart in your eyes. You do not grieve for that Tommy who was bad, do you? You know him when you are yust a child. It does not hurt still, does it?"

She looked away, not wanting to face him. "Please, Papa."

Jake sighed. "He was never our kind, Yudith. Too much money his family had. Now they are dead, but I still remember they look down their noses and call us 'dirty Dutch' even when we are clean. I know. They said it in town and it was told to me. His mama does lots of talking when she was alive. She blame you because he breaks into a store and steals money and goes to reform school."

"He wasn't alone that night!" Judith cried. "I know he wasn't! There must have been others and he wouldn't tell on them!"

"Others do not excuse him," Gina Udema said, her lips tightening. "You tell yourself there were others, Yudith. Then it is not so hard to believe when you think others were bad, too."

"Please!" Judith put her hands over her face.

"Enough, Gina!" Jake's voice was sharp. "We say no

more. We forget the name 'Tommy.' I have a little present for you, Yudith. We buy it because today is your birthday. We buy it for you because you work so hard and ask for nothing. We buy it because we love you. Stand up, Yudith, and close your eyes."

Obediently she stood with her eyes closed until he said, "Now — look!"

She saw the big diamond shining blue-green. It seemed strange in the shabby kitchen with the bare floor that had been scrubbed white. She had never seen such a ring, not even on the hand of Tommy's mother when she poured tea at a high school party given for the senior girls.

Judith felt tears sting her eyes. So much of their needed money — Papa's long hours working in the field; Mama's long hours milking cows, making butter to sell to people like Tommy's mother. *And still we are Dutch,* she thought, *and we are big and have red faces.*

"Something hurts you?" Jake asked anxiously. "Tears come in your eyes. We do not want you to cry. We want you to be happy."

She kissed them gently, first Gina and then Jake. "It is too much," she said. "You should have saved the money; there is pastureland to be put in grain. You should have taken a trip — had fun."

Gina shrugged her broad shoulders. "Fun, what is that? Our fun is having you happy, Yudith. You hurry now and take off the tight pants and put on the dress. Hilder comes soon and takes you to the dance. You look nice for Hilder."

Judith went to the bedroom and put on the blue dress. It was a very plain dress. One does not look so big and awkward in something plain, she thought. She heard Hilder's voice in the living room, but she didn't hurry. After she combed her hair and put powder on her face, she went to the open window where the starched curtains swung in the soft spring wind. She could hear the river murmuring against the willow-shaded bank.

Once Tommy had driven his big car to the river and they had sat under the willows that night. He had held her hand against his cheek and said, "Whenever I hear a river, it will bring you back to me, Judith. You are so clean—so clean—and all bubbling magic inside, like the water." Then he had laughed awkwardly and said, "Funny, I never talk this way to anyone else. With the others I play jokes and dance and try to show off. With you, I want to be quiet, and when I speak say only the things I really feel."

Tommy had always said nice things to her. And he had always been kind—like the time when they were in fourth grade and she made him a valentine. She hadn't the money to buy valentines and she didn't want to tell Gina and Jake she must have a valentine for Tommy. She'd borrowed red paper from the teacher and cut out red hearts of varying sizes. She'd found a piece of heavy string in her lunchbox and pasted the hearts on the string. Then, when no one was looking, she hurried to the big valentine box in back of the schoolroom and stuffed the hearts into it.

The afternoon dragged. She waited impatiently for the teacher to hand out the valentines. It started at last, and as name after name was called, Judith's heart beat louder and louder. Then the teacher held up the long string with the hearts dangling awkwardly and said, "This one has no name. Who made it? Who is it for?"

There were titters and whispers. Judith cringed in her seat. She saw how crude and cheap her valentine looked compared with the beautiful white-frilled hearts on Tommy's desk, for all the girls had given Tommy valentines.

The teacher's little dark eyes seemed to bore right through

Judith. The teacher said, "You, there. Didn't I lend you some red paper like this? Who is the valentine for?"

Judith's face turned crimson. She ducked her head and barely whispered, "I made it for Tommy."

There were more titters and whispers. Then Tommy got up easily, as he always did, walked to the front of the room and said, "It's my valentine." Gravely he smoothed the red hearts, turned to smile at Judith and said, "Thank you, Judith." No one had snickered then.

There was a sharp rap on the bedroom door. "Yudith! Hilder gets tired of waiting. Hurry! Hilder has a birthday present for you."

Judith picked up her coat and went into the living room. Hilder was tall and blond, his red face shining as though it had been scrubbed hard with soap. He thrust a big box at her, laughing loudly and saying, "You can use these. I should have brought you candy to sweeten you up, though. Have to be careful with you now — your old boyfriend's back in town."

Judith felt the color leave her face. *Tommy,* she thought. *Ah, Tommy with the hair like a blackbird's wing. Tommy with the warm smile and the dark eyes.*

"Open the package," Jake said gruffly, staring at his daughter.

Her fingers felt numb as she untied the strings. There were boots inside — big, thick-soled boots with long laces.

"Figured she needed them," Hilder said, smiling as though pleased with himself. "For heavy work, she needs heavy boots."

"Where is your tongue, Yudith?" Jake said sharply. "Don't you trouble to say thank you to Hilder?"

Judith closed the box and set it on the table. "Thank you," she said dully, and thought, *already he sees me as a big horse of a woman helping with chores.* With Tommy there would have been magic even if the box had been empty. Tommy would never give her ugly boots for her birthday. Tommy would —

"I'll bake the cake while you are gone," Gina said. "When you come from the dance we all have birthday cake together. It is best fresh. Papa and I sit up Saturday night. We pretend maybe we go dancing too."

Hilder touched Judith's arm. "Come on. We're late now."

"Show him the ring," Gina said. "It is birthday present, too."

Hilder stared at the ring and whistled. "Fancy," he said. "But not very practical for a girl who milks cows and runs tractor."

Jake cleared his throat. "For Yudith we do not care about the practical," he said. "We only try to make her happy."

Hilder nodded and urged Judith toward the door. All the way to town she kept thinking of Tommy, and Hilder kept talking about Tommy. "People aren't falling all over him like they used to," Hilder said. "He's no big shot now. I don't know what he figures on doing around here. Who'd want him when he has a reform school record behind him?"

Judith stared at the road, her hands tightly clenched in her lap.

"This is a small place," Hilder said. "People don't forget things. Once a thief, always a thief. If he'd been smart, he'd have stayed away."

Judith's lips drew tight. She saw the town lights coming close. Hilder kept turning his head to look at her as he talked on and on. "Does he think anyone would be fool enough to give him a job? His money's gone, you know. His mother was broke when she died. They flew too high, Tommy and his mother. His dad was always talking big, too. Well, they are both gone and who does he have to come home to in Riverton?"

They drove up Main Street and parked at a dance hall.

"What I don't understand," Hilder said, "is what made him want to look people in the face again?"

Judith said, "It is very tiresome, your talk, Hilder. You say the same things over and over. It makes my head ache." She got out of the car then and they walked into the dance hall.

The music was fast and the crowded room was warm from the breath of dancing people. Hilder put his arms around Judith. He held her too tight, and he worked her arm up and down like a pump handle. They danced and danced, only trading twice, and Judith kept looking toward the doorway.

They were waltzing near the orchestra when Hilder said, "I knew he would show up here. That kind are always bold as brass."

Judith looked over Hilder's shoulder and the strange aching began inside her and the lump grew large in her throat, for Tommy was there in the doorway — Tommy with his tumbled black hair and his long, dark-skinned face.

The music stopped and he stood there alone. A few people walked past him and nodded, but no one went to speak with him; no one held out a hand.

The aching in Judith became a wound that lay open as though flicked raw by a whip. Where were the girls who always crowded around him, hanging on his arm, laughing up into his face, saying the bright, clever words she could never say? Where were the boys who used to run onto the football field to slap him on the shoulder when he was captain of the team? Where were all the ones who knew him when he drove the big car and everything about him was gay and reckless and shining?

But still he stood there, his shoulders squared, forcing a stiff smile, trying to hide the hurt on his face. Judith quivered. It was like when she first went to school in town, she thought, and she stood alone on the playground, trying to show the girls she didn't care when they walked past her. It was like when she walked to her desk and her shoes made a noise like the hoofs of a work horse, when her hands dropped the pencils and fumbled with the book pages. It was like when they laughed and called her Dutchy-with-the-red-face. *Oh, Tommy, Tommy.*

And then she was going to him, half running the length of the dance floor while everybody stared. She held out both her hands, and she couldn't speak as she touched his fingers.

She stared hungrily at his face as he said, "Judith — the same Judith. Nothing changes you. Nothing ever will." And he tried to smile the warm smile, his face twisting in a grimace.

He is the same, she thought, *and yet not the same. He is older — a man instead of a boy. And what has happened to his eyes? There is no twinkle in them now. The mouth has lost the gentleness; it is a bitter mouth.*

She was aware then of Hilder standing beside her and saying coolly, "The music has started, Judith. Let's dance."

Judith turned to him, her eyes pleading with him to be kind. "You remember Tommy, don't you, Hilder?"

Hilder's red face turned redder.

Tommy laughed, a short brittle laugh, and said, "Don't bother, Hilder. It's all the same with me." He turned and walked out of the dance hall.

"Let him go," Hilder said.

Judith stared at Hilder. She said, "I'm getting my coat and going after Tommy. I shall return your boots, Hilder, for I would never wear them. Good-bye, Hilder."

Tommy was half a block away, walking slowly, under the yellow street lights. Judith ran after him, calling his name. When she caught up with him, she put her arm through his, saying, "Come on, Tommy, we will walk toward our farm. It's good to walk in the night. You do not have to talk. Just smell the earth and think about it being spring. Everything starts over in the spring, Tommy. New life, new hope."

They walked silently after that, leaving the town behind them and coming into the the open country where the smell of burning brush and fresh earth was on the wind. Judith held his arm firmly, matching her long stride to his.

After a while he said, "It was all very foolish and wrong. And it started as a joke."

"You were always playing jokes," Judith said.

"A bunch of fellows dared me to break into the store, Judith. I intended to put the money back. All I wanted was to show them I had got it. When I came out of the store that night, a cop was waiting for me." He kicked at a loose rock on the roadside.

"Someone was cheap," Judith said with sudden fierce anger. "Someone told the cop so he would be there."

"Yes."

"Who were these boys? Tell me their names, Tommy."

"No. It would do no good now. Water under the bridge, Judith. I tried to tell the cop it was a joke. He never believed me. Guess I shouldn't have expected him to."

They came at last to the river and sat down on the bank to rest. The dark willow branches moved above their heads. A night bird called. The water moved, talking softly against the shadowy bank. A short distance away, Judith could see the light in Gina's kitchen. *Mama is baking my cake,* she thought. *What will they say when I bring him to the door? Will they turn him away?*

"Tell me what it was like — at that place," she said, taking his hand in hers. "It will help now to speak of it, Tommy."

For a long time he was silent, and then he said, "At night it was terrible. I'd never been shut in. It was like screaming inside and not making any noise. Then I learned to think of you, Judith. I could see you, so tall and strong and alive. It was like resting against a warm shoulder. It was like being home."

Her fingers tightened on his hand. *Let him say it now,* she thought. *Let him say it and maybe some of the hurting would stop.*

"After a while it wasn't so bad there," Tommy said. "The man in charge was a good man. We became friends. There's a farm the boys work and I learned to like farming, Judith. The earth felt good in my hands. The sun was good on my face."

I know, she thought; *it was that way with me, too. When I came home from school, hurt, I could walk in the field or I could work in the field, and it made me easier inside.*

"After I got out," Tommy said, "it was a long time before I could find courage to come back here. I was afraid to face people, to know when they looked at me they thought I was a thief. Well, I guess I was, but I never meant to be. Only you can't make people understand things like this, Judith. You saw it tonight. Nobody believes in me, Judith."

She put her arms around him then and pulled his head against her breast. "I believe in you, Tommy. I'll always believe in you."

She felt the shudder run through him and then he was crying like a child, and she felt the dampness of his tears go through the thin silk of the blue dress and lie against her flesh. She didn't move or speak, but only held him and waited for it to be over. And while she cradled him against her, she thought of the beautiful yellow cat she had owned when she was a child. She could see the cat now, the long fluffy yellow fur, the tail waving like a bright plume. Then one day the cat went into the field and was injured. Judith saw her crawling slowly toward the house, the beautiful tail limp, the fur matted with blood, the eyes glazed with pain. *But we loved her,* Judith thought, *and we cared for her. She was healed and only a scar remained—her tail hung limp, never again waving so proudly. And we got so we never noticed the drooping tail, for she was loved and knew it, and became beautiful again.* It would be like that with Tommy; with enough love the scar might still be there, but it wouldn't show.

He drew away from her, fumbling for a handkerchief. Judith got to her feet, squared her shoulders and looked toward the lighted window. Reaching down, she grasped Tommy's hand and pulled him up to stand beside her.

"We have our coffee and some cake now," she said. "Mama will have it ready."

"No!" Tommy cried. "I can't go in your house, Judith!"

"Yes," she said firmly. "Don't be a coward. I cannot care for a coward, Tommy." And holding tightly to his hand, she began to walk toward the house. *Please, Papa,* she thought, *please be kind. Make him feel wanted. Do not let him be a stranger and afraid.*

When she walked in with Tommy at her side, her parents were sitting in the living room. Gina had on her best dress and Jake had carefully combed his hair. *Maybe tonight they thought that Hilder would propose,* Judith thought, *and they are fixed up for the occasion.*

Gina half rose from her chair, staring at Judith and Tommy. A little sound like a moan came from her lips. Her stricken face said plainly, *Yudith, Yudith, why do you bring a thief to our door?*

Judith looked at Jake. Jake looked back at her. Then he turned to his wife and said loudly, "I think of your Uncle Richta in the old country. Seems my mind is full of Uncle Richta."

"Is that so?" Gina asked stiffly.

"Lots of geese Richta always had in his barnyard," Jake continued, talking loud. "Lots of geese for the table too, and someone asks, 'How is Richta always keeping so many and eating so many at the same time?' You hear me, Gina?"

Gina's face was flushed. "I hear you," she said. "You sound like I'm deaf. And you talk too much. Talk, talk, talk. Magpie, that's what you are."

"I talk to remind you about Uncle Richta," Jake said. "I remind you he sometimes stopped by a neighbor's barnyard at night and came home with a goose under his arm."

Gina's eyes blazed with sudden anger. "Och!" she cried. "He throws up my family again! And I remind you, Jake Udema, your cousin, Pete, steals horses from my father, and my father is so mad we wait a year to get married and my wedding dress is covered with dust."

Jake began to laugh. He went to Tommy and Judith and put a big arm around each of th . "Sometimes it is good to think of Uncle Richta and my cousin Pete. We keep from narrowing the mind — eh, Yudith!"

"Yes, Papa," she said softly.

"Now, Tommy," Jake said, "you are very thin. Gina makes good cake. It will stick to your ribs and make you fat maybe." He glanced at his wife and shouted, "Gina! You cut cake for Tommy!"

Gina put her hands on her broad hips. Her face was very red now and she was panting a little. "Am I to fetch to him like he cannot move? He is one of the family, isn't he?... Tommy, you march to the kitchen with the rest of us!"

Judith saw the slow smile come over Tommy's face. She lifted her chin. *We are all big Dutch people with red faces,* she thought with sudden pride. *Yes, we are big, and big people have lots of room for love. That is magic.*

"OSAGE GIRL" WAS PEGGY Simson Curry's first work to appear in the *Saturday Evening Post* (June 1947) and her husband, William S. "Bill" Curry gets credit for inspiration.

Bill, an instructor and later chairman of the English department at Casper College from 1946 to 1973, belonged to the Casper Literary Club, whose members gave hour-long programs. Bill's presentation was a recollection of travelling in Illinois with his uncle, a colorful and well-known harness-race driver. Peg read Bill's finished paper and was immediately interested. He supplied additional detail and background, and she developed the plot.

The story was later anthologized — and was the only piece by a female author — in the collection *Twenty Two Stories About Horses and Men,* compiled by Jack B. Creamer (New York: Howard-McCann Co., 1953).

Walt Disney Studios holds a television option for "Osage Girl," but no screen play has been produced.

OSAGE GIRL

WHEN I REMEMBER my Uncle Jed, I always see him the way he looked that day in Springfield, sitting easy on the sulky behind Osage Girl as she paced a half length ahead of a field of nine. That was the greatest race I ever saw Uncle Jed drive.

My Uncle Jed was a big man. He was over six feet tall and he weighed two hundred and ten pounds, but he walked lightly. There was nothing clumsy about Uncle Jed. He had a round red face and hair that was white even when he was young. His eyes were blue, and when he looked at horses they softened the way some men's eyes do when they look at a beautiful woman.

When he drove his pacers and trotters he always wore a black silk jacket, a black silk cap and a Windsor tie. He was a handsome man, my Uncle Jed, and no other driver looked the way he did on a sulky. Not even Will Blaine, who had been driving the grand circuit for years.

Uncle Jed could have married any girl in Dewitt County, but he wasn't in any hurry to be tied down. He waited until he was past thirty-five, and then picked Aunt Lucy. He didn't know how she was going to act about harness racing until it was too late.

The summer I was fourteen I went to live with Uncle Jed

and Aunt Lucy on the farm. It was a good farm, one hundred and sixty acres of Illinois black land, but Uncle Jed liked horses better than corn, and he farmed with only half his heart.

The frame house needed painting. There was a big yard where the chickens were always scratching under lilac bushes. Sometimes the hogs came through the sagging picket fence and rooted up Aunt Lucy's flower beds.

"Your Uncle Jed," she would say, shaking her head, "sees nothing but horses. He hasn't time to fix the fence or make a place for his chickens." And she would get a hammer and pound at the fence, muttering under her breath. Aunt Lucy had big gray eyes and gold-colored hair. Uncle Jed said she was like a Charles Dickens heroine. Other people said she was pretty, but set in her ways. When a woman stayed single until she was thirty years old, they said, she was bound to have a strong will.

Uncle Jed said it wasn't Aunt Lucy who had the strong mind, but her mother, Mrs. Brown. Mrs. Brown claimed she had been born with the veil and could look right into the future. "Having a vision," she called it. And soon after Aunt Lucy and Uncle Jed got married, Mrs. Brown had a vision telling her Uncle Jed must quit harness racing and tend to his farming.

Right away Aunt Lucy and Uncle Jed started having trouble. Aunt Lucy said Uncle Jed should quit driving and buying race horses. "You farm," she said. "It's safer."

"Clete Harkins fell off the wagon the other day and broke his arm," Uncle Jed said.

"Mother knows what you should do," Aunt Lucy said. "She has visions to tell her."

"I don't hold with visions," Uncle Jed said. "And I don't think light of the supernatural, either. Why, electricity is supernatural as anything. But I don't believe in any vision your mother ever had."

Aunt Lucy was getting mad. "My mother has second sight," she said, "and you're too dumb to know it."

Uncle Jed got mad then too. "Even the Almighty couldn't send your mother a vision," he said. "She makes up her mind first and hangs a vision on last. My farming doesn't suit her and she aims to change it."

Uncle Jed's farming wasn't in a class with his harness racing. Anyone could see that. He said the only reason he bought the farm was that it was across the road from the Dewitt County fairgrounds, and he could work his horses out on the track.

It seemed that Mrs. Brown always managed to have her husband drive her over on the days the hogs were on the rampage or the wind had blown the shingles off the roof. She would step out of the buggy, look around the place, and then come into the house with her long black dress rustling. She always wore black, rustling clothes. "Gives me the creeps," Uncle Jed said.

She'd lift her veil from her small pale face and say, "Lucy, this farm's falling into ruin."

Then she would look up at her husband, Silas, as though she expected him to back her up, but he never said anything. Uncle Jed said Silas Brown was so quiet because he never had a chance, living with a phonograph like Mrs. Brown.

Aunt Lucy was under her mother's "spell," as Uncle Jed called it. She believed in the visions and tried to shape her life to fit them. "Why," Uncle Jed would say, "your ma would have visioned you right out of marrying me if I hadn't carried you off to Clinton one dark night and got a ring on your finger fast." Then he would grin until his eyes crinkled into blue slits. "That's once I beat the old girl's time!"

Then Aunt Lucy would get mad and speak sharp right back at Uncle Jed and remind him about being respectful toward his elders.

One June morning Mrs. Brown came up to the farm before we had finished breakfast. Uncle Jed, Clem and I were sitting around the kitchen table. Clem was Uncle Jed's swipe and he loved horses the way Uncle Jed did. A swipe's duty was to take the horses to and from the track, but Clem did other things, like keeping the barn clean and helping Aunt Lucy when she went on a painting spree.

Mrs. Brown was all afluster that morning. "Lucy," she said breathlessly, "I had a vision last night."

"Coffee?" Uncle Jed said to Silas Brown. Mr. Brown came timidly to the table.

Mrs. Brown looked right square at Uncle Jed and said, "I saw you lending money — a lot of money — to a man from Atlanta. Then he couldn't pay you back, so he gave you a mare, a big black mare."

"Money!" Aunt Lucy cried. "Why, we haven't money to lend! Look at this farm. And I need clothes, too!"

"You certainly do," Mrs. Brown said. She squinted at Uncle Jed. "What do you think of my vision, Jed?"

Uncle Jed stopped pouring sorghum over his pancakes. "It's no vision," he said shortly. "It's the truth."

Mrs. Brown looked triumphantly at Aunt Lucy. "He admits what I visioned was true."

"Only you didn't see it," Uncle Jed said sourly. "Someone told you. I understand you've got poor relations in Atlanta."

"Jed," Aunt Lucy's voice was stern, "you never told me about lending money or getting another horse."

"Was coming to it," Uncle Jed said. He took out his pocketknife and began flipping the blade open and shut with his thumb, the way he did when he was upset about something.

"And that's not all," Mrs. Brown said. "The mare's no good. She's jumped through the fence at the start in every race she's been in. She's worthless."

Uncle Jed stood up, big and quiet. "I suppose a vision told you that, too. I know a good mare when I see one. Osage Girl is a winner. All she needs is a driver who understands her."

"If you were as smart on a sulky as Will Blaine," Mrs. Brown said, "you might straighten her out."

"Will Blaine's not smart," Uncle Jed said. "He's been lucky and he's had plenty of money to buy good horses."

"And money to take care of his wife, too," Mrs. Brown retorted pointedly. She looked back at Aunt Lucy as if to say, "Why didn't you take Will Blaine when you had the chance?"

"It's bad enough to risk your neck for a good horse!" Aunt Lucy cried. "But a worthless mare! Jed Blanchard, I think you're touched in the head."

"Maybe I'm about to have a vision," Uncle Jed said dryly.

Mrs. Brown began to sniff into her handkerchief and finally squeezed a few tears out of her eyes. "I won't stand for it," she said with another sniff. "I won't have my divine gift smirched by a wasteful harness racer who keeps my daughter in poverty."

Silas Brown didn't say anything. He just drank his coffee and looked sadly at the floor.

Uncle Jed walked out of the house, hitched his bay mares to the buggy and drove away.

"He's in a huff," Mrs. Brown said. "Never mind, Lucy. Just remember your home is open to you any time. Come back to us if he doesn't treat you right." She rustled out to the buggy, followed by Silas and Aunt Lucy.

"Mothers-in-law!" Clem said in disgust.

Uncle Jed didn't come home for two days, and Aunt Lucy began to look down in the mouth. She spent most of her time staring out the front parlor windows, watching the road.

When Uncle Jed came, he brought Osage Girl. She was the prettiest mare I had ever seen, but Aunt Lucy wouldn't even come out to the barn to look at her. Clem ran his hands over the horse and then stood back.

He cut off a chew of plug tobacco and said, "She's perfect, Jed. Darned if I ever seen such a mare."

"She's a winner," Uncle Jed said, and his eyes got warm and bright. "Knew it the minute I looked at her. This fellow in Atlanta needed money. Wouldn't sell her, though. I scraped up all my spare cash and made him a loan. I took her as security. Knew he couldn't pay up. He's one of those men that let money run through their hands. He can't drive, either. That's why she got to going through the fence. He didn't handle her right. She's high-strung."

We stood quietly then, admiring Osage Girl. She was shiny coal black, and the only mark on her was the white star on her forehead. Her legs looked thin and frail for such a big, strong body.

It was cool in the barn. There was a driveway between the stalls where Uncle Jed kept his sulkies. The sulkies were painted black and the wire spokes in the wheels were yellow. The racing harness hung in a special room. When Uncle Jed got wound up he would point with pride to sets worn by famous horses he had owned and driven.

"That's the bridle Bingen Azof wore at Charleston," he would say. "He was a great horse. I hated to retire him to stud…. And that's the harness Daisy Bell wore when she took first at Clinton."

He would always end up by talking about Sparkling Boy, who had won many races and was almost good enough for grand circuit. "I sold him to a man from New York. Later he was bought by the Russian Czar for racing on ice. That's the way they do it in Russia."

That afternoon in the barn Uncle Jed didn't talk about his favorites. He kept looking at Osage Girl with that warm light in his eyes. "This girl's going to Springfield come August," he said. "I aim to drive to win."

"But that's grand circuit!" I cried.

"Osage Girl was born for grand circuit, son."

Things were pretty strained around the house the next two weeks. Aunt Lucy didn't say much. "She's broody," Clem said, "and your Uncle Jed don't act right, either. Old Lady Brown has sown the seeds for trouble."

Uncle Jed tried to act natural. He worked and worked with Osage Girl, but he never took her onto the track. He just drove the training sulky around the pasture or walked her up and down, talking to her all the time. He kept his voice low and gentle. After a while, when he would come into the barn after being gone, Osage Girl's black ears would move forward and back. Then she'd nicker softly. Uncle Jed would laugh, go up to her and stroke her, murmuring words that ran together until we couldn't tell what he was saying.

Two weeks before the state fair at Springfield, Mrs. Brown came for another visit, although she'd sworn she'd never set foot in the house again. She came in the evening and it was still hot from the day. We were sitting at the kitchen table eating cold chicken and big red tomatoes from Aunt Lucy's garden.

Aunt Lucy got up and went to greet her folks, but Uncle Jed just sat still and went on eating. Mrs. Brown rustled over to a chair and sat down. Silas followed with his hat in his hand.

"Lucy," Mrs. Brown said, "I had a vision last night."

Uncle Jed made a strangling sound in his throat. Mrs. Brown looked at him with cold, greenish-blue eyes. "I suppose you've told Lucy you're driving at Springfield."

Aunt Lucy dropped her knife. "Why, Jed!" her lips parted. "That's grand circuit!"

"It's still just driving," he replied.

"And he's driving that no-good mare, Osage Girl," Mrs. Brown said. "In my vision, he had a spill in the third heat."

Aunt Lucy's face turned white. "What did you say, Mother?" she asked in a flat voice.

"And he was killed," Mrs. Brown said solemnly.

There was a moment of silence, and then Aunt Lucy cried out, "No! No!"

"I've come to protect you, both of you," Mrs. Brown said. "Jed, I must ask you to give up harness racing now. I must ask you to withdraw your entry at Springfield."

Uncle Jed banged his big fist down on the table. The dishes jumped and rattled. "Go home!" he roared at Mrs. Brown. "Go home and leave us alone. You and your visions! You've held them over Lucy and her father all their lives. It's your way of getting what you want! But you'll never stop me from trying grand circuit."

Mrs. Brown stood up. Her face got as red as Uncle Jed's. "You—" her voice shook. She swept from the room with a final rustle, and Mr. Brown walked timidly in her wake.

Uncle Jed took out his pocketknife and began clicking the blade back and forth real fast. "Lucy," he said sternly, "I aim to drive at Springfield. I aim to try and make grand circuit, if it's the last race I ever drive."

Aunt Lucy stood up, too, and her face was very white. "I love you, Jed," she said, "and I don't want to see you killed. If you don't withdraw from that race, I'll—" She swallowed and lifted her chin. "I'll leave you."

They looked at each other for a long time. It was so quiet in the kitchen that we could hear the tick of the grandfather clock in the front parlor.

"Lucy," Uncle Jed said, his thumb working the knife, "I aim to drive."

Aunt Lucy's face crumpled. She ran from the kitchen. We

heard a door slam and the lock click on. Uncle Jed walked out through the back porch, still flipping the knife.

We waited a long time for Uncle Jed to come back. After a while, I washed the dishes and Clem wiped them. We didn't say anything. Then we went out to the barn. Uncle Jed wasn't there and the training sulky was gone.

"Listen," Clem said.

It was a warm night, and still, except for the crickets. The fireflies darted among the lilac bushes. No wind stirred the drooping elms. Then I heard it. The sound of singing wheels. The sound a sulky makes coming down the stretch.

We ran from the barn and across the road to the fair-grounds. The moon slid out from behind a cloud and we saw the big dark horse rounding the far turn and we heard Uncle Jed shout, "Ha-a-a-a! Ha-a-a! Ha-a-a!" He was driving Osage Girl. It was a picture, him bringing her down the stretch, with the wheels singing and the empty bleachers white in the moonlight.

"She's fast," Clem said. "Faster than Bingen Azof that time at Charleston."

We watched him drive Osage Girl around the track again. When he took her back to the barn, we ran behind the sulky. Clem cooled her out, rubbed her down and blanketed her. Uncle Jed didn't say a word. He just ruffled my hair with his big hand. We went to the house and I got ready for bed. I heard Uncle Jed knocking on Aunt Lucy's door, but she wouldn't answer.

The next day Aunt Lucy left. She sent Clem with a message to her folks, who lived twelve miles up the road. Her father came and got her suitcases and the boxes filled with her things. Uncle Jed didn't come near the house while they were packing her belongings out to the buggy. He stayed in the barn and helped Clem curry Osage Girl. After they left, he came to the house and stood by the front parlor windows, looking up the road for a long time. He looked awfully sad and didn't say anything.

It was hot that August and the woman Uncle Jed hired to cook didn't know how to fix things so they would appeal to a man's appetite in hot weather. Uncle Jed ate hardly anything, and each morning Clem and I would find him out behind the barn, flipping his knife and staring across the cornfield.

"It's a bad sign," Clem said. "Your Uncle Jed's not right. He's got the blues, and a man can't drive to win when he's low in his mind. I wish your Aunt Lucy would come back."

"Maybe we ought to send for her," I said.

"It wouldn't hurt, son. She might come."

When Uncle Jed took Osage Girl across the road to the track, we went into the house and started a letter to Aunt Lucy. Clem couldn't write, so I put down what he told me. "Tell her your Uncle Jed's not right in the head. Tell her he has spells and looks at the corn like he was in a trance." Clem said we better finish the letter by saying Uncle Jed would be killed in Springfield for sure if Aunt Lucy didn't come home.

Clem slipped up to the Brown farm that night after dark and gave Aunt Lucy the letter. The next morning we were out in the barn working with Osage Girl when Clem said, "Looks like someone's pulling into the yard."

Uncle Jed lifted his head. He looked past the house, and his eyes began to shine. "There comes your Aunt Lucy," he said softly. "You better go talk to her."

"She didn't come to see me," I said. "You better go."

"We'll both go," he decided.

When we got to the house, I saw that Mrs. Brown was there, too, rustling all over the kitchen. Aunt Lucy walked up to Uncle Jed, stood on tiptoe and kissed him.

"How are you, Jed?" she said.

"Can't complain," he said.

"I decided to come home," Aunt Lucy said. "I thought maybe you'd want me to go to Springfield, since it's your first time driving grand circuit."

"Why, honey, I'll be happy to take you to Springfield. Now I know I can win."

Mrs. Brown stopped pacing back and forth. "You can't win," she said shortly, "not with Will Blaine driving Starlight against you."

Uncle Jed scowled. "Will Blaine will eat dust off my wheels. No horse is going to beat Osage Girl at Springfield. I don't care who's driving."

"You're very sure of yourself," Mrs. Brown said.

"I am," Uncle Jed retorted.

"Then I'll make you a proposition," Mrs. Brown said. "If you lose, will you promise to stop harness racing?"

"Last time you were here you told me I'd be killed driving at Springfield," Uncle Jed said, his eyes glinting.

Aunt Lucy looked at her mother and then back at Uncle Jed. "Mother had another vision last night after I — after I said I was coming home."

"I see." Uncle Jed was thoughtful. After a while, he said, "All right, if I lose I'll quit harness racing. If I win, you quit having visions. Is it a deal?"

Mrs. Brown chewed her lower lip. I could see lots of things were going through her mind. Aunt Lucy looked perplexed.

"If it's fair for me to give up harness racing, then it's fair for you to give up having visions," Uncle Jed said. "I'm offering you a straight proposition. Take it or leave it."

"I'll take it," Mrs. Brown said.

"But, Mother!" Aunt Lucy cried. "You can't just—" She stopped short and looked away. I knew right then that Aunt Lucy understood about her mother's visions. She knew what

Uncle Jed had known for a very long time.

Uncle Jed was very happy that night after Mrs. Brown went home. The hired woman got supper, and for the first time Aunt Lucy went out to look at Osage Girl. Osage Girl moved her black ears forward and back and nickered softly.

"She's talking to you," Uncle Jed said. "She wants to be friends."

Aunt Lucy laughed and patted Osage Girl on the neck. After supper, Jed held Aunt Lucy on his knee and sang songs. They sent me to bed an hour earlier than I should have gone, but I didn't mind. I was too happy about having Aunt Lucy home again.

When we went down to Springfield for the fair, the corn was tall and the dust was deep. The day before the race was hot and Clem began to worry about rain. Uncle Jed squinted up at the sky and said the weather would hold for a day yet.

Mrs. Brown and Silas came down for the race, and Aunt Lucy went with them to their box, but I stayed at the stables with Uncle Jed and Clem. All the farmers in Central Illinois had flocked to town with their wives and children. The men came back to the stables to look at Osage Girl. Then they would go to the other end of the barn and look at Starlight and talk with Will Blaine. Starlight was a big bay and he looked stronger than Osage Girl, but Uncle Jed said he wasn't so fast.

Uncle Jed stroked Osage Girl and talked to her in a low tone. She moved her black ears forward and back just as if she knew every word he said. Clem had worked on her coat until it shone like the front-parlor floor after Aunt Lucy had polished it on her hands and knees.

Will Blaine came to Osage Girl's stall and said to Uncle Jed, "Jed, I've got a lot of money behind me in this race."

"That so?" Uncle Jed didn't stop stroking Osage Girl.

"I'll split with you if you'll let me win," Will Blaine said in a low voice.

Clem looked up then, but Uncle Jed paid no attention.

"There's a lot of money in it for you," Will Blaine continued. "More than double the purse. What do you say, Jed?"

Uncle Jed turned around then and looked square at Will Blaine. "Will," he said, "I've never sold out to any man. I don't intend to start now. I aim to drive to win."

Will Blaine looked funny then. His long, thin face got sort of red. He cleared his throat. "I've got to win, Jed."

"There's another thing, Will," Uncle Jed said. "You've got a reputation for being a rough driver. Don't crowd me. I wouldn't want to drive over you."

Will's face got redder. "I wanted to make it easy for you," he said harshly, "but you made your choice." He turned and walked away.

Uncle Jed took out his pocketknife and began flipping the blade back and forth. I knew he was worried then. Clem said, "He doesn't act very sociable, does he?"

"Someone's given him a lot of money to beat me today," Uncle Jed said, "and I think I know who it was."

"You think the old lady would go that far?" Clem asked.

"She aims to make me quit harness racing," Uncle Jed said. "She's bound to have her way, no matter what it costs. Get the girl ready to go." He closed his knife and stuck it in his pocket.

We led Osage Girl to the track, Clem on one side and I on the other. Uncle Jed walked behind the sulky, dragging his whip in the dust, his black silk cap in his hand. The people in the stands recognized him with his white head and his black silk jacket. They shouted his name, "Jed Blanchard! Jed Blanchard!" The applause thundered across the sultry afternoon and my heart felt big enough to burst with pride.

The starter and the judges were in their box directly across from the grandstand. On the performer's platform the entertainers had just finished the bicycle-and-trapeze act. Men could be heard placing their small bets all around us.

Up in the stands, the people were drinking pink lemonade and eating ice cream sandwiches. I looked over the rows of faces, and then I saw a small figure holding a pink parasol.

I caught Uncle Jed's arm. "Aunt Lucy's over there," I pointed. Beside her, I could see Mrs. Brown and Silas.

Uncle Jed straightened until he stood very tall. He looked over toward the grandstand and smiled. Then he turned back to Osage Girl and slid his hand along her neck.

He said to Clem, "You want to warm her up?"

Clem shook his head. "You better, Jed. She's keyed high. I might get her off."

Uncle Jed put on his black silk cap. "Rein her up," he said. He climbed onto the sulky and began slowly. He came by the starter's stand three times before he let Osage Girl lengthen into her stride.

The starter shouted, "And now for the first heat of the Two-twelve Pace. Two — Osage Girl has the pole! Five — Harris H. is second! Seven — Rosebud is three! One — Starlight is four! Three — Firefly is Five! Eight — Gray Dawn is six! Nine — Maisy Maid is seven! Six — Patches is eight! Four — Kentucky Lady is nine! All turn and come together slow! Don't come ahead of the pole horse!"

The sulkies turned. The dust floated up like a gray fog. The starter yelled, "Hold back Starlight!" He waved his arms. The gong rang three times. "No chance! No chance! Go back and score again!"

"Will Blaine's in a helluva hurry to get started," Clem said, and cut off a piece of plug tobacco.

"Now all turn! Come up with Gray Dawn! Now all together!"

The horses hit a nice even stride as they came under the wire. Osage Girl was in front by a head. They were nicely spaced.

The starter shouted, "Go!"

Osage Girl moved out fast, holding a half-length lead. Gray Dawn was in a pocket. Starlight was behind Gray Dawn. The others didn't count — not yet.

"Osage isn't in her stride," Clem said. "Looks like she might break."

I felt my heart sink. I looked toward the grandstand, but I couldn't find Aunt Lucy. All the faces swam together in a blur, and I knew there were tears in my eyes. I didn't want Osage Girl to let Uncle Jed down.

Osage Girl broke on the near turn and Starlight took a half-length lead. She broke again on the backstretch, and Starlight moved to the pole position. I began to feel as though I had drunk too much pink lemonade. The heat crowded down over me from the low gray sky.

Then, at the three-quarter turn, something happened. Osage Girl lengthened out and hit a perfect pacing stride. And as they came around the far turn, Uncle Jed swung out for the stretch drive. The crowd screamed his name. His black silk jacket billowed out behind him. Osage Girl moved forward like the wind, her slim hoofs moving in perfect precision. No horse could match that flying pace.

Uncle Jed moved forward, driving straight ahead. And above the singing sound of the yellow-spoked wheels his voice rang out, "Ha-a-a-a! Ha-a-a! Ha-a-a!" And he touched Osage Girl with the whip. Just once. She moved up neck and neck with Starlight. She came under the wire a nose ahead to win the first heat.

Clem and I ran onto the track. "Starlight's tough," Uncle Jed said, "but Will didn't crowd me any."

Clem spat on the dusty ground. "Waitin' for the next heat," he said. "Then look out."

Uncle Jed walked over to the starter's stand while Clem and I unhooked Osage Girl, put her harness on a peg and gave her a rubdown. In a few minutes Uncle Jed came back to the barn, and Will Blaine was with him.

"Think it over," Will said. "It's your last chance, Jed. I win and we split everything, purse included."

Uncle Jed swung around. He looked as if he would hit Will Blaine. "The hell with you and your money," he said shortly. He turned to Clem and said, "Harness her for the second heat. Tighten the hobbles one notch. I don't believe she'll break then. Those breaks almost cost me that first heat."

We were all set for the second heat, and Osage Girl looked good. The horses got off to a smooth start the first time they scored. Osage Girl was out in front, but before they rounded the near turn, Starlight was creeping up on her.

"Will Blaine's crowding," Clem said. Starlight was pushing closer and closer to Osage Girl. I saw Uncle Jed turn his head. He knew what was happening as Starlight swung close beside him at halfway round the track. Starlight was moving ahead and a long sound like a deep sigh went up from the grandstand. Uncle Jed wasn't driving to win now. He was driving to keep from having a spill. The distance between the two sulkies widened, but Uncle Jed lost ground in moving over. Starlight forged ahead and took the heat, with Osage Girl pacing second.

When we went onto the track, Uncle Jed's face was white. "He aims to spill me," he said in a tight voice.

I couldn't say a word. I was sick all over. Sick and mad. I hated Will Blaine and I hated Mrs. Brown. Between them they were going to ruin my Uncle Jed.

Osage Girl was nervous and it was all we could do to

quiet her down. Will Blaine walked by our stall, but Uncle Jed never said a word to him. Clem cut off another chew of tobacco and spat on the floor. He didn't say anything either.

"She can't win," I said, and my lip began to tremble.

Uncle Jed put his big hand on top of my head and ruffled my hair. "Takes three heats to decide this race, son. It's the last one that counts today."

When they took position for the third heat, Starlight had the pole, since he had won the second. Osage Girl was in second position. The horses scored three times before the starter shouted, "Go!" Starlight swept out ahead and Uncle Jed pulled right in behind him.

Clem chuckled and slapped his leg. "That's the trick, Jed! Look, son, he's letting Starlight break the wind. He's saving Osage Girl for the stretch drive. He's all right if they don't catch him in a pocket."

The grandstand was quiet, waiting and watching. Sweat ran down my forehead. I couldn't seem to breathe. Starlight held the lead right up to the far turn. It looked as though Osage Girl would never get out of second place. Then, suddenly, Uncle Jed leaned forward and swung out just as they came into the stretch drive. Osage Girl lengthened her stride, her powerful legs reaching out, cutting through the thick, dusty air. Uncle Jed and Will Blaine were sitting side by side on their sulkies. Starlight and Osage Girl were neck and neck. The crowd screamed and then was still. The sound of singing wheels rose in the silence. The horses' hoofs beat out the perfect rhythm.

Clem caught my arm so tightly it hurt. "Blaine's crowding again. He knows he can't win, and he aims to spill Jed."

I saw the distance between the sulkies narrow. Blaine was moving over. Wheels moved closer to spinning wheels. I was afraid to look, but I couldn't take my eyes away from those turning wheels.

Uncle Jed leaned forward, driving straight ahead. This time he wasn't going to give an inch. Above the singing of the wheels his shout rang out, "Ha-a-a-a! Ha-a-a! Ha-a-a!" His whip flicked Osage Girl each time he shouted. He was calling on her for all she had, and Will Blaine was crowding closer with each turn of the wheels.

The quiet roared in my ears. Everyone could see what was happening, but there was no stopping Will Blaine now. Uncle Jed was gambling — gambling everything on Osage Girl. The sulkies seemed so close together it looked as though the wheels must lock. Again Uncle Jed flicked Osage Girl with the whip and shouted. In that second everything seemed to hang in balance. And then Osage Girl went forward fast and a great shout rose from the grandstand. Faster and faster she paced until the dust from the sulky wheels flew back in Starlight's face. She came under the wire, her black coat wet, her pointed ears set forward.

People stood up and screamed. Men threw their hats in the air. Women tossed their parasols on the ground. My Uncle Jed sat on his sulky like a king.

Clem and I stepped onto the track, and when we looked into Uncle Jed's eyes, they were shining with something more than pleasure. He put his shaking hand on Osage Girl's hot, damp neck.

"A queen!" he said.

Her black ears moved forward and back. She nickered softly.

Aunt Lucy came running from the grandstand and threw her arms around Uncle Jed's neck. "I'll never ask you to quit driving again," she said. "Never!"

That's about all there is to tell, except that Silas Brown got mad for the first time anyone ever remembered and told his wife off in front of everybody. It seemed she not only paid

Will Blaine to drive to beat Uncle Jed but she also bet all their spare cash on Starlight.

After that, Mrs. Brown never had any more visions. She took up tea-leaf reading instead. But Silas wasn't impressed by the tea leaves and spent the last twenty years of his life having a wonderful time.

TWO YEARS AFTER HER *Saturday Evening Post* debut with "Osage Girl," Peg placed a second horse story there. "Night of Champions"—also set in Illinois—appeared in December 1949 and owes its origin to a visiting friend.

As he left the Curry home with his bride to continue their honeymoon trip, Donald Splain, an old family friend from Illinois, mentioned he would shortly be judging a horse show where there would be "roadsters with appointments." Peg wedged herself between him and the door and said, "Donald, you can't leave now. I want to ask you some questions."

Soon she knew that the roadster class is not a horse race, but is instead a show class that depends on a combination of style and horsemanship. As they circle the track, both driver and horse must make a fine ring showing, after which the driver displays before the judge his "appointments," items considered standard equipment for a gentleman in horse and buggy days: a razor, shaving lotion, a flask, comb, horse brush, bottle of horse liniment, and an extra horseshoe.

Armed with a wealth of other detail, Peg began writing the story of King Barton who drove his sleek mare, Lulu Belle, to show rings from Denver to Kansas City to Chicago. Always concerned with accuracy, Peg mailed her story to Splain, the horse show judge, and he returned it, having found no errors.

"Night of Champions" was mailed off to the *Post* and was quickly accepted.

NIGHT OF CHAMPIONS

Maybe you've seen King Barton drive at the Kansas City Royal, the International in Chicago, or the Western Stock Show at Denver. He drove racing pacers and trotters around all the big tracks, but it was in the roadster class that he was really famous.

A roadster isn't like a race horse. A roadster doesn't compete in races, but he's got to win the judge over in a ring showing; he has to trot with the greatest possible amount of action and yet be smooth in doing it; and he's Standardbred and must look like a million dollars worth of fancy horseflesh.

King Barton always drove roadsters with appointments — the dress-up roadster class. He liked to step to the back of his buggy after he'd finished driving, open the buggy box, and spread out before the judge his kit of appointments: shaving lotion, silver whiskey flask, horse brush, comb, razor, a bottle of horse liniment and a horseshoe — those things which might be required by a gentleman making an overnight trip in the horse-and-buggy days. Roadsters with appointments carry more prestige than any other class and that's what King liked — prestige.

King doesn't show roadsters any more. Doesn't race, either. He's still got good horses, but if anyone asks him when he's going to drive again he just smiles and looks away like

175

he is thinking about something. Maybe he remembers that
night he took Lulu Belle out in front of the fair crowd in his
home county. Or perhaps he thinks about his son, Dave, and
Lindy Ames, the blacksmith's daughter.

No one in the county hated King Barton more than old Zeke
Ames. There was a time when Old Zeke shod all the horses for
the county fair, but once he put shoes on a trotter of King's and
she lost the race. King blamed it on the shoes. He claimed old
Zeke had shod the mare too heavy. Old Zeke blamed King's
driving. This happened after King's wife, Kathleen, left him and
some folks said he'd hit the bottle before the race.

"Wasn't the mare's shoes," old Zeke said the next morning when King cursed him. "Your hand wasn't right on the
reins, for you got soaked up with rotten liquor the night before. You got soaked up because you lost a good woman by
acting so high and mighty and not takin' time to love her. You
always did think more of your drivin' than of her."

King hit him then. Hit him hard. Might have been King
was still drinking. Nobody saw the fight, but that's the way
old Zeke told it. And old Zeke didn't shoe any more horses
for county fairs. King always hired a blacksmith to come in
and do the work and saw to it that folks patronized the
stranger. Most people did what King said, for he had everything under his fingers — farms, the bank at the county seat,
and more livestock than you can imagine.

"Someday," old Zeke Ames said, "a feller'll come along
and knock him plumb off his throne. I hope I live to see it."

Didn't look like that would ever happen. King kept right
on climbing up the golden ladder until he was famous all over
for his roadster driving. About the time he was on top, Kathleen was killed in a train wreck down South. King went after
his son. Dave was twelve years old then and King hadn't seen
him since he was a baby.

King started the boy out helping him with horses. They kept busy, and if King grieved over Kathleen's death, he never showed it. He got more arrogant as the years went by and he didn't take much notice of Dave, who was growing up and getting blue fire in his eyes when he looked at horses.

The boy was built like King—tall and lean with wide shoulders. But he looked like his mother. He had hair black as midnight. He had Kathleen's blue eyes and her wide, sensitive mouth. But his chin was stubborn.

The summer Dave was twenty-one he fell in love with Lindy Ames, old Zeke's daughter. They knew how things were between their fathers, and for a long time no one knew that they were meeting after dark.

About a month before the county fair there was a dance in town and Lindy was one of the girls nominated for fair queen. Dave came late to the dance. He arrived just in time to see Blaney Coolidge kiss Lindy out on the porch of the old dance hall.

Dave forgot all about keeping their love affair quiet. He waded into Blaney with his fists. Finally the crowd came out and somebody pulled them apart. Dave's lip was cut and bleeding. Blaney had a black eye.

Dave shouted so everyone could hear, "You leave her alone! She's my girl."

Blaney didn't believe it and said so. Then Dave turned to Lindy. "Tell him, honey," he said.

She was a tall, slim girl. Her hair was the color of bright gold and clung to her head in soft swirls. She looked at Dave and then at Blaney Coolidge. "I'm not saying," she replied quietly. "Go on inside, Blaney." She drew a deep breath and said to Dave, "You shouldn't lose your temper like that."

When the others had gone, Dave said roughly, "Why did you lie?"

"You know what will happen when your father and mine hear about this," she said. "I just wish you hadn't acted so headstrong."

"And I don't like the way you lied — as if you didn't know me at all," Dave said hotly.

Lindy turned and left him there on the porch to cool his temper.

By morning the story had gotten around town, and the next afternoon when old Zeke met Dave on the street he said, "You stay away from my daughter. My daughter ain't havin' no truck with the son of King Barton."

"You don't have to hold my father's mistakes against me," Dave said.

"One Barton's same as another to me," old Zeke said coldly.

King said, "Dave, keep your hands off that yellow-haired filly of old Zeke's. She's common stuff."

Dave's eyes got that hot blue look. "She's no common stuff," he replied shortly, "and don't you ever say it again — not to me."

King's pointed white brows lifted a notch higher. He smiled that disdainful way of his. "Since when did you tell me what to do? Let's get a few things straight. When I die everything I have goes to you. Get contrary and I'll cut you off without a dime."

Dave turned and walked away. He got in his old cut-down car and drove into town and right up to old Zeke's house. Old Zeke was down at the blacksmith shop and didn't see him.

Lindy came out, looking scared. "Why, Dave, what's the matter?"

"Get in," he said. "From now on, we're seeing each other in broad daylight."

He drove her up and down Main Street three times and

then headed for their meeting place by the river. He lifted her out of the car and held her in his arms for a moment.

She leaned against his chest soft as a kitten. "Dave," she said, "when are you going to leave King and amount to anything?"

"Who said I didn't amount to anything?"

"My father," she replied. "He says you're nothing but a swipe for King — someone to run at his heels, curry his horses, jump when he shouts."

"That's just his idea," Dave said.

"He's not the only one that's said it," Lindy continued, turning her face away. "Lots of people think you're never going to do anything on your own. They say King's grinding you down — the way he did your mother."

"I'm all he's got," Dave said. "Am I supposed to go off and leave him? I know he's hard. But underneath he's lonely. If you'd seen him looking at that painting of my mother —"

"But he keeps on acting mean," Lindy said. "You don't see him giving any business to my father. My father could have made good money if it hadn't been for King Barton."

"I'm not saying he hasn't done wrong. I said I felt sorry for him. That's why I didn't leave long ago."

Lindy stepped back and looked at him. "But you can leave him now." Her chin came up and her wide gray eyes filled with points of light. "In fact, I'm asking you to leave him now, Dave."

"Lindy, I can't. You see, I'm like my mother. I love him in spite of his weaknesses. Besides, he needs me. He's not able to train all those good horses himself. And there's Black Shamrock — he says she's worthless, but I know better."

"What you're really saying is that a broken-down mare is more important to you than me."

"Never. I'm telling you I wouldn't be happy away from horses — and my father needs me."

Her eyes grew bright with anger. "If you're so smart with horses, why don't you drive them? Why don't you show people you're not just a dumb—" Her voice broke. "Go on back to him! Stay on his farm till you rot! I don't want to see you again!"

She turned and started running. Dave ran after her and caught her. He pulled her roughly into his arms and kissed her. Lindy slapped him. Then his temper exploded. "All right!" he shouted. "I'll show you! And old Zeke too!" He got in his car and drove away.

When Dave reached the farm, he saw some horses in the corral and a truck waiting to be loaded. King was leaning against the corral fence. Dave looked at the horses and saw Black Shamrock.

"What are you doing with these horses?" he said.

"Killers," King replied. "Sending them to Rockford. They'll make good horse meat."

Dave stared at him incredulously. "But not Black Shamrock! She's only a four-year-old! You've got her in with a bunch of broken-down work horses."

King scowled. "She's Standardbred and cost me plenty. I might as well have thrown the money down a hole. She never had any speed. You saw me start her when she was a two-year-old."

"And I said you were crowding her. I said she'd come slow."

"Too slow," King said shortly. "I get sore every time I look at her. Get her out of my sight."

"I'll keep her," Dave said.

"Who's running this place?" King shouted. "Load her for Rockford." He turned and strode toward the house.

Dave went into the corral and whistled. Black Shamrock came prancing up to him, her dainty hoofs moving up and down like they were set on springs. Her velvet-soft nose brushed his hand. Dave put his arms over her neck and patted her affectionately. He took her into the barn and left her there until he loaded the killers. Then he walked slowly to the house, where King sat on the front porch.

King said sharply, "Send those killers to Rockford?"

"All but one," Dave said quietly.

"What!"

"I kept Black Shamrock."

"I told you to ship her!" King shouted. "When I give orders I expect them carried out."

"Listen," Dave said in an even tone, "you've never let me own a horse. I've worked them out, taken care of them, loved them — but they always belonged to you. You don't want Black Shamrock. Let me have her."

King stared at his son, the red on his high cheekbones spreading up his temples to the roots of his thick white hair. "What do you want with a horse of your own?" he asked harshly.

Dave shrugged. "Doesn't every man want something of his own?"

King was silent for a long time. Then he said, "Keep the mare if you like. Only don't get any fancy ideas. You can run her legs off on the track out there, but don't get any notions about showing her."

A few days later Dave went into town. It was late afternoon when he stopped by old Zeke's blacksmith shop. Old Zeke was working on a wagon bolt. He glanced up, saw Dave, and went on hammering sparks from the bolt.

Dave started to tell old Zeke how he felt about Lindy.

"Look," old Zeke said, "don't come spouting soft soap about my daughter. She's done with you, Dave, and it's better thataway. She's just gone to the drugstore with Blaney Coolidge. They're celebratin' her election as fair queen."

"I saw them," Dave said slowly. "I told her I was proud

she was going to be queen. She wouldn't speak to me."

Old Zeke nodded. "Knew she wouldn't. Like I said, she's done with you. Your high-and-mighty pa couldn't keep my girl from being queen, and that's something." His faded brown eyes lighted with pride. "I'll be there on final show night when she hands out the silver trophy to the first-class roadster with appointments."

Dave swallowed. "I hope it'll be me," he said quietly.

Old Zeke's hand went idle on the hammer. "You mean you're drivin'?"

Dave nodded. He looked at the old man, hoping for some small sign of approval. Old Zeke smoothed the front of his leather apron.

"Made my entry this afternoon," Dave said.

Old Zeke turned back to his work. "Don't make no difference to me whether it's you or King," he said. "I hate that Barton name. And it won't make no difference with Lindy, either."

"I'm doing it for her," Dave said.

"Go on!" old Zeke shouted impatiently. "Can't you see I'm busy?"

When Dave got home King was pacing up and down on the front porch. "Where the devil have you been?" he demanded irritably.

"Town," Dave answered briefly.

"That all you got to do — run to town?"

"Just decided to go today."

"That so? Why?"

Dave forced himself to meet King's penetrating look. "I entered Black Shamrock in the roadster-with-appointments class at the fair."

King's face went white. "You fool!" he shouted.

"I want to drive," Dave said, his voice very low. "And

I've always known you didn't want me to. Did you think you could keep me swiping forever?"

"You can't drive," King said contemptuously. "You've had no experience in a show ring. Lots of men are good trainers, but they can't put a horse through the big show."

"This isn't anything big," Dave replied. "It's just the county fair."

"But it leads to other things," King said harshly. "I know. I've seen thousands of kids like you. They end up broke and swiping for the men who can drive, or they end up drunken bums because they've eaten their hearts out over horses. I'll do the driving in this family. You can help train. Stay away from the shows."

"Black Shamrock's built to show and she's got lots of action in her trotting," Dave said evenly. "I've watched you drive. I know all your tricks — and some of my own. I'm driving Black Shamrock, and when Lindy hands out that trophy it's going to be mine."

King threw back his head and laughed. It was an ugly sound. "Cocksure of yourself, aren't you? So it's her that's back of all this?" The glittering gray-blue eyes narrowed. "I ought to tan some sense into that thick hide of yours. But I won't. There's better ways to beat men than with fists."

Dave felt a chill run down his spine. "What do you mean?"

King's jaw tightened in a resolute line. "I'll enter and drive against you."

Dave stared incredulously at his father. He said hoarsely, "You wouldn't — you couldn't. Why...you haven't driven at a county fair for eight years. You're big time."

"The choice is up to you," King said coolly. "You drive and I drive. You stay out and I stay out."

Dave's eyes hardened. "Now I believe what I've never wanted to believe," he said. "You're cruel and egotistical. You don't want me to drive because you want to keep all the glory for yourself."

The thin smile touched King's lips. "Maybe."

Dave's hands doubled into fists. "I'll stay and train Black Shamrock," he said, "but when the fair's over, we're through."

King Barton entered the roadster show the following day. Then the wild speculation began. "The kid's stood up to him at last," people said. "And that kid knows horses and driving."

The next morning crowds leaned over the rail at the farm track. They saw King working out the sleek bay mare, Lulu Belle, who had been shown at the Kansas City Royal. And they saw Dave driving Black Shamrock.

Old-timers said King had never been in better driving form and that Lulu Belle had her usual impressive style. But when they looked at Black Shamrock they shook their heads. "She's built beautiful," they said, "conformation for a winner. If all she had to do was stand still, she'd knock the judge's eyes out. But the way she travels! She's a wide-going horse behind and she'll never square up and go smooth in the ring. The kid hasn't got a chance. Damn shame, isn't it?"

The last night of the fair, when it was nearing time for the roadsters with appointments to show, a silence settled over the grandstand. The lights burned white under an ominous sky and the track looked black.

Down front in the grandstand, in a box draped with blue and white crepe paper, sat Lindy Ames, looking like a small, fair-haired ghost. Old Zeke sat beside her, shuffling his feet and glancing nervously toward the entrance gate.

The high school band began to play and the announcer lifted his hard black hat and shouted, "Ladeez and gentlemen! The event of the evening! The highlight of the fair! The cream of driving skill! Ladeez and gentlemen! Roadsters with appointments!"

The band rhythm quickened. A wind of excitement rose in the crowd. Roadsters began to jog through the gate. Russ Longpre driving Heat Lightning. Bill Wallace driving Royal Archer. Skeet Stanton driving Braw Bess. Hugh Arnold driving Kentucky Joe. And then — King Barton, in his famous red silk shirt, driving Lulu Belle. He half rose, swept off his rakish red hat, pressed it against his heart and inclined his head in a bowing gesture. The crowd, as always, broke into thunderous applause.

There was a momentary hush. Everyone looked toward the gate. And in came Dave and Black Shamrock. An exclamation of surprise rose from the grandstand, for Dave was wearing green trousers, a white jacket, and a green snap-brim felt hat. Surprise was followed by shouts of approval.

Dave's lips tightened in a grim smile. His entrance, at least, had caused as much fanfare as his father's. He eased Black Shamrock to the right, going the wrong way around the track as was the custom in warming up.

Judge McLennan, standing in the center of the track, gave him a faint smile. Thunder growled in the distance and a blue chain of lightning laddered down the eastern sky.

Five times Dave passed with the others around the blocked-in track before the judge. Then he saw the judge's arm go up and heard the shout as it fell. "Turn on!"

Drivers jockeyed to the left, turning the horses the right way of the track. Wheels scraped wheels, and then King Barton's famous cry rose in a great "Wa-ooh!" The crowd came to its feet. King sparred for an opening and shot through, passing Dave and Black Shamrock, flaunting Lulu Belle's speed before the judge and the grandstand.

I'll cover him up, so help me! Dave thought fiercely. *I'll fix it so Judge McLennan can't see that mare!*

As he flicked Black Shamrock with the whip she acted as

though she'd amble. "Oh, Lord!" he muttered. "Don't let her break into pace." He held her down the straightaway, but when she came to the turn she almost galloped.

Someone shouted, "Look out, Dave. She can't trot a turn."

Black Shamrock seemed to rock awkwardly and Dave knew she was trotting wider than usual and away to the right. He began to feel sick inside. If Black Shamrock didn't travel smoother, the judge couldn't give him enough points to matter.

He brought her back to the straightaway. King Barton crowded past him, coming so close the spectators gasped.

Dave tightened up on the reins as Black Shamrock pounded toward the curve, but he felt her breaking—breaking. He shouted hoarsely, pulling hard on the reins. Then it happened. She threw a shoe. Dave pulled her up as the judge signaled for the showing to stop.

"Blacksmith!" the announcer shouted. "Bring on the blacksmith!"

Dave looked frantically toward the crowd, noting that King had stopped beside him.

King said, "Too bad. The blacksmith went to the hospital this afternoon. Appendicitis." And he smiled that thin, sardonic way of his. "Old Zeke's on duty tonight."

"Blacksmith!" the announcer repeated.

Dave looked toward the box where Lindy and old Zeke sat. The track dust was thick in his throat. The grandstand blurred before his eyes as he saw Lindy rise to her feet. And then he saw something else and his heart thundered against his ribs. Old Zeke was running across the track, his leather apron flapping, and a boy ran behind him with the shoeing kit.

"Seven minutes!" the announcer shouted. "Seven minutes to shoe her!"

King Barton laughed harshly and said, "Old Zeke never could shoe a horse in less than twenty minutes."

But the blacksmith was already trimming away the right hind hoof where it had broken when Black Shamrock threw her shoe.

Dave bent toward old Zeke, saying, "She's trotting way wide behind and to the right."

"Saw that," old Zeke grunted. "She never was shod right in the first place. I know how to weight a mare where she needs it. Gimme that felt, boy. There's only one way to narrow a horse's way of trotting behind, and that's to add weight to the inside of the shoe. I'll build up the break and add the weight here where she needs it." He gave Dave a momentary glance. "And don't get the idea I'm doin' this for you. You're still a Barton to me. But you can drive. And I'd sell my soul to see King Barton get beat."

"Four minutes to go!" the announcer shouted.

Old Zeke slapped the felt padding into place and reached for a shoe.

"Nails!" he shouted. The hammer beat a quick tattoo.

"Three minutes!" the announcer said.

The rasp slid down, grating in the silence.

"One minute!"

"Finished!" Old Zeke panted, straightening. "Now, watch her square up when she starts to trot!"

He looked across at King Barton and a stream of tobacco juice squirted down the front wheel of King's buggy. Then he ran from the track, the boy helper at his heels. Dave climbed back on the buggy seat.

"Turn on!" Judge McLennan shouted.

The roadsters stretched out, lengthening into a trotting stride. Dave pulled in behind his father. King Barton sat easy on the buggy seat, his proud head tilted back, a disdainful expression on his face.

Dave felt Black Shamrock steady into her stride. He felt

her go swift and smooth, her slim legs flashing out in powerful trotting action. She wasn't trotting wide behind any longer. She was squared up like a champion.

Wild excitement surged through Dave. Recklessness possessed him. He shook the reins and leaned forward. "Yeah, girl!" he yelled. Delighted, the crowd repeated him. King Barton sent a startled glance toward his son.

Dave crowded close, shoving past Heat Lightning and Braw Bess, pushing forward and forward until he covered up Lulu Belle and displayed Black Shamrock's trotting before the judge. Then with another wild "Yeah, girl!" he matched King Barton down the straightaway for speed.

A flash of lightning ripped open the clouds above the track as Black Shamrock hit her top stride. Drops of cold rain struck Dave's face. He eased Black Shamrock past Lulu Belle and the crowd cheered him. Black Shamrock took the turn at a perfect trot, swinging back into the straightaway with her long tail streaming in the wind.

Dave caught a glimpse of his father's face. It was white and tired, but the stubborn pride was still evident in the uplifted head, the tilt of the chin and the disdainful smile.

Recklessness fired Dave's driving skill and he drove as one possessed, squeezing through the smallest possible openings and taking again and again the best showing position before the judge. The crowd saw the king of track showmen crowded to the wall by a young black-haired boy.

Judge McLennan signaled for the showing to stop. The drivers brought their horses forward, lining up before him. And each driver stepped down and to the back of his buggy, lifting out his kit of appointments and spreading it open on top of the buggy box.

Dave let the reins fall to the ground and Black Shamrock stood proud and motionless, her feet braced in a perfect showing stance. He tossed aside the green blanket and opened his kit, laying out the silver whiskey flask, the horse brush, a black comb, a bottle of shaving lotion, a safety razor, a bottle of horse liniment and a small silver horseshoe.

Judge McLennan moved from buggy to buggy, carefully inspecting the appointments. He paused beside Dave, touched the silver horseshoe and smiled. "Most of them just carry an ordinary shoe, Dave, but a few folks with imagination put in one like this. I like it. Where'd you get it?"

"Lindy Ames sent it to me."

The judge nodded, his smile deepening. He finished his round of inspections, wrote on a slip of white paper and handed it to the announcer.

The announcer's words were drowned out by a loud clap of thunder, but the crowd saw Dave Barton driving toward the fair queen's box and applauded. He stepped down, lifted Lindy and the silver trophy out of the box and into the buggy. Black Shamrock trotted toward the entrance gate.

Then King Barton, a showman to the last, flicked Lulu Belle with the whip and raced across the track, pulling up beside them. There was a strange broken look on his face, but he stepped from his buggy and stood holding out his hand in a gesture of congratulation.

Slowly Dave's hand moved down to meet his father's.

"Dave," King said, "you were born to show horses. I knew that from long ago, but I tried to keep you from it." He paused, his mouth twisting. "Don't make the mistake I did. Don't let show business mean more to you than her." And he looked at Lindy Ames.

Then King Barton got into his buggy and drove out. When he reached home he burned his red silk shirt and red hat. He walked into the wide carpeted hall and stood staring at the oil painting of Kathleen.

That was where Dave found him. King turned and looked at his son, and a faint gleam of hope kindled in his eyes. "Well, Dave?"

"Could you use a beautiful swipe," Dave asked — "one with gray eyes and gold-colored hair?"

The thin, sardonic smile flickered across King's mouth. "No law against it," he replied, trying to keep his voice cool and steady. "But I need a driver, too." He looked searchingly at his son.

Dave nodded. "I'd want my own blacksmith," he said. "A blacksmith can be very important around race and show tracks. Especially when he knows how to weight a mare to win."

Color came up in King's pale face. "Well, bring them in!" he shouted. "Don't stand there all night!"

King's still got the best horses in Illinois. You can see them any time you drive past the home farm, west of town. But he won't drive them. And when you ask him if he'll ever take a roadster into the show ring again, he just smiles and looks away — like he is thinking of something else.

THE THIRD STORY set around Illinois harness racing, "Gypsy Trainer" appeared in *Boys' Life* in March 1974.

GYPSY TRAINER

AROUND THE ILLINOIS harness-racing stables, you'll hear the story. Some of what you hear will be true but most of it will be hot air. I'm the only one who can tell it the way it really was.

Take my name for instance. They call me Coonhound Johnny but that's only a nickname. Illinois is a great place for nicknames, especially when it comes to men who work pacers and trotters. Like Duke Callahan. Nobody ever speaks of him as Kevin Callahan, which is his real name. He's "The Duke" to the thousands of people who watch him drive to win, one of his great horses pacing a half length ahead of the field.

I'd never have had the nerve to challenge him if it hadn't been for my past history. While I was in the orphanage I read everything I could get my hands on about harness racing. And the day I was fifteen and ran away, I met up with an old gypsy trainer named Hoot Jamison. I bummed around with him for two years, going to all the county fairs in summer and helping him train his horses to a jog cart in winter.

Like all gypsy trainers, Hoot Jamison didn't have money for fancy horseflesh. He bought cull colts, old horses, and broken-down horses. He raced them in overnight events at the county fairs. These are the races for horses that aren't fast enough to qualify for the stake races.

Hoot Jamison believed in all sorts of far-out things: colts foaled in full moon could pace faster, river mud would heal sores on a horse that nothing else could heal, horses were smarter than humans and sometimes they talked to you. I got so I believed everything he said. I even started dreaming he was my father. When you've never known blood kin of your own, you can have a lot of wild dreams.

Then came the spring when he was short of cash. We'd had a bad summer before winter set in. His last two horses didn't win any prize money at the fairs. He sold one to an Amish farmer for a quiet life pulling a buggy and the other one to a man from Canada. They have harness races on ice in Canada and don't mind buying older and slower horses. It was April when he told me he figured on settling down to farm work for a while.

I didn't want to work a tractor. They don't warm under your hands like horses. So I took off on my own and hitched a ride down country with a paint salesman. He let me out one afternoon by a big white farmhouse. "That's the Duke's place," he said. "Might be he could use you."

I looked at the pasture with a curve of river going through one side. The grass looked a lot more prosperous than back where Hoot and I had grazed horses on the infield of the county fair tracks. And the big farmhouse and barns were mighty fine compared to the old trailer Hoot and I shared. But I walked toward the front door, holding my head up high and telling myself I was a real gypsy trainer and knew horses better than my name. And I reminded myself that my duffel bag held more than just a few faded clothes. In it I carried my license to drive pacers and my driving jacket. When you get your colors for your jacket, they're yours for a lifetime and I was mighty proud of my green and white.

My hand shook when I knocked on that front door. Then

it opened and I looked up at this tall man who didn't have any extra flesh on him anywhere. His hair was thick and black and turning white at the temples. He looked just the way such a man would look—proud and sure. Only his eyes made you feel like squirming. They were the color of a clean, cold winter sky. I pushed my beat-up bag behind me and tried smoothing down my red hair. It sprang up rough and wild under my hand the way it always does.

"Well," he said. Not a question but not a word to encourage you, either.

I reeled off about a ten-minute autobiography of my life with horses and Hoot Jamison. "I expect you know Hoot," I finished.

"Never heard of him," Duke Callahan said.

"Him and I seen you drive lots of times. He's got magic with horses and—"

"That's what all gypsy drivers think," he cut in. "If you need a job, I could use another swipe."

My pride took a bad spill. With Hoot I wasn't a swipe. I was a trainer and driver. We shared the chores. "I've got my license and my colors," I said quickly.

"You won't need them."

I was of a mind to move on but I only had $2.45 in my jeans and I was hungry. I vowed I'd stay only two weeks at this fancy place. "Okay," I said. "They call me Coonhound Johnny. Hoot named me that because I liked to prowl around and pet his horses in the night."

Something glinted in those cool eyes. I wasn't sure whether he was laughing at me or not. "Okay, Coonhound," he said, "park your stuff in the room at the end of the first barn." Then he shut the door, practically in my face.

The room was as fine as I'd ever hoped to settle in. Big bed, red leather chairs, a desk, red linoleum on the floor, and pictures of some of the Duke's horses on the walls. I sat down and took off my shoes and started dreaming I belonged there.

In a few days I was well acquainted with all the swipes and trainers and a million dollars worth of fancy horses. They were all Standardbreds and the Duke's favorite was Magic Ben, a two-year-old he'd nominated as a colt for the great Illinois stake race at the state fair.

I didn't know he'd paid the fee and the other payments to nominate another two-year-old—a black mare. I didn't hear about her for a week and only then because I happened to go into a barn where I never worked and saw her shut up by herself. "Who's she?" I asked the swipe who was hosing out a stall.

"They call her the black jinx, but her real name is Princess."

When I moved toward the stall I understood why. She wasn't gentle like the other horses but reared up and snorted. The swipe moved up beside me and told me she wouldn't even lead right. "Sets her feet like she was sunk in concrete," he said. "Besides, she's got a split left-front hoof that won't heal and up above it is always swollen and full of infection. The Duke's gonna sell her to a couple of killers from Chicago. They'll make dog food outta her."

I stood there staring at the black mare. Her head swung around and she looked right at me. Something happened then. I could feel a part of her reach out to me. And part of me went out to her. I knew we belonged together. Maybe I felt this deeper than some because I'd never had my own blood kin to care about me. I started into that stall.

"Don't go in there!" the swipe yelled. "She'll pound you to a pulp!"

But I wouldn't have stopped if he'd stuck a gun in my face. I moved right up to the mare and she stood shaking, her eyes rolling. I felt my hands tingle when I touched her, gently, the way you touch someone you love. "Princess," I said, "you're a champion."

I felt her change under my hands. It was as though all the rough, tough things in her smoothed out and flowed quiet as deep, peaceful water. And I knew then I was a real gypsy trainer. I had that special magic in my hands that the great gypsy trainers have always had.

It was at that moment that the Duke came walking up with two pasty-faced men. I could tell what they were at a glance. I leaned against the Princess. I wanted to pour all my hard seventeen years of growing into her and make her strong and perfect. "You're a champion," I said again. "You were born to be a champion." Then I turned and faced those pasty-faced men. "You can't have her!"

They all stared at me. The Duke's jaw sagged and his mouth fell open. Then he pulled himself back together. "What do you mean, kid?"

"She's got to have her chance. They've no right to her until she's had her chance. I'll heal her and drive her."

His face hardened. "She's had her chance — cost me a fortune. She's had all the fancy hot baths I ever heard of. I hired a special horseshoer from Kentucky and an expensive veterinarian from Chicago. I've kept making payments on her in case she might heal. It's all been a waste and a heartbreak. Besides that, she's got a rotten disposition."

"She'll outpace your Magic Ben!" I cried. "Listen, I'll make you a bet. I'll drive her against Magic Ben in the first county-fair race you enter. If she loses, then you can sell her to these men. I'm betting her life against your favorite."

He looked shocked. One of the pale men from Chicago gave a kind of nervous giggle. "Are you afraid to call my bet?" I challenged him. "Are you afraid your great Magic Ben might lose his first race?"

He still stared at me as if he couldn't believe what I was saying. "There might be some things about horses you don't know, Mr. Duke Callahan," I finished.

That did it. I saw that his dander was up by the way the light flicked up in his eyes. "You're crazy," he said, "but I'll call that bet. And when you come leading a cripple onto the race track maybe you'll learn to keep your mouth shut." He turned and walked away. The killers trailed after him like two whipped curs at the heels of a master.

I stood there in the stall beside the Princess for a long time after they were gone. I talked to her and petted her. And when I was all talked out, I closed my eyes and held hard to the thought that she might be healed. It was a kind of praying, I guess.

I didn't get to eat the noon meal, for it had come to me what I would do. And I knew I had to start right away. I coaxed the Princess out of the stall, and she followed me as if I had been leading her around since she was a colt. I picked up a shovel and led her down to the river bank in the pasture. I found a place where high water had left a wet, swampy place. I dug a mud hole and tromped it up sticky and dark and warming in the sun. I coaxed her to stand in it, being sure that bad hoof was well covered with a mud poultice.

It wasn't long until the Duke came down there and stood over me, his face like a thundercloud. "You fool around with her on your free time," he said. "You don't neglect your real work."

I dug my big cheap watch I used to time Hoot Jamison's horses out of my pocket. "Yes, sir," I said. "I got ten minutes. I'll be at work at one o'clock just the same as I always am."

"When do you expect to eat?"

"I don't," I told him and saw something flicker in his eyes.

And that's how it was. I kept on missing the noon meal, for I wanted her in the mud when it was warm. I got thinner than I'd ever been before. My pants hung loose and I had to cut two extra holes in my belt. And every day I'd count off how many days were left until the fairs started in July.

One noon, after I'd been working with the Princess about six weeks, the Duke came back to the mudhole. He carried a plate with four ham sandwiches, a bag of potato chips, and three boiled eggs on it. "Blast it!" he said. "Eat something."

"Thanks," I said and got it all down mighty fast while he stood looking off into space.

Then he said, "How's she coming along?"

"She's coming along," I said and led the Princess out of the mudhole.

He bent down and took a long, careful look at the hoof and the leg above it. His face was something to see. He shook his head as if he was all mixed up in his mind. Then he walked away.

I'd had her in the mud two months, every day since early April, and I decided I had to start training her and she was ready. One evening after I had done my day's work, I hooked her to the jog cart and took her onto the Duke's training track just to see what kind of action she might have. I didn't put any hobbles on her, for I figured I was just limbering her legs up this first go-round. She stepped right out into a natural pace. My heart pounded hard enough to burst. I knew then she was one of those horses you don't find very often — a free-legged pacer. She'd never have to wear hobbles like most of them.

The Duke was there waiting when I brought her in. He looked at the mare and then at me and there was awe in his voice when he spoke. "A free-legged pacer!"

"And a coming champion," I said.

I began hitching her to the jog cart three days a week and to the sulky two days a week. I only got to use the track after hours, when the Duke wasn't working Magic Ben or his trainers working other horses. I took the Princess around the track early in the morning or while it was still light in the evening so I could time her every eighth of a mile. A lot of nights I didn't get to the supper table. And a lot of times men came from other horse farms to watch me work the Princess out. I guess by that time everybody for miles around knew about my bet with Duke.

There came a morning when the Duke was waiting for me as I turned off the training track. "You're up mighty early," I said.

"I heard those sulky wheels singing," he said. "It's a comforting sound when a man lives alone without wife or kids."

I stepped down from the sulky seat. I felt close to the Duke there in the cool still morning when you could smell the grass and the earth. It was the first time he'd mentioned his wife and kid, but I knew the story. Both of them had died in a car wreck long before I came to the place.

"You've brought that mare a long way," he said.

"Not as far as she's going," I replied. "She'll beat Magic Ben."

"Not according to my watch," he said. "I've kept time on her. I plan to start Magic Ben at Chester. It's a small fair but they've got a mile track and we won't have to go two heats like we do at the half-mile tracks most of them have."

"Fine," I said. "That's as good a place as any."

"Johnny," he said in a strange, quiet way, "I don't want you to drive at Chester. We'll race some other time."

"The agreement was the first race," I said. "I don't aim to chicken out on the bet."

"I'm asking you not to drive against me yet," he said.

"Why?"

"When I drive, I drive to win. I'd never hold back a horse that's trained to be a champion."

"I aim to drive the same way," I said. "Let's let it go at that."

He got mad then. His face turned red and then white.

"When I drive, I drive to win," he said again. "And that means driving rough if I have to. I have to win. That's the way I am. Johnny, I don't want a kid to get in my way of qualifying Magic Ben for the state-fair stake. I have to race him in two county-fair races to qualify him for the state fair. I don't drive losing horses. I intend to win at Chester."

"So do I," I said stubbornly.

He drew a deep, hard breath. "Okay, if that's the way you want it."

When I saw him taking Magic Ben around the track later that day, I began to feel sick inside. He went like a champion. He was fast—faster than the Princess. I started working her every chance I had. I even took her out at night, driving her around the training track under the stars. I got thin and jumpy and I could feel the Princess tensing up tight and high, the way I was. We were both strung to a pitch that was scary, and that was going to hurt us.

"You're going at it too hard," the Duke told me. "It's bad for you and the mare, too. Better slow down."

He might as well have told a kettle to stop boiling. And after that one warning he didn't say another word. He just seemed cold and distant and he didn't watch me driving the mare any more. When we went over to Chester for the fair, he was still cool and distant. I wondered if he was getting ready to fire me when the race was over. I'd come to think of his farm as home. And I'd come to feel close to the Duke. I knew that was wrong. When you're a loner like me, you don't dare let yourself feel close to somebody who's never going to want you.

The morning of the two-year-old stake at Chester, I started sweating the Princess out at eleven in the morning. The race was set for two in the afternoon. I jogged her around and around the track, keeping her warmed up. Then I washed and blanketed her and took her out to jog again. Thoroughbred horses don't have to be warmed up. They can start right out and run, but Standardbred pacers and trotters have to be sweated out thoroughly before a race.

I kept telling myself I had luck on my side. I'd drawn the pole position for the Princess. The other drivers sweating out their horses waved at me and some of them shouted, "Get in there and drive, kid. The Duke never wants to get beat and you've got him scared."

It seemed time went by too fast. Then I was driving up to the starting line, wearing my colors. My heart thudded under my ribs and my mouth was so dry I couldn't have spit if I'd wanted to. The grandstand crowd was yelling loud enough to make a man deaf. And then we were off, the Princess pacing fine and free, her tail streaming. As we rounded the near turn the wind tossed the track smells in my face — dust, frying hamburgers, popcorn, heat and horses.

I began to settle down a little, holding the Princess steady. It was the last eighth of the mile where she had to turn on and do her best. I could hear the singing sulky wheels and the pound of the pacers behind me. I don't know how far we'd gone before I felt someone drawing up close. Next thing I realized there was a horse right there pacing neck and neck with the Princess, trying to go past her and take the pole position. And I saw the spinning wheels of another sulky so close you couldn't put a handkerchief between them and mine. *Magic Ben and the Duke*! The great horse pacing to win and the Duke driving to win.

We came into the stretch and the wind was in my eyes so I couldn't see anything clear any more. Sweat ran down me like a shower of warm water. Then I chilled. There was only a breath between the Duke's wheels and mine. "*I aim to drive to win. That means driving rough if I have to.*"

I knew now what rough driving meant. You were scared

half to death. One wrong move and your sulky could be spilled and all those horses behind you would pound up over you. You either stuck in there and took your chances or you eased up and let the Duke take the race. I made my decision. I leaned forward and touched the Princess with the whip for the first time. "Ha-a-a-a!" I yelled. "Ha-a-a, girl! Go, girl, go!"

For a second nothing happened and then like the champion mare she was, she began to draw away, pacing faster and faster. We were clear, free of those menacing wheels! The finish line blurred right there before me. A roar like thunder came from the grandstand.

I passed the finish line and went quite a way up the track before I could find strength in my arms to stop her. I got off the sulky and walked unsteadily to her head and put my arms around her and laid my cheek against that hot, wet, black neck.

I don't know how I happened to look down but I did. And I saw she held up that front hoof and blood was oozing down over it. I knew then she'd never go on to race for the championship at the great Illinois stake. It would take two or three months to heal that hoof again — and maybe it could never be healed for always. I'd worked her too hard or maybe there wouldn't be blood on her now.

I dropped down there in the dust of the track and took that hoof in my hands. I didn't care that somebody was flashing a camera at us. I just held the hoof and cried. Then the Duke was in the dust beside me with his arm tight around my shoulders.

"You beat me fair and square," he said. "You drove a great race and she's a great mare." His arm drew me closer. "Let's take her home now and take care of her. That's where I want you both to stay."

Home. It was a word he spoke like he was my own blood kin. I knew right then I was one gypsy trainer in Illinois who was never going to go wandering again.

ONE WINTER PEG PRESENTED a program in Worland, Wyoming, for the Wyoming Council on the Arts. While she was there, she learned of the local tradition of using teenage students as school bus drivers. One of the bus routes ran out to a place called Gooseberry Creek, according to Bill Curry, and so was born a story.

"Gooseberry Run" appeared in *Boys' Life* in December 1970.

GOOSEBERRY RUN

D ENNY O'KEEFE WAITED impatiently in the driver's seat of the small yellow school bus. The sky was low and gray. The air had a strange, damp stillness to it.

Denny worried about driving his bus route. Gooseberry Run was the longest bus route serving the town school system, a seventy-mile road through lonely Wyoming prairie country to the foot of the mountains where his parents had a small ranch. He made the trip twice a day; with the stops for passengers, it took him two and a half, maybe three, hours each way.

But today it'll take longer, Denny thought, shifting nervously. Today he had the extra Christmas groceries for the ranches. He'd been excused from his last class at school to go downtown and load all the things besides passengers he had to carry out Gooseberry Run. The mail sacks, newspapers and Christmas groceries were packed in the back of the bus.

Now the Three Wise Men came jostling out the front door of the grade school building. Their purple and yellow and red robes fell from under their heavy coats, trailing color on the snow. They were followed by Mary, splendid in voluminous white, her coat hooked to her shoulders like a cape. She carried a cradle in which the baby-doll Jesus was tucked under a blue blanket. Behind these leading characters of the grade school pageant came other passengers for Gooseberry Run—

a pushing, squealing, laughing group laden with popcorn balls in plastic sacks and Christmas gifts with wrappings carelessly folded around them.

Denny's attention shifted to the high school building. *Where was Billy Martin?* Several times in the last month Billy Martin had deliberately lingered, making Denny late in starting. And there were other methods Billy used to annoy him. Twice he had brought mice on the bus, loosing them as Denny drove along the lonely prairie road, sending the little girls into hysterics. Another time Billy had carried a rattlesnake in his hat. It had taken Denny a while to convince the smallest passenger the snake was really dead.

As Denny went outside to greet them, the grade school kids scrambled aboard, voices rising in chorus, "Hiya, Denny!" A sack of popcorn balls fell to the floor. Feet crunched over it. "Where's Billy?" someone shouted. Then, when Denny again sat in the driver's seat, the group yelled in unison, "Go without him! Go without him!"

At that moment Billy Martin sauntered from the high school and moved at a leisurely pace toward the bus. Tall, dark-haired and thick-shouldered, he swung a bright-red stocking cap in his hand.

He came aboard, paused by the driver's seat and looked at Denny with bold black eyes. "Better stay in town, Denny. Old Shifty told us last night a bad blizzard was gonna break this afternoon."

Old Shifty was a dreamy and drifting man who moved from ranch to ranch, doing odd jobs. Many thought Old Shifty had strange powers of looking into the future. The people of Gooseberry Run had superstitious faith in Old Shifty's predictions.

"I checked with the weather bureau," Denny said. "Only light snow flurries predicted." *But,* he thought with a twinge of uneasiness, *Wyoming weather doesn't always behave according to weather predictions.*

Billy smiled in a superior way. "You don't say," he drawled, sliding into a seat behind Denny. The kids giggled at the sarcasm.

Denny felt the flush crawl up the back of his neck. He was seventeen and sensitive. And, although he was a senior in high school, like Billy Martin, somehow Billy always made him feel like a child.

"Listen," he said, easing the bus away from the school buildings, "I wish you'd lay off me. It's not my fault I got this job instead of you. I took a year of special driver training, worked with the highway patrol and the police. You didn't. All you did was ask for the job and ignore the requirements."

"We've got a dumb school board and superintendent," Billy said, "They don't think we know anything out on Gooseberry Run. I was drivin' when I was ten years old. I've forgot more about handlin' a car than you smart guys from California ever knew."

Denny tried to ignore him, driving carefully along the six blocks of main street, moving under the sagging green ropes and mute red bells of Christmas decorations. He headed the bus out of town and took the country road toward the distant blue-white smudge of the mountains.

"You dudes don't know this country," Billy went on. "You been here two years and—"

"I know," Denny cut in bitterly, "we're dumb. We don't understand the cattle business, the country or the people. You and your folks haven't helped us any. Some neighbors, the Martins!"

"We call the shots like we see them," Billy replied. "Your folks buy a two-bit ranch at the end of Gooseberry Run and think they can make it go. You go over to town and smart off to the school board and the superintendent and take a lot of fancy courses in how to drive."

From the back of the bus Mary, still holding the cradle, shouted, "You think it's gonna snow, Billy?"

He turned around. "Sure. Old Shifty don't miss a prediction. We're not gonna make it to your ranch. And the Three Wise Men won't get home for supper either."

"That's enough!" Denny spoke sharply. "Don't try to scare the kids."

"Okay," Billy said pleasantly. "But you still got time to turn around and make it back to town." He took a transistor radio from his pocket and turned it on loud. The passengers began to stomp and clap to the jangly Western music.

Looking up the road, Denny assured himself that nothing was going to happen. He remembered how proud he had been when he got the job driving the school bus. The school superintendent had said, "You've got a tradition to uphold. For eighteen years we've had student drivers on our bus routes and we've never had an accident. And remember, it's a special honor to drive Gooseberry Run."

Now Denny wasn't so sure, not when he had a Billy Martin bucking him all the time. He glanced in the front mirror and saw that one of the Wise Men was brandishing a plastic baseball bat. Denny raised his voice above the loud music, "Bring that bat up here."

Billy Martin turned down the radio. "No law says he has to."

"I say he has to." Denny's thin jaw tightened.

Grumbling, the boy brought the bat up front and dropped it near Denny's feet. "It was the present I got at the school party today."

Denny made his first stop, getting rid of three passengers, a sack of mail, a newspaper and a box of groceries. He drove on, looking anxiously toward the mountains. He couldn't see them now; a gray-white curtain lay between him and the peaks.

"They just issued an emergency weather bulletin," Billy Martin said, his transistor at his ear. "Blizzard comin' in fast from the west. Travelers' and stockmen's warning. Temperature dropping. Old Shifty read the signs right."

Denny didn't answer. He didn't know whether Billy was telling a lie or the truth. He wasn't going to ask questions and make a fool of himself. A cold knot grew in his stomach as he watched the white curtain move closer across the prairie. By the time the light was thickening, he had gotten rid of all of his passengers but Mary, the Three Wise Men and Billy Martin. *Only ten more miles to Mary's place,* he thought. *If I have to, I can stop there....*

A few big flakes of snow drifted across the road. *Only a flurry,* Denny reassured himself. *The weather man knows more than Old Shifty.* And then, suddenly, the snow came thick and fast, like a white wall breaking and tumbling over them.

Denny stared toward the side of the road where a wire fence marked off prairie pasture land. He could barely see that fence. He slowed the bus, driving slowly and carefully. Cold sweat began to gather under his arms and on his forehead. He switched on the headlights. They didn't help much.

The bus was crawling now. Denny peered desperately ahead. The windshield wipers scarcely moved the heavy snow, slicing slowly back and forth to make two arcs of cleared glass that quickly clouded over again. Denny stopped the bus. "This is as far as I'm going," he said. His hands trembled on the wheel. His knees shook.

"What's the matter, Denny?" Billy Martin's voice was soft and mocking. "Scared of a little snow?"

"I can't see the road. It's not safe to drive."

"I'll drive. I know this road in the dark." Billy Martin came up beside him. "Get up and let an old pro take the wheel."

"No," Denny said firmly, "It's not safe. Nobody moves my bus."

Billy Martin yanked him out of the seat. For a moment they stood in the narrow space. Blinding anger swept over Denny. He struck out, his knuckles scraping off Billy's chin. Then a big fist rocked him. He went down hard, hearing a scream before his head struck something sharp and numbing.

Denny came slowly out of darkness. He was conscious of motion. *The bus was moving.* He tasted blood and felt something gentle and soft against his mouth. His vision focused on the Three Wise Men. One was holding a handkerchief against Denny's cut lip. He struggled to his feet. Billy Martin was in the driver's seat and the bus was going steadily up the road.

"Stop!" Denny's voice sounded strange and hoarse.

Billy Martin laughed and kept on driving.

Denny moved toward him. Then the bus started sliding — down, down, down. It plunged faster, slipping sideways. Denny grabbed for a seat and hung on. There was a hard jar. The bus stopped. Denny looked back at his passengers. "Everybody all right?"

The Three Wise Men, white-faced, clung to seats. Mary was down in the aisle, crying. Denny hurried to her. "Are you hurt, Mary?"

"My arm—"

Denny knelt beside her. examining the arm. "Just bruised, honey. You'll be okay." He patted her tousled blond hair.

Billy Martin was trying to back up the bus. The motor roared. The wheels spun. Denny reached him as Billy shut off the motor. He turned and looked at Denny. "We ran off into a ravine," he said.

"You wrecked my bus," Denny said. "I'll hold you responsible."

Billy Martin got out of the driver's seat. His mouth had a tight look to it. Beyond him Denny saw the windshield closing over with snow — *like a thick, cold fur,* Denny thought. It seemed to Denny in that moment that the bleak country, the indifferent sky, the fierce storm and Billy Martin all joined in one great force to defeat him. *Why had his parents ever come from California to bring him to this?*

As he stood there, staring hard at Billy, he could feel the darkness coming — coming quickly and coldly, bringing its shroud of white. He saw Billy start, as though from a sudden scare or shock. Then Billy spoke. "We gotta do something." And Billy's head swung toward Denny as if he asked for help.

"Yes," Denny said, the word spoken through the pain of his lip. He flipped on the lights, driving back the shadows crowding inside the bus. He looked at the Three Wise Men. "You boys take off your costumes. Tear them up and make a cloth rope. Get Mary's costume, too. We'll fix a curtain over the rope, shut off the front part of the bus up here near the heater. That'll keep most of the warm air in a small space." He turned to Billy Martin. "You got a pocketknife?"

Billy Martin nodded.

"Rip up some bus seats. Pack the stuffing on the floor and around the doors. Mary, get the newspapers in back."

"What for?" Billy asked curiously.

"Insulation. You kids pack the newspaper under the outer layer of your clothes. Gather the plastic sacks scattered around. Take off your shoes and put on the sacks — then your overshoes. Your feet will stay warmer." Denny went to the back and looked over the packages in the mail. He found three big boxes and ripped them open. There was an electric blanket, a tablecloth, and three large bath towels.

"That's against the law," Billy Martin said, "tampering with other people's mail."

Hysterical laughter bubbled in Denny's throat. *Billy Martin, defier of rules and regulations — Billy Martin telling him about breaking laws!* He carried his loot up front and strung the cloth rope made by the Three Wise Men. Then he draped the things over it, creating a makeshift curtain. By then the bus was cold. Denny started the motor and turned on the heater. "We'll only run it a little while at a time," he said. "The gas has got to last."

When the bus felt warm, he cut the motor and the interior lights. Now it was very dark. He heard Billy Martin's transistor. The dance music stopped. Weather reports came on, warning stockmen and travelers, announcing blizzard conditions. It was ten below zero in town and the temperature was expected to keep dropping. Billy Martin shut off the radio. It was very quiet in the darkness.

"Why don't we tell stories?" Denny said. "One person start and everybody join in. I'll begin: Once upon a time there was a fat red rooster...."

When Denny finished, Billy Martin took up the story, his voice calm and soothing in the darkness. He made the story funny and the kids giggled. Denny was grateful for the humor. After a while the bus grew cold again. Denny ran the heater as long as he dared. When he turned it off, Billy Martin started singing a cowboy song of his own. "Oh, I come up from Texas on a dusty-devil roan, and a-hangin' on my saddle was a sack of Indian corn...." The small passengers joined in as he taught them the words.

The next time Denny tried to start the engine, it coughed and stopped. He tried again, and again it sputtered and stopped. "What's wrong?" he asked anxiously.

"Exhaust pipe's clogged with snow," Billy Martin said. "We can go out the back, through the emergency door. You've got a shovel, haven't you?"

They left the curtained-off space and went to the back of the bus, Denny carrying the big flashlight he kept by the driver's seat. They found the shovel, got the emergency door open, and stepped down into the snow. Denny was shocked at how deep it was. He wallowed in it to his knees. Wind struck his face in an icy blast. He handed the flashlight to Billy and began shoveling.

"I'll spell you," Billy said.

Denny gave him the shovel and took the flashlight. He was sweating and shivering at the same time.

"That's it," Billy said. "I got the end cleared, but that exhaust will drift back. We oughta get it farther away from the bus. It's not safe this way."

"We could make a kind of funnel out of newspaper," Denny said through chattering teeth. "No, that won't work. Paper will be soggy in a little while."

"Must be something—" Billy muttered. "I got it! That plastic baseball bat! Cut off two ends and fit one open end over the exhaust pipe. The bat's hollow in the middle—they all are."

They went back in the bus and cut the plastic baseball bat. When they took it out and tried it on the exhaust pipe, Billy gave a shout of triumph. "Works like a charm!" Wind blew over them in a sudden, fierce gust. "It's rising," Billy said. "Be worse before morning."

Denny didn't answer. He didn't want to think about it. Back in the curtained-off space, he had to run the heater again. It was very quiet in the bus now. When he shut off the heater, he turned on the flashlight. The Three Wise Men and Mary were huddled close together and asleep.

Billy said, "I quit using the transistor. Didn't want them to hear any more about the bad weather."

"That was good thinking, Billy."

"I'm sorry I slid off the road, Denny. I shouldn't have taken the wheel. But I was scared. I saw how bad it was getting. I figured I might reach the next ranch."

Denny heard the rush of wind against the bus. Billy spoke again, "What do you think, Denny?"

"It could clear by morning. It's got to clear if —" He swallowed to ease the tightness in his throat.

"If it clears, we can burn the spare tire," Billy said. "It'll make a lot of heat and black smoke. They'll find us — if they can see the smoke."

Mary wakened and began to whimper about being cold. Denny took the flashlight and helped her to the other side of the curtain. "Walk fast up and down the aisle—then run."

"I can't, Denny —" she was crying. "I'm cold — and scared!"

He gave her a little shove. "Walk, Mary! Faster — faster! Run! That's a good girl." When she was panting, he took her back to the front of the bus and held her in his lap. "See, you're okay now."

"Is there anything to eat back there?" Billy asked.

"Take a look," Denny replied. Then he added, smiling, "It's a crime to take other people's groceries. It's stealing."

Billy Martin laughed and suddenly they were both laughing, too loudly and too freely. Denny finally managed to choke it off.

Billy returned with apples and oranges. "The lettuce is freezing," he said. "Well, I never did care for salad anyhow." They went into another round of wild laughter. Now the Three Wise Men were awake and they began to laugh, too. Mary joined in. Afterward they all seemed more relaxed, Denny thought.

Billy Martin made a joke of serving slices of apple and segments of orange, imitating an Irish waitress. talking in a shrill brogue. The youngsters giggled. After they had finished eating, Billy said, "This café's gettin' chilly."

Denny moved the flashlight, sliding its beam over the windshield. Frost covered the inside, glistening in the light. Billy hadn't had to see it; Billy knew that they had to have some heat. Denny ran the heater, hearing the wild howling of the wind. He didn't check the gas gauge. He was afraid to.

The hours dragged by. Periodically they walked and ran in the aisle of the bus, coming back to huddle in the small space behind the makeshift curtain. It was five o'clock in the morning when the gas ran out. For a while Denny shivered, then began to feel a strange sleepiness. His head came down on his arms, resting over the steering wheel.

Someone shook him violently. He felt the hard *slap-slap* against his face. "Get up!" Billy shouted. "Get up, you fool!"

Denny spoke slowly, thickly, "Leave me alone —"

Billy Martin pulled him to his feet. "You've got to move! You'll freeze to death!"

It was all anguish. It was like struggling to waken from a bad dream. He slowly became aware that it was light in the bus. He saw Billy Martin's face, drawn and old-looking. Billy said, "I was looking out for the kids. I didn't know that you — are you all right, Denny?"

The gray light changed to purple. Denny's stomach felt as though it were falling away. "Sick— I'm going to throw up."

"You can't!" Billy shook him again. "We've got to burn the tire."

Then the Three Wise Men were clinging to him, looking up into his face. "We gotta build a fire, Denny."

My passengers, he thought vaguely. *I'm responsible —* "Sure," he said through lips that felt huge, "sure. Gather some papers and—" His hand moved stiffly, numbly into his pocket and found his knife.

Billy Martin dragged the spare tire up front and they sat down beside it and began to whittle rubber shavings. It was slow and tedious work. The Three Wise Men collected paper. Mary brought the cradle she had used in the pageant and Billy Martin broke it into pieces.

Denny's hand was suddenly still as he held the pocketknife. "I don't hear the wind."

"It stopped," Billy said. "Stopped snowing, too." He drew a harsh breath and added, "It's just — cold." He got to his feet and went to the bus doors. "We gotta break a path away from the bus — to where it's safe to start a fire. Can you help me, Denny?"

Denny stood up. He felt sick and empty and dizzy. "Sure."

They got the bus doors open. The icy air made Denny gasp. He didn't recognize anything he saw. All around them the land was white and strange.

They broke trail through the snow, staggering, falling, using the shovel to get through the highest drifts. They cleared away snow at the end of the trail. "Enough," Billy Martin said, his mouth hanging open, his breath drifting from it like smoke.

It took a while to get the tire to the end of the trail. Denny piled up papers and rubber shavings. Billy set the pile afire. They eased the tire over it. The small flames began to grow. Denny fanned them with his cap, and a drift of black smoke moved skyward. Heat from the fire spread, melting the snow. Denny went back to the bus and brought Mary and the Three Wise Men along the narrow trail to the fire.

The droning sound came from the east — that way lay town. Nobody said anything. Denny stared at the sky. And then it was there, a small plane flying low over the vast white land. It came on toward them, guided by the tower of smoke. Billy Martin shouted wildly, waving his arms. Mary and the

Three Wise Men screamed and jumped up and down. Denny could only stare as the plane dipped low over them, circled, and flew away.

"He saw us!" Billy cried. "Somebody will come!"

Denny looked down at the fire. He didn't want them to see tears in his eyes. It was awhile before he had ahold of himself.

The wait by the fire went on. As the flames died down, the cold crept up around them until they were shivering again. And then there came another sound, like the faint buzz of a power saw. It grew, swelling into an angry humming.

"*Snowmobiles!*" Denny shouted. He swung Mary up in his arms and hugged her.

Later they stood like soldiers in a row, watching the line of machines winding up Gooseberry Run. They came on, up close to the dying fire, and stopped.

For a moment it seemed to Denny the quiet was enormous. Then people came around them in a rush of love and concern. Denny's father put an arm around Denny's shoulders and held him close.

Denny struggled to speak, to find words to tell everybody how great Billy Martin had been, to say Billy Martin had kept him from freezing to death. He tried to talk about the small brave people, Mary and the Three Wise Men. But he could find no words; it was all too big for words.

Then he looked at Billy Martin. Billy was looking at him, the bold black eyes warm with respect and admiration. "Merry Christmas, Denny," Billy Martin said.

As PEG AND BILL CURRY traveled between Casper, Wyoming, and Walden, Colorado, to visit relatives, they passed a small cabin which seemed to be deserted, yet there were always bright geraniums blooming in the two front windows. They often remarked to one another that they should stop and see who lived there, but finally decided to leave it a mystery. They began referring to the cabin as the "geranium house."

Eventually, Peg wrote "Geranium House," the story of an indigent married couple, Melora and Sam, who move into an abandoned homesteader's shack. When the story was completed, however, it contained a scene she thought some readers might find offensive. She considered this a literary work "not meant for popular readership."

As noted in her writing text, *Creating Fiction From Experience,* she rewrote the story "...but it still bothered me. I then switched to bystander point-of-view in which the outcome of [the scene] was subtly planted and hinted. The story came off with a fine tone and unity when related by the minor character in third person.... I am certain I could never have published this story had I insisted on...third person, major character viewpoint."

"Geranium House" was first published in the anthology *Frontiers West* (New York: Doubleday, 1959). In 1966, Peg adapted it to a three-act play, which was presented in Casper by the Paradise Valley Players.

This fine story was anthologized a second time twenty-five years after its first publication. "Geranium House" was included in *Westward the Women* (Garden City, New York: 1984), a collection of western stories by women writers such as Dorothy M. Johnson, Mari Sandoz, Willa Cather, Leslie Silko and others.

219

In 1988, the story captured the interest of Gretchen Wheeler, Theater and Communications instructor at Casper College, who adapted it for a Readers' Theater production, with the permission of Bill Curry.

"Geranium House" received several awards as a Readers' Theater production: a first in regional competition in 1989 at the Ricks College Invitational at Rexburg, Idaho, and a second in competition at Northwest Community College in Powell, Wyoming.

"I fell in love with this story," said Wheeler in an April 1990 interview. "I wanted to play all the parts." She found it easy to adapt "because Curry wrote wonderful dialog."

GERANIUM HOUSE

WE HEARD ABOUT them long before we saw them. News traveled fast in those days even though we didn't have telephones in the valley. Old Gus, the mailman, gave us the full report. "They come in from Laramie in a two-wheeled cart," he said, "him ridin' and her walkin' beside the cart and the old sway-bellied horse pullin' it. That cart was mostly filled with plants, and she was carrying one in her arms, just like most women carry a baby."

"Where they going to live?" my uncle Rolfe asked.

"They moved into that old homestead shack on the flats," Gus said. "Been there since the Indians fired the west range, that shack. Used to belong to a man named Matt but he died a spell ago, and I guess they're welcome to it." He sucked on the end of his drooping brown mustache and added, "Him now, he don't look like he'd be much — his pants hangin' slack and his shoulders humped worse than my granddad's. But her! You'd have to see her, Rolfe. What she's got ain't anything a man could put words to."

As soon as Gus finished his coffee and started back to town in his buggy, my mother mixed a batch of bread. "We'll take over a couple of loaves and a cake," she said. "A woman deserves better than that dirt-roofed cabin on the flats."

My uncle Rolfe stood looking out the kitchen window. He

was big and handsome in a wild, blackheaded way. He was always splitting his shirts and popping off buttons, and he never cared what he had on or how it fitted. Uncle Rolfe came to live with us and take over part of the ranch when my father died, and you'd never have thought he was my mother's brother, for she was small and neat and had pale brown hair.

"Anne," Uncle Rolfe said, "I wouldn't be in a hurry to rush over and welcome a couple of squatters. We don't know anything about them and they don't come from much when they have to put up in a dead man's shack on the flats. What's more, they won't stay long."

The color flew high in my mother's cheeks. "You don't understand about a woman," she said. "You don't know how much it helps to have a friend of her own kind in this big lonesome country. You've been a bachelor too long to see a woman's side of things, Rolfe Annister."

"Well," he said, "I aim to leave them alone."

But the next morning when we were ready to go, Uncle Rolfe got in the buggy. "Won't hurt me to meet them, I guess." Then he turned to me and smiled. "Billy, you want to drive this morning?"

I was thirteen that spring morning in the mountain country, and nothing ever sounded better than the clip-clop of the horses' hoofs and the singing sound of the buggy wheels turning along the dirt road. The meadowlarks were whistling and Uncle Rolfe began humming under his breath, the way he did sometimes when the sky was soft and the grass coming green.

It was six miles to the homesteader's cabin and we were almost there before we saw it, for it sat low on the flat land among the sagebrush and was the same silver-gray color. The river ran past it but there weren't any trees along the water, only a few scrubby willows still purple from the fall, for they hadn't leafed out yet.

First thing we noticed was the color in the windows of the old cabin, big blossoms of red and pink and white. My mother stepped out of the buggy and stared. "Geraniums!" she exclaimed. "I never saw anything so beautiful!"

The two-wheeled cart was beside the door and so old and bleached it might have been part of the land. And we saw the horse picketed in the sagebrush. Like Gus had said, he was a pack of bones with a belly slung down like a hammock.

My mother carefully carried her box with the cake and the bread to the front door and knocked. She was wearing her new gloves, the ones Uncle Rolfe had bought her in Denver when he shipped the cattle.

The door opened slowly and all I saw that first moment was the woman's eyes, big and dark and shining. She was young and her hair was so blond it looked almost white and was drawn back tight until it made her eyes seem larger and blacker. She was brown-skinned and tall and she looked strong. Her dress was clean but so worn my mother would have used it for a rag.

"I'm Anne Studer," my mother said. "We're your neighbors. This is my brother, Rolfe, and my son, Billy."

The woman seemed to forget my mother and Uncle Rolfe. She bent over and put her hand on my head and smiled down into my face. "Billy," she said, and her hand stroked my head and I could feel she loved me, for the warmth came right out of her hand.

She asked us to come in and then I saw the bed on the floor near the stove and the man there in the blankets. His face was thin and gray and he sat up, coughing. "Sam," she said, "we've got company — our neighbors."

He didn't try to get up but just lay there, and I thought how terrible it was he didn't have any bunk or bedstead, only the floor under him. Then he smiled at us and said, "The trip was too much for me, I guess. We've come a long way. Melora, will you put on the coffee?"

The woman went to the old stove that had pools of velvety-looking rust on the lids and she set a small black pot on it and filled the pot with water from the bucket. Her arms were soft and rounded, but strong lifting the bucket.

No one said anything for a few moments and I could hear a rustling that seemed to come from all the corners of the room.

"You've got lots of mice," my uncle Rolfe said.

Melora smiled at him. "I know. And we forgot to bring any traps."

Mother looked around and drew her skirts close to her, her mouth pinching into a thin line. I saw her touch the shiny lid of a tin can with her toe. The can lid was nailed over a hole in the rotting wooden floor.

Melora cut the cake, saying what a beautiful cake it was, and glancing at my mother, who still had that tight look on her face. Then she poured coffee into two battered tin cups and three jelly glasses. "Billy," she said to me, "if I'd been expecting you, I'd surely have fixed lemonade and put it in the river to cool." She stroked my head again and then walked over to one of the geraniums and I could see her fingers busy among the leaves. Her hands moved so softly and quietly in the plant that I knew she was loving it just as she had loved me when she touched me.

We didn't stay long and Melora walked to the buggy with us. She shook my mother's hand and said, "You were good to come. Please come back soon — and please bring Billy."

Driving home, my mother was silent. Uncle Rolfe finally said, "I knew we shouldn't go there. Makes a man feel low in his mind to see that. He's half dead, and how are they going to live?"

"I'm going to ride over with mousetraps," I said. "I'll set them for her."

My mother gave me a strange look. "You're not going alone," she said firmly.

"No," my uncle Rolfe said. "I'll go with him."

A few nights later we rode to the house on the flats and Uncle Rolfe set twelve mousetraps. Sam was in bed and Melora sat on an old spice keg, her hands folded in her lap. We'd just get started talking when a trap would go off and Uncle Rolfe would take it outside, empty it, and set it again.

"Sam's asleep now," Melora said. "He sleeps so much — and it's just as well. The mice bother him."

"Isn't there any other place you can go?" Uncle Rolfe asked, a roughness in his voice. "You can't live off this land. It won't grow anything but sagebrush."

"No, we haven't any other place to go," Melora replied, and her strong shoulders sagged. "We've no kin and Sam needs this climate. I've got more plants coming from Missouri — that's where we used to live. I'll sell my geraniums. We'll manage — we always have."

She walked out in the night with us when we were leaving. She put her arm around me and held me hard against her. "So young," she said, "so alive — I've been around death a long time. Sam — look at Sam. And our babies died. We had two. And now, now I'll never have another child — only the geraniums." Her voice broke and I knew she was crying. Her arms swept me closer and there was something about the way she clung to me that made me hurt inside.

"Come on, Billy," Uncle Rolfe said gruffly. I pulled away from Melora and got my horse. I could still hear her sobbing as we rode away.

We were riding quietly in the dark when my uncle Rolfe began to talk to himself, as though he'd forgotten I was there. "Beautiful," he said, "and needing a strong red-blooded man to love her. Needing a child to hold in her arms — and there she is tied to *him*. Oh Lord, is it right?"

A week later my uncle Rolfe wrapped a piece of fresh beef in a white sack and rode off toward the flats. My mother watched him go, a frown on her forehead. Then she said to me, "Billy, you bring in the milk cows at five o'clock. I don't think your uncle Rolfe will be back by then."

The next morning I saw a pink geranium on the kitchen table and a piece of brown wrapping paper beside it. On the paper was written in strong sloping letters, "For Anne from Melora."

It wasn't long till everybody in the valley spoke of the cabin on the flats as "Geranium House." On Sundays, before haying season started, the ranchers drove out in their buggies and they always went past the cabin on the flats. The women stopped to admire the flowers and usually bought one or two plants. They told my mother how beautiful Melora was and how kind — especially to the children.

"Yes," my mother would say and get that pinched look about her mouth.

One morning in early August when Gus brought the mail, he told us Melora had been driving all over the valley in the cart, selling geraniums and visiting with the women. "And she's got a new horse to pull the cart," he said, "a big black one."

That afternoon my mother saddled her horse and, taking me with her, went riding through the horse pasture. "I'm looking for the black gelding," she said. "Seems to me I haven't noticed him around lately."

We rode until sundown but we didn't find the gelding. I said he might have jumped the fence and gotten out on the range or into one of the neighbor's pastures.

"Yes," she said, frowning, "I suppose he could have."

She asked Uncle Rolfe about the black gelding and Uncle

Rolfe let on like he didn't hear her. "Well," mother said tartly, "there's such a thing as carrying good will toward your neighbors too far."

"You haven't," he said angrily. "You never bothered to go back. And she must be lonely and tired of looking at a sick man every day."

"She hasn't returned my call," my mother said, her chin in the air. "I'm not obligated to go there again. Besides, there's something about her — the way she looks at Billy —"

"You've forgotten, Anne, what it is to hunger for love, for a child to be part of you — for a man's arms around you in the night."

Tears came into my mother's eyes. "No, Rolfe! I haven't forgotten. But I've got Billy — and when I saw her eyes and hands on the geraniums — Rolfe, it isn't that I don't like her. It's — it hurts me to be around her."

Uncle Rolfe put his hand on her shoulder. "I'm sorry, Anne. I shouldn't have said a word."

"If she comes here," my mother said, "I'll make her welcome, Rolfe."

And then one warm morning I saw the two-wheeled cart driving up in front of the house, and I saw that the horse pulling it was our black gelding.

"Billy!" Melora called to me. "How are you, Billy?" And she got out of the cart and put her arms around me and I could feel the warmth coming from her body and covering me like a wool blanket in winter.

My mother came to the door and asked Melora in. "How's Sam?" she said.

Melora put her hand to her eyes as though she wanted to brush something away. She was thinner than when I'd last seen her and her eyes burned bigger and brighter in her face that now had the bones showing under the fine tanned skin.

But she still looked strong, the way a wire is tight and strong before it breaks. "Sam," she said, "Sam's all right. As good as he'll ever be. It's a weakness, a sickness born in him—as it was in our babies. Anne, I didn't know Sam was a sick man when I married him. He never told me."

Uncle Rolfe came in with his black hair looking wilder than usual. The color burned in Melora's cheeks and her eyes lighted. "Hello, Rolfe," she said, "and thank you for being so kind to Sam."

"That's all right," Uncle Rolfe said gruffly.

"I went to town to see the minister," Melora said, still looking at Uncle Rolfe. "I asked him to find me a baby I could adopt—like you suggested. He said 'no'."

"He did!" Uncle Rolfe sounded shocked.

"He said I had nothing to take care of a baby," Melora went on. "He said I had my hands full now. I begged him to help me, but he just sat there with a face like stone and said it wasn't my lot in life to have a child."

"The fool!" Uncle Rolfe muttered.

My mother set food on the table and asked Melora to stay and eat with us.

Melora shook her head. "I'm going home and fix something for Sam. He can't eat much in this hot weather, but I tell him he must try. And he gets so lonesome when I'm gone."

My uncle Rolfe went out and helped her get into the cart. He stood for a long time looking down the road after she left.

Two weeks later we saw the buggy of Gus, the mailman, coming up the road. It wasn't the day for bringing mail. The horses were running and a big cloud of dust rose behind the buggy. My mother and I stepped onto the porch just as Uncle Rolfe rode in from the haying field with a piece of machinery across the saddle in front of him. My uncle Rolfe dismounted and waited for Gus. The buggy rattled to a stop. The horses were panting and sweating, for it was a hot morning.

"Melora's taken Sadie Willard's baby," Gus said, "and drove off with it."

"Oh, no!" My mother twisted her hands.

"Happened a little while ago," Gus said. "Sadie went to feed the chickens and when she came back she saw Melora's cart going over the hill in front of the house. She thought that was strange. She went into the house and looked everywhere and the baby was gone. She sent the sickle grinder to the hay field after Jim, and just as I left, Jim come in and said he'd get the neighbors and they'd go after Melora. It's a terrible thing and Jim's about crazy and Sadie sittin' cryin' like her heart would break."

Uncle Rolfe looked at my mother. "Anne, you take the lunch to the meadow at noon for our hay hands. Billy, you come with me." He jammed his big hat lower on his black head and we started for the barn.

The heat waves shimmered all around us on the prairie as we rode toward Geranium House. When we got there our horses were covered with lather, but there wasn't any sign of the cart or Melora. Everything looked still and quiet and gray except for the flowers blooming in the windows and around the outside of the cabin.

Uncle Rolfe pushed the door open and Sam was propped up on some pillows, reading an old newspaper. There were two bright spots of color in his thin cheeks. "Hello, Rolfe," he said. "Thought you'd be making hay."

"Where's Melora?" Uncle Rolfe asked.

"Melora? She left me a lunch and said she was going to drive up to the timber and get some water lilies. A lily pond she found a while ago, I guess. I don't know where it is, though."

"I do," Uncle Rolfe said.

"Folks are lookin' for her," I said, my voice rising with

excitement. "I bet they're goin' to—" Uncle Rolfe's big hand covered my mouth and he shoved me toward the door.

"What's wrong?" Sam said. "Has something happened to Melora?" And his face twisted like he was going to cry.

"No," Uncle Rolfe said gently, "nothing's wrong with Melora. You just take it easy, Sam."

It took us a while to reach the timber, for it was so hot we couldn't crowd the horses and there was no wind moving to cool things off. The smell of pines was thick, almost clogging my nose, and I could see big thunderclouds building up behind the mountains.

I didn't know where the pond was, but Uncle Rolfe rode right to it. It was a small pond and very smooth, with blue dragonflies hanging over the yellow lilies. Uncle Rolfe got off his horse and I followed. He took a few steps and stopped, staring.

There sat Melora under an aspen tree, holding the baby against her breast and her eyes closed and her mouth smiling. She didn't look like any ordinary woman sitting there. She looked like the pictures of saints they have in Sunday School books.

Uncle Rolfe said, "Melora—"

She opened her eyes and looked at us. Then she said in a small frightened voice, "I only wanted to have him a little while to myself—to feel him in my arms. I meant no harm to him." She got up then, holding the baby carefully. "He's asleep and don't you bother him."

"They're looking for you," Uncle Rolfe said. "Melora, you shouldn't have done this. The women will never be your friends again."

Melora bowed her head and began to cry. The sun came through the trees and made her hair shine until it looked like a halo. "I only wanted to hold him," she said. "I only wanted to have him in my arms for a little while."

"Hush!" Uncle Rolfe said roughly. "Where's the cart?"

"I hid it in the trees."

Then Uncle Rolfe took hold of her arm and said to me, "You bring the horses, Billy."

Melora cried all the way through the timber until we reached the cart. Then she sat stiff and quiet, holding the baby. I rode along behind, leading Uncle Rolfe's horse.

When we got to the cabin on the flats there were several buggies and saddle horses there, and men were standing by the front door, their faces dark and angry. Inside the cabin I could hear Sam shouting hoarsely, "She meant no harm, I tell you! She's good, a good woman with no mean thing in her!"

Uncle Rolfe took the baby and gave it to Sadie's husband, Jim Willard, and the baby wakened and started to cry. Jim Willard stared at Melora, his face ugly. "You get outta this country!" he shouted. "We've got no place for baby stealers in the valley. If you ain't gone by tomorrow night, I'll burn this shack to the ground!"

Melora shrank back, pressed against the wheel of the cart, her eyes filled with a terrible look of pain and her lips moving but no words coming out. The men began to mutter and shift restlessly and someone said, "Why don't we load their stuff and start 'em out of the valley now?"

Jim Willard kicked at one of the geranium plants that set beside the cabin door. His big boot ground the blossom into the dirt. Melora gave a little cry and covered her face with her hands.

"That's enough, Jim!" Uncle Rolfe's voice was cold. He moved to stand close to Melora, his shaggy black head lifted, his fists clenched. "You men go home and leave her be. She's got no other place to go and her man's sick. I'll take care of things. I'll be responsible for her — and for him, too."

One of the men moved forward toward Melora and Uncle Rolfe's big hand grabbed him and shoved him aside, spinning him away like a toy man. There was some arguing then but Uncle Rolfe stood silent with that fierce look in his eyes. After a while the men got on their horses and in their buggies and went away. Melora walked slowly into the house and we could hear Sam half crying as he spoke her name, and then her voice, soft and warm, "I'm here, Sam. Now don't you fret. Sleep now, and when you waken, I'll have supper ready."

"Come on, Billy," Uncle Rolfe said. His voice sounded old and tired. We rode slowly toward home.

It was black that night in the mountain country, black and sultry, the window curtains hanging motionless. When I went to bed it was too hot to sleep and I could hear thunder rumbling in the distance. Lightning began to play through the house, flashing streaks of blue and red, and I heard my uncle Rolfe moving in the bedroom next to mine. I heard his boots on the floor and then his steps going to the kitchen and a door closing. I got out of bed and ran through the dark house and when the lightning flared again, I saw my uncle Rolfe walking toward the barn. A little later, when the lightning glowed so bright it made me shiver, I saw my uncle Rolfe ride past the window, his hat pulled low on his black head. He was headed toward the flats.

I was awake a long time, for it was hard to sleep with the thunder getting close and loud and the lightning popping all around. When the storm broke I got up again and closed the door of Uncle Rolfe's room. A little later my mother came into the kitchen and lighted a lamp and heated some milk for us to drink. We sat close together in the kitchen until the storm went over and a cool wet wind began to blow through the house.

I never knew when Uncle Rolfe got home that night but

the next morning he was at the breakfast table. And all the rest of the summer he didn't ride toward the flats again.

It was far into fall and I was going to country school when Gus came one Saturday morning and brought my mother two large red geranium plants with the penciled message on brown wrapping paper, "To Anne with love, from Melora."

"Pretty," Gus said. "Never did see such geraniums as are in that house now. And Melora, she's bloomin' like the flowers."

Uncle Rolfe put down the local paper he'd just started to open and turned to look at Gus.

"Yes, sir," Gus went on, "she always was a woman a man had to look at more than once, but now she's downright beautiful. Sam, he's not much better. Might be he'd die tomorrow and might be he'd live a few years yet. Never can tell about things like that. And I guess if he did die, somebody would look out for a woman like Melora."

"I expect so," my mother said, pouring coffee for Gus.

"The Lord's favored her, make no mistake about that," Gus went on, "for she's going to have that baby she's been hankerin' for. The women, they've all forgiven her for what she did and been up there with baby clothes and buyin' her geraniums again." Gus sighed and sucked at the end of his drooping brown mustache. "Only the Lord's doing would give a woman a baby when she needed it so bad and didn't have but a shell of a man to love her."

My mother lifted her head and stared at my uncle Rolfe, a strange softness in her eyes and around her mouth. My uncle Rolfe looked back at my mother and it seemed to me they said a lot of things to each other without speaking a word. Then my uncle Rolfe opened the local paper and began to read the news.

LIKE MOST WRITERS, Peg didn't take too kindly to major editorial tinkering. When a *Saturday Evening Post* editor changed the title of her story "Night of the Red Surf" to "Heal a Wounded Heart," Peg was outraged. Her son, Mike described her reaction in a letter in July 1990: "I distinctly see her stomping around the house, fiercely dragging on a cigarette, saying, 'Those SOB's want to change my title to something sappy like that! Can you imagine that, Bill?... Have you ever heard of such a shitty deal?'"

The story did appear, however, under the new title in the *Post* in January 1961.

She discussed its origin in an article — "Genesis of a Story"—published in the *Writer* magazine in December 1962.

She noted the linking of several disparate memories, altered by time, which assumed new dimensions and merged: her feeling after her father's death, her trip to California where she was invited to the beach to watch the grunion run and her first experience talking with a group of young children about writing poetry.

Also unique to "Heal a Wounded Heart" is the fact that its main character is a writer Peg called John Durham; the story is set in California.

HEAL A WOUNDED HEART

JOHN DURHAM LAY ON the sand and felt lifeless. It was as though a curtain of glass had been drawn between him and the world. He could look through it, but he could not break it. He heard the surf, but it didn't really reach him; it was like something happening in a faraway tunnel. His hand moved under the beach towel and touched the bottle. He had not used it. He had scorned it as he scorned the pills the doctor had given him. But now, in the warm, sea-moist afternoon, he took hold of the bottle and raised it to his lips.

"That's bad for you," a small, flutelike voice said.

He knew the voice. She had been by every afternoon, and he didn't bother to look up. Her feet were in his range of vision, small, brown feet stained with tar that washed in with the waves. *Why didn't her mother ever get those feet clean?* he wondered crossly. And then something sharp and terrible happened inside him; he saw the feet that had been his daughter's — white, delicate, awakening in him a queer tenderness. *Put your shoes on, honey. You'll get stickers in your toes.*

In the mountains it had been — high Montana. His wife had rested in the curve of his arm as they lay under the pine shade. Their child had played near them, her shoes and stockings cast carelessly aside. John Durham pressed his arm across his eyes. *I can't bear to remember,* he thought. *I don't*

235

want to remember. He spoke harshly, "Go away — go away and leave me alone."

But the dirty, tar-stained feet didn't budge, and the maddeningly clear voice went on, "Don't be so nasty."

He heaved himself to a sitting position, the taste of warm whiskey sickening in his stomach. He forced himself to look at her. She was as she had been that afternoon a week ago when he'd first come to the beach. Her brown, freckled face was alert with mingled curiosity and reproof. The faded blue bathing suit clung to her thin hips and rode the mound of her stomach as she stood, back arched, sturdy legs spraddled. Her sun-bleached blond hair was straight and thick, and suddenly he wanted to put his hand on it.

"What's your name?" he said, trying to control the convulsive movements of his stomach.

"I told you the first day. It's Mary Ann." She eyed him critically. "You don't remember much, do you?"

His lips moved in a tight, bitter smile. "How right you are. What grade are you in?"

"I told you that, too. I'm in second. I'll be in third this fall."

Younger than Judy — if Judy had lived.

"She would have been in fifth," he said to the dead sand and the dead sky and the dead ocean. And her hair wasn't sun-bleached blond, like late-summer grass — it was red. The same color as her mother's. *My lovely, my loved — Irene, my wife.* And he thought with foolish clarity that if Irene had been alive now, she'd have worn her hair in one of these new styles — like a beehive maybe. A beautiful red beehive.

John Durham began to shiver. His fingers dug in the sand and worked frantically.

The child before him said, "My teacher would scold you. We try to keep our hands quiet — especially when someone's talking to us."

"School's out," he said thickly, groping for something, anything to say to this pest of a girl. "It's June, you know — well into June."

"But I'm back in school. I'm in a special program. We go three weeks. We take all sorts of things — Spanish, art, dancing —"

I don't give a damn what you take, he thought, closing his eyes. *Just go away.*

"Are you a teacher?" Mary Ann asked.

"No, I am not."

"Oh. Then what are you?"

"A writer," he answered automatically, and then thought, *past tense. Was. But not now; now I am nothing. Never again anything.*

"I'll bring my teacher to see you," Mary Ann said. "I know where you live."

"You know everything." He spoke crossly again. "And I do *not* want to meet your teacher or any teacher. I don't want to meet anyone."

"You," Mary Ann observed, hands on her thin hips, "are not friendly."

"Togetherness," he replied, "is a word that makes me gag." And he turned face down on the beach towel and lay with the sound of the surf, dull and strange, in his ears. He knew after a while that Mary Ann had gone away. He felt the heat diminish and the air take on the evening coolness. At length he slept, and when he wakened it was dark and the rising tide had moved closer, the breakers flinging cold drops of sea across him.

He got up and fumbled into his shoes and, carrying the big towel over his arm, walked across the narrowing strip of sand and up the steep, dusty slope to the top of the bluff that hung above the sea. He passed lighted windows where people smiled at each other across dinner tables. Music drifted out the open doors. Children played under the strange blue trees that were in blossom. *Jacarandas,* he thought. *I should use them in a story; I've never written a story with a California setting.* And then desolation swept over him. In two years he had written nothing. Months of blank pages. Because he couldn't bear to remember; because he had shut off a world he had known and because he couldn't find his way into a new one. *My name is John Durham,* he thought, *and once I was famous — or at least successful. Now I am nothing.*

The beach cottage that belonged to an old college friend was dark. He welcomed darkness. He sat down in the sand-filled swimming trunks and stared into blackness. His college friend had written, "Come and stay in my place. We'll be gone for a month. Nobody will bother you. I won't tell the neighbors who you are. And maybe out here in the salt air, and with the sea around you...."

John Durham began to laugh soundlessly in the darkness. His friend hadn't reckoned with a snoopy little girl from the second grade. Everything else had been so carefully taken care of — no toys of his friend's children left around as reminders, no clothes of his friend's wife hanging in the clothes closets. *Had they buried all evidence of love and living in some cave along the shore?* But despite the careful planning, there had been Mary Ann with her bleached thick hair, her tar-stained feet and her habit of searching him out on the beach that was supposed to be so private.

Now he was shocked to hear her voice again, coming from the flower-scented night outside. Her voice and another voice, soft and feminine. He swore. He jumped, ready to bolt for the bathroom and lock the door, but it was too late. The screen banged, and Mary Ann spoke, "He's in here. He never turns on any lights for hours." And he heard her hand scratching along the wall for the light switch.

"Stop that, Mary Ann," he said wearily. "You remind me of a bat." And he moved quickly to flip on the lights.

Mary Ann still wore her swimming suit, and her feet looked dirtier than before. But the young woman who stood beside her was clean and cool and very slender. Pale blond hair was drawn back into a prim knot. Her face was plain, John Durham thought, but there was something about the wide, sensitive mouth — a need, a hurting. The white linen dress was simply cut and unwrinkled.

"I'm Miss Chamberlain, Mary Ann's teacher," she said. "I teach in the little town here by the beach."

Her voice was low, and John Durham had the feeling that it was much too controlled. *One of the remote ones,* he concluded, *but that was better than the chatty let's-get-to-know-each-other type.*

"Hello," he said. "I'm not going to ask you to sit down. I—"

"Oh, I didn't expect—" A flush came into the pale-tan cheeks. "I only came to ask you to lecture to my second graders."

His jaw sagged. He stared at her. John Durham lecturing — yes, that was what she had said — *to children*! John Durham, who had never spoken to any group except top writers or college students. He couldn't help it. He began to laugh. He laughed until moisture ran down his cheeks while the plain, prim-looking girl with the sensitive mouth stood awkwardly with an expression of shock in her wide gray eyes. He kept on laughing even as he noticed Mary Ann's small face twisting in what looked like pain while she rubbed one stained foot against the other.

At last he could control himself. With a gasp, he said, "Pardon me. I couldn't possibly lecture to second graders."

"But there's no writer around here," Mary Ann began, her voice no longer high and clear, but shaken and thick. "We've had artists and musicians talk to our class — and — and I promised the kids. I promised Miss Chamberlain you'd come. I said...I said you were my friend." Her lower lip began to tremble.

"You say too much, Mary Ann."

Then Miss Chamberlain spoke. "I'd never have thought a writer of your caliber would consider yourself too good to —"

"Too good!" He began to laugh again. This time it was a hollow, bitter laughter. "Go outside, Mary Ann. I want to talk with your teacher."

To his surprise, Mary Ann went away. John Durham looked at Miss Chamberlain. "Have you ever been in love?" he said.

She swallowed hard, and the quietly clasped hands moved in a gesture that was at once defensive and protective. "No — I, well, I had to take care of my mother until last winter. And then — well, in winter — I —"

"Winter? What's that got to do with it?" He drew his breath sharply and shouted at her, "It can happen any time — winter, summer, daylight or dark. Anywhere. Any moment. When it happens, you live, see? You stand in the sun. And when it's gone, you're dead and you don't write. You don't feel a tree or a sunset or a blade of grass. Do you understand?"

She nodded, the gray eyes bigger than before.

"And worse," he said, his voice becoming harsh, "you don't see into people anymore. You don't care about their hearts. You don't give a damn about anything. That's why I can't talk to your second graders — because I don't give a damn. Because I'm dead and have been for two years. I'm all washed up. I haven't written a line, and I never will again. Now, will you go outside and get that kid by the hand

and take her home and leave me alone?"

Miss Chamberlain turned and marched away, her slim back very stiff and straight. Outside he could hear the murmur of her soft voice, but not what she was saying. Then he heard something else. Mary Ann was crying. And at last the sound of her sobbing died away and there was only the stillness of the night.

In a little while Miss Chamberlain came back. He looked up and saw her standing there, just inside his front room. "You hurt Mary Ann," she said. "You don't think of anyone but yourself."

He moved slowly from the chair, and the words came out of him, pulled from deep inside, brought forth in mingled pain and anger. "Two years ago my wife and my child were killed in a car accident."

For a long moment the wide gray eyes looked steadily at him, and then Miss Chamberlain said, "But because you were hurt is no reason to hurt Mary Ann. And you had love — you knew what it was. You had the best." Then she was gone, and he rushed to the window in time to see the white dress going down the street and hear the sound of her running steps.

He tried to sleep that night and couldn't. Again and again he heard the soft, controlled voice saying tightly, "You had love — you knew what it was. You had the best."

When afternoon came, he again lay on the sand and waited for Mary Ann. He kept telling himself that he couldn't have hurt her much, that she was a brassy, bragging little girl and any moment she'd be along to pester him. But afternoon moved into evening and the soft darkness fell over him and Mary Ann didn't come. The moon rose red and full over the Pacific. He thought the surf sounded like shattering glass. And at last he got up, stiff and hungry, and made his way up the steep slope and past the lighted houses along the bluff.

But this time he stopped at each house, saying, "Does Mary Ann live here?"

And then at last, at the end of the row, in a house that looked shabby, the yard overgrown with weeds, he faced a woman with thick, graying blond hair. The eyes that looked so sharply at him told him what he wanted to know. "I'd like to speak to Mary Ann," he said.

"I think she's gone to bed."

"Please, I must speak to her."

He waited at the door, and at last she came, the blue shorty pajamas riding on her rounded stomach. He saw that her feet had been scrubbed, but some of the tar stain had stayed. He cleared his throat against her proud, withdrawn look and her silence. "Mary Ann, I'll speak to your class. When can I come? Tomorrow afternoon?"

"We only meet in the morning," she said with dignity. "You may wait while I call Miss Chamberlain."

He sat on the sagging front step. After a while Mary Ann came and stood beside him. "You may come at eight-thirty in the morning. Here's the address. Mamma wrote it down for you." And she handed him a slip of paper.

He took the slip of paper. "Thank you," he said gravely. "Good night, Mary Ann."

He spent another sleepless night. He lay filled with fear. What did a man who'd talked with college professors, editors and newspapermen say to second graders? In his novels he'd reached the masses of men and women who read best sellers, but what could he say to reach Mary Ann and her friends? Thousands of words raced through his mind — words from lectures, big and impressive words, and words from his stories; words of tenderness and hatred, of pain and joy. None of them seemed the least meaningful when he thought of Mary Ann. *If I were as I once was — before the curtain of glass fell between me and the world—I could find words; they would come to me.*

The fear was still with him the next morning when he drove up before the schoolhouse. He saw children and teachers gathered beside a flagpole. Two small boys worked with a rope, and then the flag went up and uncurled in the wind. Small hands moved to cover hearts, and voices murmured in unison. "I pledge allegiance to the flag of the United States..."

John Durham got out of his car and stood at attention and spoke silently with the children. And then across the clean, warming morning came the singing. "My country 'tis of thee, sweet land of liberteee..." And for a moment John Durham was back in a country school in Nebraska, and beyond the narrow windows the wheat fields flowed to the world's horizons.

Teachers and children began moving toward the open doors of the school building. John Durham stood uncertainly, suddenly aware that he was a big, thick-shouldered man in wrinkled slacks and a sport shirt he'd rinsed out in a washbowl. His hand, a strong and long-fingered hand, moved hastily to smooth down his rough, dark hair and then to touch his jaw. *I forgot to shave,* he thought, and he felt miserable. *For Mary Ann I should have shaved.* A sense of inadequacy overwhelmed him. Then he saw Miss Chamberlain hurrying toward him. A blue dress this morning, a cool and quiet dress—plain as the girl who wore it. No, she had said, she had never been in love. A pity. A waste of life.

"I'm so glad you came," she spoke with warmth.

He felt as small as a pebble on the playground. "I look— I didn't even think—"

Her hand touched his arm. "Forget it. Now, these are selected pupils of high intelligence and this is an enriched summer program. It's not only for the pupils, but for teachers, too. It's a workshop course for them. Several teachers will sit in the back and observe while you talk to Mary Ann and her friends. You'll have around twenty minutes to speak. Mary Ann is very intelligent, and she has asked to introduce you."

He walked beside the slim, cool girl into the building. He felt like a slob. "The children are from several different schools in neighboring towns," Miss Chamberlain continued. He followed her into the classroom and sat down in the chair she indicated. He judged there to be forty small boys and girls before him. *Second graders*, he thought in panic. Miss Chamberlain moved away from him, across the room, and sat behind her neat desk. He wished she would come close. He was terrified.

Wriggling motions in the seats were subsiding. Mary Ann got up and carefully smoothed her skirt. She walked slowly, head high, to the front of the room and faced the class. "This is Mr. John Durham. He is a professional writer. Mr. Durham will tell us how to become writers." She turned toward John, inclined her head and smiled, and walked carefully back to her desk.

John Durham stood up. He saw the children's faces. He saw the dozen visiting teachers sitting quietly in the back of the room. His knees shook. He glanced toward Miss Chamberlain, and she was so quiet and remote. Then he thought he saw something come to life in her eyes. Faith? Trust? Excitement? He turned to look at Mary Ann, and her sea-tanned face beamed at him. It was a completely trusting little face. *Like Judy's,* he thought, and pain came up all through him until his flesh felt raw and his bones ached. *I must not,* he thought desperately, *I cannot remember. It will kill me.*

The morning sun came in the window and touched him like a blade of gold, slashing deep. And the strange blue tree across the playground was shivering with wind like a jagged piece of sky. His eyes found Mary Ann's again, and it was like finding Judy, his daughter. And even as he tried not to remember, he knew he must. John Durham began to talk then, speaking as he thought he would never speak again, saying words he had once said to his little daughter while he held her in his arms before a winter fire.

"When you want to be a writer, you say what you feel. You say what a color says to you — like red is hot, and you want words that are hot and bright and crackle. And you listen to everything as if it were the last time you would ever hear anything — and you know rain sounds one way on a tent and another hitting a tin roof. And spring doesn't come first in the grass that turns green. It comes in the sky."

John Durham turned to the blackboard and picked up a piece of chalk. "In winter, clouds are like this." And he drew flat lines on a blackboard. "They're skinny, like hungry people. But when spring is ready to start, clouds are like this." And he drew circles on the blackboard. "Fat, that's what they are. They say it's spring before anything else — before rain or grass or birds."

He put the chalk down and looked at Mary Ann. "Tell me what colors mean to you, Mary Ann."

"Brown is sad," she said. "Purple is dreamy."

A boy in the back row put up his hand. "Green is cool, like lime sherbet."

"Very good," said John Durham. And then he asked how they would write about a friend if they wanted a stranger to know the friend. "What would you say?" he asked.

A little girl with eyes like dark pansies said she would tell what her friend looked like and wore and the kind of house she lived in. Mary Ann added, "I'd tell if my friend was happy or sad most of the time and what made her happy or sad."

A chubby, red-faced boy held up his hand and said, "I

want to tell you I like best the way trains sound at night. It's like I'm going away somewhere special, by myself, and I'm lonesome, but I feel good, too."

It went on and on, John Durham speaking to the children and the children speaking back to him, and he saw the visiting teachers nod and smile. And then he saw the clock had ticked past the time when he should have stopped talking. He stepped to the blackboard once more. "This is all — just to show you one more thing, the difference between a good writer and a poor writer. This is a kite." The chalk made the box and then the angling tail. "Here is the tail of the kite. And this square is a house and this is the road going up the hill behind it. Look at the road and look at the tail of the kite. A poor writer will say, 'The road went up the hill.' But a good writer will say, 'The road went up the hill like the tail of a kite.'" He put the chalk down and walked from the room. He stumbled along the empty hallway, pain and remembering filling him. He stepped into the hurting sunlight.

"Wait! Mr. Durham — John!"

He turned and saw the blue dress and the sensitive mouth and the arms that moved in a gesture that called him back to her, but he could not bear it. "No!" he said. "Leave me alone." And he stumbled on to the car, got in and drove slowly toward the beach cottage, for all the houses and the sky ran together as though the rain washed over them and their colors flowed into one another. He went into the house and lay face down on the bed, and the sheet grew wet beneath his cheek. And at last he slept.

He wakened to hear Mary Ann calling, "Get up! Get up! The grunion are running!" And her hand tugged hard at his shoulder. He saw the light was on, and behind her stood Miss Chamberlain.

Miss Chamberlain was wearing a white sweat shirt and

very short blue shorts, and she carried a bucket and a lantern. "Hurry," Miss Chamberlain said. "The moon is right. The grunion are coming in from the sea to spawn on the sand."

Mary Ann handed him his swimming trunks. "And you better put on a sweater. It'll be cold in the water."

Strangely, as in a dream, he went down the slope to the beach. Fires were burning and people were standing at the edge of the sea. Some carried flashlights and others held lanterns. Most of them had buckets. Children ran laughing and shouting along the sand. The moon hung red and full over the ocean. Then someone screamed, "I saw one!"

Mary Ann pushed him forward on one side and Miss Chamberlain on the other. He was running into the surf. Beside him, Miss Chamberlain shouted, "They're little fish—like trout. They come in with one wave, burrow a hole and lay their eggs, and go out with the next wave. You have to be quick!" And she pressed the bucket into his hand. "Scoop them up!"

She swung the lantern high. The surf rumbled toward them. He saw the long wave, dark and specked with foam. It broke eddying around his knees, and as it drained away, he saw the wriggling silver shapes of the fish. He plunged toward them, bending quickly, but they were gone, and he scooped only sand and water. The next wave smacked him, soaking him. He gasped and laughed. Stumbling toward the shore, he saw Miss Chamberlain was laughing too. Her blond hair had come loose from the neat knot and streamed untidily over her shoulders. The wet blue shorts clung to her long, beautiful legs. Her mouth was tender.

He dropped the bucket, and his hands went out to touch her shoulders. "What?" he said.

"You were so wonderful—today at school."

"You *are* wonderful—now!"

The sensitive mouth moved, looked shaken in the light from the lantern she still held high. He took the lantern and set it on the sand. Beyond them the beach fires leaped up like small tigers in the dark. He saw the light of the reddish moon riding the breakers in liquid flame. He put his arms around her and held her hard against the wet, cold sweater, but he felt warm. "I don't even know your first name," he said.

A wave came in, splattering them, soaking them. He remembered the lantern and then saw that Mary Ann had run back to where the beach was dry and was holding the lantern in her hand. She peered toward them, frowning, and reminding him of a small, brown owl. "You won't get any grunions," she said, "not doing *that*."

"You are my grunion," John Durham said, smiling at her, still holding Miss Chamberlain in his arms. And his hand moved to trace the outline of the face so close to his and felt the fine bones of her cheeks.

"I don't even know your first name," he murmured again, "but there's plenty of time — all of time — to find out that and everything else I need to know." He kissed her then and heard the surf crashing all up and down the shore, crashing like the final shattering of thick glass.

ALTHOUGH IN THE LATE 1950s and early 1960s the word "beatnik" was a common term, today it is seldom used. What is a beatnik?

Writer Jack Kerouac once said the Beat Generation "includes anyone from fifteen to fifty-five who digs everything." Those who were not "beat" or "hip" were "square." Not a formal movement, it came about as groups of young people from eighteen to twenty-eight rejected conventional attitudes, conventional dress, developed their own slang speech and "dug" all forms of artistic expression.

Beat heroes included such diverse figures as the poet Dylan Thomas, actors James Dean and Marlon Brando, singer Elvis Presley and jazzman Charlie Parker.

Kerouac's novel, *On The Road*, published in 1957, outraged the critics but seemed, to some, to typify the search for identity of that first generation to inherit The Bomb. On college campuses far from San Francisco and Greenwich Village, coffee houses sprang up where writers recited their protest poetry, sometimes to jazz accompaniment. Few dormitory rooms of that era were without the requisite candle-in-a-wine-bottle. The works of Kerouac, Norman Mailer, poets Gregory Corso and Lawrence Ferlinghetti and other "beats" are now required reading on college campuses.

While little is known about the sources of "The Professor is a Beatnik," its setting does resemble Casper College. Fictional art teacher Dan Montgomery is clearly a person who, in his own way, upsets the status quo.

The story appeared in the *Saturday Evening Post* in February 1961.

THE PROFESSOR IS A BEATNIK

WHEN HE CAME TO teach in the small junior college, he arrived in an old car with a lean dog riding beside him on the front seat. They got out and stood together in the amber sunlight of September. And it was as though the feel of impending autumn touched man and dog; it was as though the nostalgic air and the haze on the near mountain said, "They've come a long way, and they've been looking for something for a long time."

The dog, mostly hound, put his thin cold nose in Dan Montgomery's hand, and the man smiled and murmured, "Good boy." Then they went up the front steps and into the one-story building, the dog padding softly beside the man. They walked along the polished halls to the office that was partly open to the hallway, with windows that could be closed at night.

Dan Montgomery was thirty, but he had the kind of face that said he could be forty and that he probably would look the same at sixty. The lines around his mouth and eyes were not bitter; they only said that life had got to him.

He looked with pleasure at the students moving about the halls, aware of their youth and their anticipation. Classes had not begun, but there was registration. He stopped at the office, looking across the broad, tablelike section that faced the hallway, leaning casually against it. He was completely unaware that he wore dusty jeans, a travel-stained blue shirt and unaware that his hair hadn't been combed for some time. His clothes clung to him as though he shaped them to himself and extended beyond them. He felt that the college hall and the office before him took on the aura of his life, for he embraced them with willing heart and spirit.

He asked for the dean of the college, and the office girl, obviously a student, said, "He's busy now, but you may see Miss Bevan. She's the registrar and the dean's assistant."

"I'm not registering. I'm teaching," Dan Montgomery said.

"Still, you better see Miss Bevan. Come into the office. Her private office is at the back." She indicated a closed door.

He moved along the counter and around the glass windows and into the office and to the closed door. The girl opened it for him and said, "Miss Bevan?"

He stepped inside with the lean dog close by his legs. He paused, and the dog pressed closer. He looked at the woman sitting behind the big desk. She stood up, and he saw that she was tall and wore very high-heeled shoes. *Either she's not ashamed of being tall*, he thought, *or she's being defiant about it.*

She was looking at him but not really seeing him. *Not beautiful*, he thought, *but with a sort of innate quality — class. Good blood, like a fine race horse. Nervous, too.* His large expressive mouth moved in a smile. "Good morning, princess," he said. "Dan Montgomery reporting. I thought the dean might like to know I got here."

"Oh, I'll tell him, Mr. Montgomery. And please put your dog outside. We don't —"

"He's a gentleman, and he enjoys college. He always attends my lectures. Sit down, Blue. Do you know the ballad about the good dog Blue? That's what he is." Blue obediently sat down. "If I had my guitar, I'd sing the ballad for you. It's a nice song."

She was seeing him now, her teeth gnawing at her lower lip. "I'm afraid I haven't time for—"

"There's always time for something like a song or a sunset." He smiled at her. "I'm going to enjoy working here. Nice to meet you, princess."

"My name is Miss Bevan," she said. "Emily Bevan."

"But you do look like her, you know."

"Like whom?"

"Princess Margaret.... Come, Blue." And he smiled at her again and wandered from the building through the sunlight to the old car. He drove across town to where he had rented a small apartment an hour before and began to unload his possessions—two battered suitcases, an easel, paints and stacks of canvases. Last, he took the guitar from where it lay on the back seat and carried it into the apartment. He sat down on the faded brown davenport and began to strum softly.

The window was open, and he could smell the warm grass and the leaves that were losing their juice. He heard the cars go by, and somewhere a child was laughing. The laughter fell around him like chips of September sunlight. The dog curled at his feet, like a thin gray-blue puddle on the dingy brown rug. Dan Montgomery's gray eyes looked far away into yesterday and into something more, into a dream he held in his heart. "Poor princess," he said to the autumn day. "So lonely and so afraid."

He remembered her black suit and the white collar and her hair so smooth and dark and shining and her face as white as the collar of the suit and the way her mouth held firmly together. And he wished he could have been an artist himself, instead of one who tried to make artists of other people. "I would paint Miss Emily Bevan," he said to Blue, and Blue opened one eye and looked at him in what Dan Montgomery thought must be pity.

He did not see her again for almost a month, because his work began in day school and he had classes in art three nights a week. He was busy, and he moved lightly through the days in a sort of gentle happiness, for he saw his students begin to understand, and he felt himself drawing out of them that which was theirs — a way of feeling and of being.

The second time he met Miss Emily Bevan — it was in the hallway — he was carrying a pile of old bones to his class- room. He paused and said, "Bones, rocks, wood, old wheels, old rusty stove lids. Basic. Wouldn't you like to sign up for one of my classes?"

"You're spilling dirt on the floor," she said, "and I'd think you could put on a white shirt for a change — and some pants that have been pressed. We're very proud of our college."

"I'd like to see you unpressed," he murmured. "I'd like to see the wind do things with your hair. I'd like to see you cry or hear you swear."

She turned and walked stiffly away, and he carried the old bones on to his classroom and let them fall on a piece of cloth that looked like tired earth. He said to his students, "Paint what you feel about this. And never, never ask me what I feel. It's you — it has to be." And while they worked he laughed deep inside about what Miss Emily Bevan had said to him, but that afternoon when classes were over he went downtown and bought two inexpensive white shirts and an iron. He scorched one of the shirts, and he worked an hour with a pair of pants. There was a tie in one of his suitcases, binding together a pile of old letters. He let the letters fall loose and pressed the tie.

The next morning he stopped by her office. The dean was talking to her. The dean was harassed-looking and wore polka-dot bow ties and liked to talk about fishing. The dean said, "I keep telling them we don't have enough room. I keep trying to convince the board of trustees that we need an arts-and-science building." He turned to Dan Montgomery. "You know it's true. You haven't room to do anything in that dinky classroom of yours."

Dan Montgomery nodded. He was still looking at Miss Emily Bevan, and at last he said, "There's a deer on the mountain, and she's very tame. She loves chocolate-covered peanuts. A taxi driver I know takes her peanuts every night about eleven o'clock. Drives up when he gets off work. Don't you want to go with us tonight?"

She stared at him, her dark eyes widening, and then she seemed to forget him. She said to the dean, "If we don't get another building, we'll lose students. We'll lose all we've worked for. Oh, the fools!" Then she looked into space and said, "I think of how we started — a dozen students on the top floor of the high school building. I think of how you've worked, and I've worked —"

Dan Montgomery turned and walked out. *Sublimation*, he thought. *She's turned all of herself into the work. The college — that's her outlet.* He stopped and stood still in the noisy, youth-filled hall and thought, *I know about sublimation too — but work's not enough. The heart has to spill somewhere — spill warm.*

That night he thought about her while he sat in the small apartment with the dog Blue resting at his feet. But he didn't think for long. Two of his night students came by to visit him. One was a bottle blond he had named Miss Vodka because of a liquid evening she'd spent telling him about her sad life. The other woman was dark-haired and needed a good girdle, but he called her Angel because she was always so pleasant and brought homemade cookies to class. Angel painted while

Miss Vodka wept quietly and talked about the husband who had left her. And, as they were both thus occupied and happy in his company, Dan Montgomery forgot them and played his guitar.

At last he looked at the alarm clock that ticked noisily on an upended apple box and said, "Come, ladies. I want you to meet Bimbo, the deer who likes chocolate-covered peanuts."

They drove up the mountain toward midnight and met the taxi driver, who was waiting with a spotlight turned on, and after a while the doe came slowly out of the timber, walking with great dignity, and accepted the peanuts. "Ain't it wonderful the way she knows I'll be here every night?" the taxi driver said.

Angel said it was and that she would burn a candle for Bimbo the next time she went to church. "So nobody will shoot her," she added.

Miss Vodka said it had been a wonderful evening, so wonderful that she couldn't refrain from throwing her arms around Dan Montgomery's neck and kissing him. "Y'know," she said, "it's your voice that gets me. It makes me feel like going out and living in sin."

Dan patted her gently on her bleached head. He wished it were Miss Emily Bevan who felt like living in sin. And while he thought thus, sharply aware of the stars and the doe and the whole blessed universe, a carload of young people went by and shouted his name. He didn't think to remove Miss Vodka's arms from around his neck until after the car had disappeared along the mountain road. And he thought of it then only because Miss Vodka was leaning so heavily that he almost lost his balance.

Miss Emily Bevan did not speak to him for several weeks. Fall moved into winter, and he kept pressing shirts and pants and he bought another tie. It was red. Then one day he met her in the hall and asked if she was going home for Christmas. She flushed and looked past him, muttering that she had work to do, and, anyhow, anyone who mattered to her was so far away.

"Blue has been asking for you," he said. "Blue invites you to have Christmas dinner with us."

Then her dark eyes flashed, and she said angrily, "Tell Blue I am sure Miss Vodka and Angel will be happy to accept his invitation. And you might also tell Blue that the dean doesn't care for Beatniks on the faculty."

Dan Montgomery replied, "And I'll add that Miss Emily Bevan is a prude. She has a heart of stone, and Miss Vodka and Angel have blood instead of ice water running through their veins." He turned and left her, and he knew she looked after him until he was out of sight. *Let her*, he thought, *let her be lonely and lost and more dead than alive. Why should I care?*

Winter seemed forever, and he went on through it — sometimes laughing aloud to see how well his students painted, sometimes thinking of Miss Emily Bevan and walking around town at midnight, stopping in strange little places where people played sad, tired music, and sometimes walking miles across the snow-covered prairie in the evening with his dog pacing along beside him. Man and dog and blue winter twilight would slowly blur into darkness.

Always he'd come home to find some of his students waiting at the apartment. The young ones cooked spaghetti, pizza and tacos for him. Angel pressed his clothes, and Miss Vodka bought him a new lamp and a pair of slippers that looked like Eskimo mukluks. Life bubbled around him and came to him, and he poured himself back into it. But when the wind blew lonely around the windows, just before the breaking of daylight, he thought of Miss Emily Bevan.

Toward the end of winter, when patches of snow pocked the prairie like a nuisance disease, he read articles in the paper about the need for a new arts-and-science building. And then, one night when spring was a green breath rising out of the land, but not yet defined in the leaves of trees or the blades of grass, the dean asked Dan Montgomery to talk to the board of trustees.

Dan bought a new white shirt and a new pair of pants and combed his rough blond hair until it was close to his head. He combed Blue, too. The dog sat beside him while he stood before the men of the board of trustees. He talked for a long time about art and science having to move hand in hand toward the future of the world. He tried to tell them that scientific discovery had to have self-discovery joined to it to make sense of a hostile world. He spoke of the college and what it might do to help young people understand this.

They listened attentively and applauded him, but later he heard them murmur, "Too much taxation now." As he was leaving the room, Miss Emily Bevan got up from a back corner and followed him out.

He stood and looked at the stars and thought ignorance could be as eternal as their light. Emily Bevan came to stand beside him and said, "I appreciate your talk. And—and long ago I appreciated your new shirts and your pressed pants."

"Thank you," he said. And he turned to her and put out a hand to touch her smooth hair. "Why do you hurt so inside, Emily? Because you couldn't find what you wanted in life— couldn't find love, tenderness, understanding?"

Silence then—silence except for the spring wind rising like soft weeping in the trees, bringing the scent of moist earth and of the river beyond town. And at last she said, "I was always too tall—a giant among the girls in grade school. The same in high school. And I never could make easy talk.

I studied hard instead. I...I have three college degrees. My father wanted me to, you see. Maybe he knew I wasn't the type — I mean, boys didn't notice me much when I was young. Later — well, later it was the wrong kind of noticing. I mean the men I liked didn't like me, except maybe if it could have been for a night or two."

"So you gave up and withered inside. You didn't keep reaching out warmly, believing it could happen. You are so wrong, Emily. I wanted to be a Van Gogh or a Matisse. I found out I couldn't, but I found I could walk where they walked, in the middle of life, in the hot full river of it. And if I had no real talent for painting, I could discover it in others. I could make life beat up in them as it did in me. I could give the best of myself to someone else who had the talent to use it."

Again the silence lay between them. He said gently, "It's never too late, Emily." There was a small choking sound, and then she was gone, running toward the street. He watched her get into her car and drive away.

"There's hope, Blue," he said, smiling in the spring darkness as they walked toward the apartment. "And we won't rush her. Coming alive is like a river moving from winter toward summer — it takes time for the ice to go out."

So he didn't try to see her. He worked hard with his students and got the dean to schedule a state art festival at the college for the month of May. He wanted to show the people of the town what art could mean in their part of the world. If the people knew, then in time the board of trustees would know. This knowledge of the people would find its way into words, and the words of the people were mighty.

On the Friday in May before the opening of the art festival he went to Miss Emily Bevan's office, his six feet of leisurely-moving frame flanked on one side by Miss Vodka and on the other by Angel. Blue trailed at his heels. An aura of paint and turpentine hung over him like a Greenwich Village halo.

"Good morning, princess," he said. "Tell the dean I'm using a live model in the hall this morning — good publicity for the art show."

"A model?" She looked alarmed, and he knew she had visions of a Junoesque girl wearing less than a bikini.

"And also tell the dean I've ordered two bales of hay from the livestock-sales barn on the edge of town."

"For your model?" Her fine eyebrows lifted. Miss Vodka tittered. Angel swung her hips and smiled.

"For my model," he said firmly. "No nudes-descending-the-stairs, princess. That's much too ordinary."

"What's more ordinary than a bale of hay?" she asked crossly.

But he only smiled at her and walked away with the two women swaying beside him. Once in the hall he paused, and a look of delight spread over his face. At the far end, before the broad windows that afforded an impressive view of town and prairie and plainly visible to all passers-by, stood a magnificent black horse. Two of his students were breaking out a bale of hay. Another was tethering the horse to a long pole that lay on the floor. Up and down the hall other students were unpacking crates of pictures and hanging them. One-man shows would be housed in some of the small rooms. Some of his class members had already set up their easels and were starting to paint the horse.

"Now," he said, "be sure to speak of this. Let it be freely and widely known that we are entertaining the artists of the state and have to pose a horse in the hall for our classwork."

During the confusion that followed, with teachers, visitors and students gathering to admire the horse, Dan Montgomery was pleased to see a photographer from the paper arrive. The photographer was followed by a reporter who asked if Mr. Montgomery would care to comment. Dan leaned against one of the broad windows. He bent to stroke Blue's lean hound ears, and then said he'd be delighted to comment. The reporter's pencil made rapid notes on a piece of paper.

The interview was terminated by a shriek from Miss Emily Bevan and some typical fisherman's language from the dean, who appeared to be choking as he reached to unfasten his polka-dot tie. What he had to say soon became coherent. Dan Montgomery was fired.

Dan squinted at the painting of one of his students. "Put in some warm shadows," he said. "Deep red would be good." Then he turned to the dean. "I won't leave until after the show tomorrow. Actually, you owe me two weeks' notice, you know. You're not being legal." And moving on to another student he said, "Let yourself go. The horse looks too much like himself."

Dan Montgomery spent a pleasant, quiet evening. His students were not so quiet. They had baked him a cake, cooked his dinner and set up a table in the living room, with candles in old bottles and a centerpiece of an old wooden bucket filled with lilacs. Miss Vodka was crying. She said the president of the board of trustees was a conformist, and when he read the evening paper he would agree with the dean that Dan should be fired. Angel said Miss Emily Bevan had gone home early, and the girl in the office said she had a terrible headache.

"I feel fine," Dan Montgomery said, looking at the front page of the paper where there was a large picture of a fine black horse, and over it the big black headline — ART STUDENTS PROTEST. The article said the students were tired of cramped quarters and quoted Mr. Dan Montgomery's theories on the stupidity of members of the board of trustees. Only the people, Mr. Montgomery said, could be counted on to save the college from ridicule and loss of students.

Dan Montgomery ate a hearty meal and went to bed. He dreamed of Emily Bevan riding like Lady Godiva through the streets of the town on a magnificent black horse. Her only digression was that she wore the dean's polka-dot tie.

He wakened to the fine May morning that smelled of lilacs and turned to Blue, who slept beside his bed. "In the beginning of things is often an ending — as the Chinese might say. But let's make the most of it, Blue."

They breakfasted on leftover pizza and strolled slowly toward the college, where the art show was opening at ten o'clock. It was then five minutes past the hour. Cars lined the street before the building and, inside, Dan Montgomery was satisfied to see crowds of people. He looked with a quickening sense of wonder at the work of his students and knew it was outstanding. At length, he came to one of the small classrooms that housed a one-man show. There were twenty-some people listening to a small, gray-haired man in jeans and runover boots. But Dan Montgomery saw only the dean, the president of the board of trustees and Miss Emily Bevan. There were very dark circles under Miss Bevan's eyes, and she had a most unpressed look about her.

"These here pictures," the little man said, "ain't mine. My wife did 'em. She painted 'em the last five years before she died. She had polio back before they had any help for it, and she could hardly hold a brush. I finally sold my cattle and just stayed near her and helped her with her painting, for I knew she was a great artist. I knew she was doin' something fine and someday other folks would see it."

Dan Montgomery looked at the pictures. He had to close his eyes. When he opened them again he knew he hadn't been having a nightmare. They were the worst paintings he had ever seen; smears of gaudy paint had tried to capture in reality the forms of barns, white-faced cattle, dogs and mountains. And worst of all was the pained posture of a bull moose drinking from a small pond.

"Like I said," the rancher went on, "I want you all to sign your John Henrys in my guest book. I'll be proud to have 'em—proud to remember sharin' Alice's work with you."

Dan Montgomery felt the stares of the dean and the president of the board of trustees. Even they, he thought, know how bad this work is. And then he looked at the old rancher. In the tired eyes was such a glow of love and pride that it went through Dan Montgomery like the glory of a prairie sunset. And he thought, *He doesn't know, he'll never know how miserable this work is.*

A haunting sadness touched him, a longing toward all those who, like himself, had wished to create beauty but lacked the ability to do it. *But the lucky ones are those who never know they lack,* he thought. *Why should it hurt me? Why do I care about this old guy who can go home in peace and remember for the rest of his days how he exhibited the pictures of his Alice?*

And then, impulsively, Dan Montgomery moved forward. "Are any of these for sale?" he asked gently. "I'm the art teacher here—was, I mean."

"Bunch is my name, Pete Bunch," the rancher said. "Son, I'm proud to know you. Now, I had no notion of sellin' these," his voice shook. "Didn't figure they'd be quite that fine, but I'd let one go to a man like you who knows about things like this."

Dan Montgomery looked at the dean and the president of the board of trustees. He felt the force of life move in him. "The moose," he said. "I'd like it. A hundred dollars, Mr. Bunch. Mark it sold."

"That's fine with me, son." The brown hand trembled as it

began to scrawl the word "sold" on a piece of paper. The face that lifted toward Dan was tender, as though the man remembered all the years of loving and living in that moment. "Thank you, son."

Blue rubbed against Dan's leg, and the two of them walked past the president of the board of trustees and the college dean and past Miss Emily Bevan, who held her fist pressed against her mouth. In the wide hall, Miss Vodka and Angel moved to meet him, and each linked an arm through his. "Hello, darlings," he said.

They had gone only a few steps when he heard her calling, "Mr. Montgomery — Dan...."

He shook himself lightly, freeing his arms of Angel and Miss Vodka. "Good-by, my lovelies," he murmured. "What I hear is my master's voice." And he turned to face the tall young woman with the dark smudges under her darker eyes.

"Oh, you knew," she said, her mouth trembling. "You saw how terrible they were. It will haunt me the rest of my life — how bad they were, how he'll never know — and the way you made him so happy."

"Sometimes," he said, looking deep into her eyes, "the thing behind a creation is much more beautiful than the creation itself. Oh, I'll never hang it on my wall. I'll keep it somewhere, quiet and secret, and sometimes I'll take it out and I'll see a monument to love and —"

"Emily," it was the dean speaking. "Don't feel so bad, Emily. We aren't going to fire Dan. Public opinion and — well," the dean cleared his throat, "all the good things you said about him and —"

"A monument to love," Dan Montgomery repeated, staring hard at Miss Emily Bevan. "The kind of love we could have had for each other if you— Ah, princess, don't cry!" He put his arms around her, and from somewhere far away he heard music. He kissed her and began to waltz her slowly around and around while the people moved back to clear a small space for them. Blue took a few steps after them and then sat down, his thin nose pointed toward the ceiling.

"I'm broke," Dan Montgomery said. "The picture — and I had to buy the black horse. Couldn't expect the dean to include him in supplies for the art department. I've nothing to offer you."

"It doesn't matter — nothing matters," said Miss Emily Bevan.

He stopped whirling her around then and held her close. "'Come live with me and be my love,'" he said, and noticing that the dean and the president of the board of trustees were standing right beside them, added quickly, "legally, of course."

THIS UNUSUAL FATHER-OF-the-groom story appeared in *Good Housekeeping* in June 1963.

Like a number of Peg Curry's stories, it deals with the search for understanding and accommodation between generations. A story with immediacy, it might have been written today.

INVITATION TO A WEDDING

H E WAS TIRED AND cross and his expensive slacks were as crumpled as though he'd slept in them. Fifteen hundred miles of hard driving lay behind him, and he looked at his wife, Willi, as though she were somehow to blame for the whole thing. She stared back at him defensively, from where she sat on the motel-room bed, the telephone in her hand. "You'd better take a shower, Matthew," she said.

"Listen," he said harshly, "if my son's gotten mixed up with a little tramp—"

"You're jumping to conclusions," she said calmly, but he observed that the hand holding the receiver was trembling. "And there's nothing much we can do about it now if he has."

This realistic statement from the woman he loved shook him more than his own bleak forebodings. "I won't assume a bit of responsibility," he said, scowling. "When I went to college it was a disgrace to be—"

"Times have changed," Willi interrupted with maddening poise. "And you haven't been asked to assume responsibility. You've been invited to a wedding." Then her face brightened and she spoke into the telephone. "Bruce! How are you, darling? I've been trying to call your fraternity house for half an hour."

Matthew McLean went into the bathroom and turned on

the shower. *Kids,* he thought, *wanting to get married. Only twenty-one, and I was thirty when Willi and I....* For a moment he forgot the present and remembered Willi as he had first seen her, sitting across the table from him at a banquet where he was the featured speaker. Willi's dark eyes had glinted mischievously at him and she had said, "The food always looks a little tired at these things." And then a warm explosion had happened inside him, and he, who had always been conservative, had said boldly, "May I take you home after the banquet?"

We only went together six weeks, he thought, startled, *but Willi was twenty-five and I was almost thirty.* He squared his big shoulders under the stinging shower. *I was mature — not like my son. I would never have called my parents without warning and said simply, "I'm getting married. I want you to come."*

He recalled resentfully the hurried arrangements before leaving home — Willi calling friends, "Sorry we can't come to dinner. We're leaving in the morning. Bruce is getting married. Oh, yes, we know the girl — met her when we were out last summer." Willi telling lies, trying to sound natural. And he, no better, looking his top salesman in the eye and saying, "Take over for me, Jim. Try to sell the Harding house before it's dead timber. We're going out of town. Bruce is getting married." And Jim blurting out, "Married! I didn't even know he was engaged." And he replying. "They've planned to get married for a year."

Now, he thought, drying himself roughly on the big towel, *who is this girl who's wrecked my son's life?* He recalled vaguely that last year Bruce had written something about "a living doll" he'd met at a dance. Then Bruce had called, shortly after college had started in September of this year, and said, "There's a girl — I might want to get married."

Matthew had laughed, not taking it seriously at all. Hadn't he let Bruce know long ago how he felt about young, fly-by-night marriages? "Don't kid me, boy! There's a girl on every corner. How's the old fight with Spanish coming along?"

In October the second telephone call had come — firm, brief, shattering. A few hours later they were on their way to the wedding.

He crumpled the big damp towel into a ball and threw it into the corner of the bathroom. *I spend twenty-one years planning, raising a son who's got a good mind, a son who could have the best—fine education, top job, travel—and one day take his time selecting that special girl from the cream of the crop. And what happens? Some little coed bats her eyes at him and—*

"Matthew! Hurry up! Bruce is coming right over and bringing Kathy-Anne."

Kathy-Anne. He strode into the other room and began fumbling in his suitcase. Why not just Kathy or Anne? He finished dressing and said, "Want a drink, Willi?"

"Please, and not too much water."

They sat silently, sipping their drinks like two strangers as they waited for their son. He wanted desperately to feel close to Willi, but he knew she was lost in her own doubts and fears. And he began to think of his son not as a college senior who would be working on a job this time next year. He remembered Bruce as a child who had once thrown a rock through a window and been punished, a child who somehow managed to get the dog in bed with him and keep Willi from finding out. He recalled other things — Bruce forgetting his part in a fourth-grade play and promptly making up a whole speech while the audience, recognizing his innovation, had burst into laughter and applause. He remembered Bruce bringing home a boy who had lost his lunch money and how the two of them had sat at Willi's kitchen table, eating peanut-butter sandwiches.

Matthew's throat tightened. Not a bad kid, he thought — a good kid, in fact. Oh, maybe a little too much like his mother at times, too impulsive on occasion, and stubborn when one least expected it; but vital and wonderfully alive. "A free spirit, Mr. McLean," one of Bruce's teachers had said of him, "like a bird, he has to fly."

But not now, Matthew McLean thought, now he's got his wings clipped. Taking on a wife when he isn't even out of college, a wife and all the problems he shouldn't have yet.

There was a knock at the door. Matthew jumped up and looked at Willi. Somewhere back on the fifteen-hundred-mile stretch of driving, Willi had begun to cry and he'd said fiercely, "Don't you worry. I'll take care of it." But now his feet felt leaden. Again there was a knock. "You go," he said hoarsely.

He saw her stand and straighten, a slim, tall woman with a streak of white through her shining black hair. She moved forward quickly to fling the door wide and then her arms. "Kathy-Anne," she said. Then, in a blur, he saw his son moving toward him, holding out a hand. "Hi, Dad. Sure glad to see you." Close-fitting pants, tan corduroy jacket, shoes that looked a little worn. But wasn't there a change? Or maybe he only imagined that Bruce's jaw looked more firm, his eyes older and graver.

"Well," Matthew cleared his throat, "how are you?" Then he turned toward the girl, his heart hammering violently, his whole body tense. He didn't see her at all as she moved to clasp the hand he held out. *Should have kissed her, but I don't even know her.* And then the room cleared, as though a fog had drifted away, and he saw her eyes. They were large green-blue eyes that looked directly at him. He stared at her, feeling confused and on the defensive. He had expected her to flush or act uncertain, but she met his scrutiny, her chin and shoulders up. And then he saw something else in those clear, steady eyes, a gentleness that was almost a pleading. It was as though she said, "Here I am. I know you don't really want me, but try to get to know me."

He said brusquely, "Well, Kathy-Anne, I guess you two have made up your minds."

"We love each other," she said quietly.

"Oh. Well, sit down, sit down. Care for a drink?"

"No, thank you," she spoke in the same contained, quiet way.

He'd thought she'd jump at the chance to feel easier in a tight situation, and somehow he admired her for not taking the drink. *Hair's sort of red*, he thought, *and she's got pretty skin — the clear, clean kind. Doesn't wear a lot of makeup like some of them.*

He glanced at Willi. Bruce was explaining the wedding plans to her. Matthew caught a few phrases — "at the church — double-ring ceremony — four o'clock tomorrow afternoon." Willi showed no emotion, but Matthew could tell by the way she lighted her cigarette, her glance darting around the room, that she was disturbed.

Willi and Bruce had been very close, so close that sometimes Matthew had felt a little like an outsider the past three years. There had been moments when Bruce was home on vacation when he'd wished Bruce was out of the house and completely on his own. He'd been ashamed of this and once had mentioned it to an old friend and the friend had said, "Well yes, I know what you mean. Two men and one woman under the same roof, it's rivalry — old as time, Matt. Natural it should happen." And now Willi was worrying about this girl who would claim her son tomorrow.

Matthew cleared his throat impatiently. "How do you two

figure you're going to make a living?" he asked. Just as well to let them know right now, to make it clear he wasn't going to be the soft touch.

Silence fell over the room. Bruce looked at him as though from a great distance. "I plan to work part time," Bruce said, "and so does Kathy-Anne. It may take us an extra year to get through, but we can do it. And her parents are going to go on helping her."

Weak-minded parents, that's what they were. When I was in college, we didn't expect parents to support us—or a wife. He noticed Willi was frowning at him.

"We've rented a little house near the campus," Kathy-Anne said to Willi. "And I have my car. I bought it from my savings. It's not new but the motor's good. And I've got most of my silver. I've been buying it out of my summer checks."

"That so?" Matthew looked sharply at her. "I thought this was all pretty sudden."

"I know it seems so to you," she spoke in the same quiet tone. "But we did see each other last year and we tried to be careful—dating other people, considering our futures. I think we knew, though, even then. And we stayed apart, worked all summer. Then this fall when school started—" She drew a deep breath. "We were sure it was real and right."

There was a long silence in the room. Willi fumbled nervously with her handkerchief. Matthew scowled and said, "How are you sure?"

It was Bruce who answered, clearly and steadily, "Our complete concern for each other, Dad—in every way. We know we'd study more if we were together, settled in the direction we want to go. We want to begin now, planning for the children we hope to have someday, the kind of life we think's important. We're willing to assume the responsibility of marriage."

Matthew looked down at the floor. Very fine, high-sounding stuff. Might have come out of a textbook on marriage and the family. Probably well-rehearsed, too. He jerked his head up, looking sharply at them. "You know we're not going to step in and foot the bills if things get tough. The world's full of parents who get caught in that trap."

Bruce answered angrily, "There are also young people who don't expect to ride the parental gravy train. They *want* to assume their own responsibilities. They want to start building the kind of world they can believe in — if the older generation will let them!"

"Mature people," Matthew said, trying to keep his voice level, "have jobs, money in the bank, security."

"Do they?" Bruce retorted. "How many people who built this country had money in the bank and security when they started out?"

Kathy-Anne stood up. "I have to be in soon, Bruce."

"Okay, honey. Just one more thing." He looked at Matthew. "If there's any real security in the world it's in the way two people feel about each other. It's the only thing *I* know you can really count on." Bruce picked up Kathy-Anne's coat and carefully helped her into it. For a moment he looked down at her, and Matthew saw an expression of great tenderness come over his face.

"Good-night," Bruce said, and Kathy-Anne's voice echoed the word in a proud, hurt tone. Willi saw them to the door and kissed them. Then she sat down on the edge of the bed and lighted a cigarette.

"You acted badly," Willi said at last. "Starting right out to talk about money —"

"I'm a realist, Willi. I've seen many parents put in a bind because a couple of kids thought they could both work *and* study."

"Now, Matthew, you could have said you were happy for them. You just stood there examining her like she might be a piece of property you were trying to find fault with. And she's so genuine — nothing phony about her."

"I'm not about to frost their cake, Willi, and don't try to change my mind."

"Bruce talked like a man, and she's no fifteen-year-old child. She's honest and intelligent and her eyes are beautiful and —"

"Then why are you sitting there looking like your heart would break?"

Willi swallowed hard. "Oh, Matthew, they're so *young!* And Bruce — Bruce and I — we can't ever be the same again. It's just the change, Matthew, for a woman — when her son marries."

He went to her and put his arms around her. Willi began to cry softly. He held her close. "Don't, don't, Willi."

He awoke from troubled sleep to hear Willi on the telephone. "But of course we want to see your house," she was saying. "That's why I called you so early this morning, Bruce. Of course your father intends to come to the wedding. Surely you didn't think —" A long silence, and then, "I know, but this has all been so sudden for us. Let's put it behind us now. You come by soon. Good-bye, dear."

So Bruce was sore, Matthew thought, getting out of bed. And what about his feelings and Willi's? He'd meant what he said, every word of it. But they didn't understand. How could they? There hadn't been a lot of money floating around in the last fifteen years. They couldn't possibly know how tough it was for us. They never saw a breadline. They've only read about depression in their history books.

Kathy-Anne and Bruce arrived in an old gray sedan. They

were polite and distant. Bruce explained they'd been excused from classes for the day. Matthew helped Willi into the back seat and sat silently next to her.

When he saw the house, he was shocked. He could have put the whole thing in his living room at home. The floors squeaked, the windows stuck, the doors didn't fit properly. A huge and sagging red chair sat in the middle of the living room. He stared at it.

"That's Bruce's chair," Kathy-Anne said, looking defensively at Matthew. "He likes it and it's ideal for studying."

"Got it at the Salvation Army store," Bruce said, his voice filling with warmth. "Only two bucks." He turned to Willi. "What do you think of it?"

Willi was chewing her lower lip. "The — ah — color seems a little vivid for these green walls."

"Oh, I intend to cover it," Kathy-Anne said quickly. "I have a sewing machine."

"Kathy-Anne makes most of her own clothes," Bruce said proudly.

Matthew glanced at Willi. "You couldn't even darn my socks."

"Still can't," Willi said.

They drove to the campus and met some of Bruce's fraternity brothers and the cook at the house. Bruce called the cook "Spirits"; she was a tall, warm-eyed woman with a twist of gray hair on top of her head. She informed Matthew that she was baking the cake for the wedding reception. "Kathy-Anne's parents wanted to have the reception at one of the hotels," she said, "but we wanted it here — for Bruce and Kathy-Anne."

They drove to meet the best man who was waiting for them outside the campus café. The best man was handsome, remote-looking, and wearing faded Levis. He drove a long, low-slung car with white leather seats trimmed in red. He looked at Kathy-Anne and Bruce and a warmth came into the cool gray eyes. "You lucky ones," he said. He shook hands with Willi and Matthew and offered his congratulations before inquiring politely about their trip.

When the best man turned back to Bruce, it was to make a joke about not having enough to do as best man. "I'm supposed to be nursing your shaking nerves," he said with a laugh. "You weren't half this calm before you asked her."

Matthew felt a flash of resentment. He didn't share any of this with us, Matthew thought, feeling left out.

Then he remembered his parents hadn't even attended his wedding. He'd met Willi in the West, and his parents lived in the East. It had been depression times and people didn't go in for big weddings. He'd merely written his parents and told them he was marrying Willi and bringing her home. He'd taken it for granted they'd understand he knew what he was doing, just as he'd taken it for granted they'd accept Willi. *It must have been a shock to them,* he thought. Still, he concluded defensively, I was a man — almost thirty. Yet, who could say at what age a boy becomes a man? Circumstances altered people.

The best man was asking politely if he might help Kathy-Anne move the rest of her things from the sorority house to her new home. Then Matthew heard himself saying, "No. I'll do that."

The three young people stared at him. He felt self-conscious and said gruffly, "Nothing else to do. Used to being busy."

And so he found himself riding alone with Kathy-Anne while the others went to pick up the rings for the wedding. He could think of nothing to say and he waited hopefully for her to begin conversation, but she was silent.

As they carried her boxes into the shabby little house he tried to ease his tension by taking charge of things. "Now," he said briskly, "I'll unpack. You put this stuff in the linen closet."

"Wait a minute," she was kneeling beside him, looking in the box. "Our linen closet is a kitchen shelf. It has to be washed and then shelf paper put on."

"You're darned particular," he said.

"So are you," she retorted. For a moment they looked at each other. Then she added, "Not that I blame you, with a son like Bruce. But there are things you don't know about him. He needs someone to care for his clothes — you should see how he throws them around the fraternity house! He needs someone to keep him from being so warmhearted and impulsive; he squanders all his study time in bull sessions. And his Spanish! I'm a language major and I intend to tutor him — although he doesn't know it yet."

She smiled to herself, looking into space. Then she turned again to Matthew. "He needs someone to be responsible for — or didn't you know he has this strong family feeling? He hated to leave home, but he wanted to stand on his own feet and that's why he came so far away to go to college. And that's why he wanted to make all the decisions about our marriage on his own. He only wanted to prove he's become an adult. He loves you so much — you and his mother. I don't know what he'd have done if you hadn't come to our wedding."

Matthew stared down at the contents of the box. The white linens and the colored linens all seemed to run together. "Get that bucket," he said. "I'll wash the shelves — if it's okay with you."

It was almost two o'clock when he got back to the motel. He took a shower and put on his best suit. A little later he said to Willi, "It's easy to go overboard on these thing, to get all covered up with emotion. But naturally I expect to give them a little wedding present. Fifty dollars, maybe. I still have my principles, Willi, and I intend to stick by them."

Willi was concentrating on fixing her nails. "Of course, dear," she said. "You're quite right."

There was a knock at the door. Matthew opened it and faced a gray-haired man and a pretty, red-haired woman. "We're Kathy-Anne's parents," the stranger said. "Just got in a little while ago. Wanted to drop by and get acquainted."

Willi was charming. Kathy-Anne's mother was charming. *In fact,* Matthew thought, *after fifteen minutes devoted to weather and roads, we're all being so darned charming something's going to explode.* He said loudly, "Let's have a drink. We need it." There was laughter, then. The tension went out of the room. And after a while, Kathy-Anne's father said slowly, "We wanted our daughter to finish college before she thought of marriage. But we like Bruce. He's fine." Willi assured him she felt the same about Kathy-Anne. They had another drink and Kathy-Anne's parents invited them to dinner after the wedding reception.

"Well," Matthew said when he and Willi were alone, "they're real good people—intelligent, pleasant."

"What did you expect, head hunters?" Willi lay down and put her arm over her eyes.

Matthew rocked back and forth on his heels. "I noticed he's trimmer than I am—still has his waistline. But my hair isn't gray and I think I look younger."

"You look very handsome," Willi said, "when you're not scowling. Matthew, I don't feel very well. I have a headache. I—I don't know if I can make it to this wedding."

"Now, Willi—" he noticed she was pale. "Take some aspirin and have a short nap."

Tears started to run down her cheeks.

Matthew brought her aspirin and a glass of water. Then he

held her gently until the tears stopped and she went to sleep.

He eased his arm from under her head, and then, restless, went for a walk. When he returned, she was dressed and smiling. "Hi, Beautiful," he said, "would you like to spend a lost weekend with me when this is over?"

"You asked me that once before — just after we met. I was shocked."

"I'd have been more shocked if you'd accepted. I —" He flushed. "I wanted you to think I was sophisticated and dangerous."

"You were quite convincing."

"I'd rather be convincing now — twenty-two years later."

Her face lighted with a lovely smile. "Thank you, darling."

As they drove toward the church, he felt time running out. If they'd only waited, if Bruce had finished college, if Kathy-Anne were a little older.... He entered the church and saw the young people everywhere, boys in their dark suits, girls in rustling dresses. He moved with a sense of unreality down the aisle to sit beside Willi. The tones of the organ fell over him. Flowers scented the air. And then he saw the bride on the arm of her father, and her eyes were as clear and steady as when she'd first looked at him in the motel room.

His son and the best man were at the altar. Everything was moving too fast. Bruce — only yesterday a sun-browned child in a summer yard, staring up at the coming storm. *"Listen to the thunder, Daddy!"* And now Bruce was saying the old familiar words that held a lifetime of implications. Matthew glanced at Willi. He had been sure she'd cry in the middle of everything, and Willi had never been a quiet crier. She put all of herself into it. But Willi looked calm, resigned. *Now everything is just her and me, back to the beginning.*

Then it was over and there was the confusion of picture-taking and rice-throwing. The crowd moved from the church to the fraternity house. After several cups of punch—strong, Matthew noted—he began to feel easy among the young people. Bruce's fraternity brothers were a distinguished lot, he decided. His daughter-in-law started cutting the wedding cake. Then she paused and looked directly at him, as though she saw only her father-in-law, Matthew McLean. He nodded and winked at her. A slow smile came over her face and she was suddenly beautiful.

Fifty dollars isn't much of a wedding present, he thought. And then he turned away, feeling foolish and confused. He found himself face to face with his son. "If you plan to stay tomorrow," Bruce said, "we'd like to take you to breakfast. I mean, we aren't having a honeymoon now. A trip later— maybe back to visit you. We have research papers for history due on Monday."

A honeymoon among the history books. Matthew blinked. It was still beyond him, part of a world he would never know, could never quite accept. But was it a world any less good than that he and Willi had known?

"Come by the motel as soon as this is over," Matthew said. "Don't forget, now."

There was a sudden hush as the young men gathered across the room in a group. They began to sing a haunting song about young love and the giving of hearts until eternity. And then from another side of the room, the young women answered, singing another love song. Bruce had gone to Kathy-Anne's side and stood with his arm about her. Matthew felt the touch of a hand on his. His hard fingers closed tightly over Willi's. What would he be without her? And what would she be without him?

He'd known there wasn't any meaning to life without her, known from the time he looked at her across that banquet table and she had spoken to him. And what if it had happened earlier, when he was in school, and Willi had said she'd work to help and there was no point in waiting?

He was aware that the singing had ended and people were leaving. He said good-bye to Spirits, the cook, who was splendid in flowing pink chiffon. He pressed her hand hard, trying to thank her for the wedding cake.

He and Willi hadn't been at the motel long when Bruce and Kathy-Anne arrived. Matthew looked at them and it came over him in a blinding rush that he wanted to do everything for them, to give them the world. He wanted to say he'd subsidize them every month, they could count on it.

But he checked his impulse, trying to see them objectively as they stood before him in their wedding finery. The garments of maturity. They had put them on, his son and Kathy-Anne, and they must have the chance to grow into them.

He fumbled awkwardly in his pocket, found the check and thrust it at Kathy-Anne. "This is for you. Please."

The brilliant green-blue eyes told him she loved him. He kissed her quickly, pressed Bruce's hand, and said roughly, "Now, get out! My feet hurt. I want to take off my shoes."

Silence again. Silence and only himself and Willi. Matthew took hold of his wife's hand. "I gave her five hundred dollars," he said.

Willi put her arms around his neck. He could feel the quick, hard beat of her heart. "I'm not really surprised," she said.

"Look," he said, his face against her soft hair, "after dinner with the new relatives, how about coming back here and packing? It's a beautiful night to drive. And I saw a little motel about a hundred miles down the highway. I'd like to start over there — you and me."

EARLY IN HER CAREER, Peg Curry wrote for romance magazines in the "pulp" field, so called because of the less expensive paper on which they were printed. After reading a number of them—though she admitted they were not to her reading taste—and noting their underlying story structure, she began writing.

After a time, she originated two delightful, middle-aged characters. Madame Olga, who reads palms and tea leaves, dresses like an opera singer in bright flowing clothes and hoop earrings. Her husband, the darkly handsome Alfonse, who assists with the fortune-telling, wears a yellow cumberbund with his tuxedo and a large turban. Traveling with them is their lovely daughter, Marcia, who participates—not always willingly—in the solution of love problems for clients.

This story was published in *Gay Love* in the June 1944 issue, in a time when "gay love" meant "happy love." It was the first story for which Peg received money. She carried around the forty-five dollar check for so long that the editor wrote to ask if she had received it. Her original title for the story was "Jack of Diamonds." An editor wrote that she recommended a title change to "Lucky in Love," but when it appeared in the magazine, it was entitled "I Woke Up Last Night."

There are at least two other Olga and Alfonse stories which were published in romance magazines. Peg credited the guiding hand of the pulp editors with teaching her the elemental aspects of plotting, characterization and story movement, and often said she "never felt the least ashamed" that she wrote for the pulps.

I Woke Up Last Night

MARCIA WAS TALL AND lithe, with shining dark hair that swung to her shoulders in a page-boy bob. Her mouth was red and full and made for laughter. But her present mood matched the sagging sky.

Walking home through the soft rain she told herself scornfully that Sergeant Cliff McMichael meant nothing to her. She told herself it didn't matter that she was only a stooge in his plan to bring his fiancée, Hilda Davis, to her senses.

Hilda was wearing Cliff's big solitaire but that didn't keep her from running around with other men — especially another man named Charlie Warren.

"I got myself into this," Marcia said aloud, remembering what had happened last night. Cliff had kissed her and she had deliberately pushed him away. It wasn't right for a man to kiss you that way — not unless he loved you. And Cliff didn't love her. He had been pretty frank about that. He had grinned apologetically and said, "That kiss didn't mean a thing, Lovely. Don't get me wrong."

Then he had told her about Hilda.

"I thought you knew we were engaged," he had explained. "Look, Marcia, I don't want to be cheap about this — but couldn't you help me make her jealous? Couldn't you pretend to be the secret romance in my life?"

Her head had lifted proudly. She had forced herself to say lightly, "Sure, I'll be the secret romance in your life. Why not? All's fair in love and war, Soldier."

Nice going, Marcia! You met a man who seemed to be something special—easy to talk to, fun to be out with. You even lied about your folks and yourself. You didn't want him to know you were only a fortune-teller, that your father read a crystal ball and your mother guided destinies by tea leaves. You wanted him to think you were a fancy package—all done up in highbrow background and classy education. You even dreamed about him—silly little schoolgirl dreams that made you warm and happy inside. And then last night—last night you woke up.

She turned off the wet street and climbed the apartment stairs. *Oh, I'm bright all right,* she told herself in quick anger. *I'm too smart to fall for him—or am I?*

She shook the mist from her dark hair, shaped her lips in a smile, and reached for the door knob. *Come on, Stooge,* she scolded, *snap out of it!*

Madame Olga was tinting her nails with red polish. She was a large, deep-breasted woman with high-piled blond hair. She used peroxide freely when she had sufficient cash. Her eyes were round and blue in a round pink and white face. She regarded her daughter affectionately. "Well, dear, how was the first-aid meeting this morning?"

"Fine." Marcia shrugged out of her coat. "I tied a splint on a soldier's arm." Her eyes looked past her mother, remembering Cliff's nearness and the hard strength of his arm beneath her fingers.

Alfonse stopped reading a pamphlet on Folsom arrowheads. He had a lean, olive-complexioned face and the lean body of an athlete, although he loathed exercise of any kind.

His black hair was silver-streaked at the temples. He had the nose of his ancestors, high bridged and thin. Alfonse looked like an aristocrat. Now his shrewd, dark eyes made a quick inventory of Marcia. "A soldier, eh?"

"Yes." She sank into a big chair and fished hopefully through a crumpled cigarette package. Alfonse watched with covetous eyes as she inhaled deeply and blew a cloud of smoke.

"Here," she thrust the cigarette toward him. "You take it. Tastes terrible on an empty stomach."

"Thank you, my child. Did you make any contacts this morning?"

Marcia's pointed, pixie-like face brightened. "Yes. Hilda Davis. *The* Hilda Davis. She got confidential over the bandages and told me she questions the attentions of a certain suitor. He swears love and devotion. She's afraid he's after her cash."

Madame Olga smiled, waving one dimpled white hand in the air to dry the nail polish. "Very typical. She's sure to be in for a reading. Then we can eat."

"Stop talking about food," said Alfonse. "I'm starving! I was just about ready to sell one of my Folsoms for a square meal. A shame, too. Arrowheads like mine don't grow on bushes."

"What's in the ice box?" Marcia said.

"One egg —" Madame Olga wrinkled her white forehead. "Oh yes, we have two slices of bread."

"Tea?" inquired Alfonse hopefully.

"Not enough. I must keep it in case some kind soul asks for a leaf reading."

Alfonse pulled a pack of cards from the pocket of his faded bathrobe. "Let's have a hand of poker for the egg. Stud or draw, Marcia?"

"Stud. Not those cards. Use these." She took another deck from the mantle over the gas fireplace.

Alfonse grinned. "You're too wise, my child."

"I never trust you with your own deck, dear." Marcia kissed his cheek affectionately.

The doorbell rang insistently. Alfonse and Madame Olga made a hasty exit to the bedroom. Marcia opened a spacious wall closet that served as a dressing room. A few seconds later she appeared in a full red skirt and a sequin-studded jacket. Her dark hair was thrust under a red bandanna. On the way to the door she pulled the heavy embroidered drapes across the windows and snapped on a corner lamp. Already she caught a whiff of incense drifting from under the closed bedroom door. *The stage is set,* she thought.

She opened the door and stared into the amused, gray eyes of Sergeant Cliff McMichael.

"Well, my little clairvoyant! So I've finally tracked you to your den!"

She felt her face burn and an annoying tremble in her knees. She forced herself to meet his eyes and said defiantly, "So what?"

He sauntered casually into the room, casting a sidelong glance at her. "Something new in spring fashions?"

"Yes," she answered dryly, "the soothsayer's ensemble."

He scrutinized the autographed photographs that hung on the walls. He examined the show cases filled with arrowheads, the fringed lamp shades, the drapes, the red cushions on the divan.

"You needn't smirk." Marcia's tone was level. "This happens to be my home."

He lifted her stubborn, embarrassed face between his hands and said, "Why did you lie to me? Why didn't you tell me the truth?"

Marcia's heart twisted. How could a man like Cliff

McMichael understand people who lived like gypsies — drifting from one part of the country to another, making a meager living with cards and tea leaves and a crystal ball?

"You're hurting my chin," she said.

"Sorry." He released her. "You needn't have been so secretive."

"Who told you about us?"

"Hilda. She got interested and traced you."

Marcia's lips tightened in anger. Hilda had made her a liar and a cheat. She could picture Hilda, beautiful and smart in her expensive clothes, saying to Cliff, "And that little dark-haired girl who put the splint on you — darling, this is priceless! She's a fortune-teller," Hilda's smooth, superior voice making the words sound cheap and shabby.

"Couldn't you have let good enough alone!" Marcia cried. "Did you have to pry into my personal affairs?"

Cliff's face reddened.

"Look, Lovely," he said, "we're friends, aren't we?"

Friends! Marcia winced. *Things had taken a pretty turn indeed. First she was a nice girl who got a kiss that didn't mean anything. Then she was a stooge. Now she was something associated with horn-rimmed glasses, baggy skirts, and flat shoes — the little pal — but definitely not romantic.*

"I don't give a damn if you tell fortunes for a living," Cliff said.

"Nice of you to say so," Marcia answered bleakly.

"Come now. Don't be so glum. I've always wanted my fortune told by a beautiful brunette." His eyes were teasing.

"I thought you preferred blonds," Marcia said coolly.

She was surprised to see his eyes kindle with something more than teasing as he said, "Not always. We had fun, didn't we? Or have you forgotten those walks in the park and all the things we did together?"

Forget them. Oh, Cliff, what do you think I'm made of? Even stooges have hearts — or didn't you know?

She picked up the deck of card with shaking fingers. She shuffled them until Cliff said, "Aren't you going to tell my fortune?"

"I hope you'll be amused," she said disdainfully and placed the deck on the card table before him. "Cut them three times toward you with your left hand and make a wish."

He leaned across the table, his gray eyes laughing at her and said, "I wish —"

"To yourself, please. I see a great change in your life. A long journey and new friends. You lie close to money. See — this is your card — you're the jack o' diamonds."

"You mean the jack o' hearts," he corrected.

The bedroom door opened. Her parents made a sudden and dramatic entrance. Madame Olga swept in like a majestic opera singer, red skirts billowing, golden hoops swaying from her ears. Alfonse had swathed his lean middle in a yellow sash and wrapped a turban around his head.

"This is Sergeant Cliff McMichael," Marcia said briefly, avoiding her father's angry eyes.

Alfonse wasn't in any town long until he knew the important names. McMichael would ring a little bell in his mind. The bell was on a cash register. McMichael. Real estate. Architects. This young man had been born with the golden spoon. The anger went out of Alfonse's eyes. Only shrewdness remained.

"Ah — Mr. McMichael — a flier, eh? So you have come for a reading. I'm certain a man of your position and intelligence would prefer the crystal ball. Of course, Madame here has recently studied palmistry under a Hindu. She is also adept with cards and tea leaves."

Cliff grinned. "You've got me wrong. I came to see your daughter."

Alfonse appraised his lanky length, noting that he wore the uniform with a certain reserved pride. Alfonse looked closely at the gray eyes, the reddish brown hair ruffled with cowlicks, and the young man's square, determined chin. "So — it is my daughter's talent you prefer."

"She's mad at me right now," Cliff said. "I came to ask her to dinner. She's been helping me promote a jealousy campaign."

"Then this is not the first time you've seen each other?"

"Of course not. Why?"

"My daughter, Mr. McMichael, is given to sudden and secret romances. They never last." Alfonse sighed. "We find it convenient and more kind to leave town."

Marcia's dark eyes flashed. Even Alfonse was conspiring against her. Making her seem like a ruthless flirt who couldn't really love anyone. She looked at Cliff. He was watching her with a surprised expression on his face. Confusion overwhelmed her. She stumbled away from the card table and deliberately turned her back on them.

"Of course," Alfonse continued smoothly, "she might accept your dinner invitation. That is, if it comes under the classification of a business deal."

"In other words," Cliff said coolly, "I must cross the palm with silver."

"We understand each other, Mr. McMichael. And what is your trouble?"

"My fiancée has given me the brushoff for a yokel from Chicago named Warren."

"Warren — hmmm. And Marcia is to appear with you tonight?"

"That was my idea. Hilda's dining at the Firefly with

Warren." Cliff tossed a crisp bill on the table. "Does that make it a deal?"

"No!" Alfonse protested. "That's too much. We aren't extortionists. We only want to eat. And didn't I hear you say you two were friends? Friendship shouldn't come so high."

"What goes on here?" Cliff demanded. "Friendship...business...I always pay my way."

"Consider it done, then," said Alfonse, smoothly pocketing the bill. "Let us talk of other matters." He began to tell the intricate plot of his most recent, unsold novel.

Suddenly the doorbell rang.

"That might be Hilda. Is there a back way out?" asked Cliff, rising from his chair.

Alfonse nodded. "I shall accompany you," he said, slapping his pockets. "I seem to be out of cigarettes."

"I'll pick you up at eight," Cliff said over his shoulder to Marcia, as the door shut softly behind them.

"Isn't it exciting?" said Madame Olga, patting her hair. "Marcia, dear, answer the door."

Marcia's heart plummeted. Hilda stood framed in the open doorway, smartly dressed in a white wool suit. The red bow of her blouse perfectly matched her lipstick. "Hello, Marcia," she said mockingly. Her eyes swept the small room. "I think this little adventure might be amusing."

Madame Olga floated toward her, her hand gracefully extended. "Sit here," she said gesturing toward the table. "Marcia, I shall begin with the tea."

Marcia was glad to escape to the kitchen. She returned with a delicate pink cup of steaming water. She watched as Madame Olga passed her hands over it, dropping in the pinches of tea. "Drink your tea, my dear," said Madame Olga. "Then we shall see your destiny."

Hilda sipped the tea. When she set the empty cup down,

Madame Olga gasped and leaned toward it. "Jealousy! I see jealousy. And you are puzzled, very puzzled by — something. I see a large room, many people." She held the cup in both her hands and turned it sideways. "Someone whose heart is false is close to you."

Hilda drew in a sharp breath. "You...you must be psychic," she said.

Marcia overcame an almost uncontrollable desire to laugh. Hilda had no way of knowing that Cliff had been there and Madame Olga had absorbed everything he said.

"Of course, I'm psychic," Madame Olga smiled. "How else could I tell fortunes by tea leaves? Tonight your questions will be answered. You will go to a place of light and laughter — possibly a nightclub." She deliberately stared at Hilda's red bow tie. "A night club...red....red...yes...red like flame...like a fire."

"Wonderful!" Hilda cried. "That's the Firefly."

Marcia flashed her mother a furious look which Madame Olga disregarded.

"Please don't interrupt," Madame Olga continued, sending a sidelong glance at her daughter, "I lose my train of thought, Miss Davis. Now remember — whatever happens tonight will come out all right. You will make a journey and meet new friends. Beware of number seven and Thursday is your lucky day."

"That's today."

"I forgot to tell you, Miss Davis — there are two men in love with you. I don't know which one you want — it isn't quite clear to me."

"Well," said Hilda, her cold eyes narrowing, "I don't intend to give up the one in uniform until I'm certain of the intentions of the other man."

Marcia's slim body stiffened. So that was the way Hilda

felt about Cliff—just someone to hang onto if she couldn't get Charlie Warren. The little cheat! Cliff didn't deserve it— Cliff was too good for her.

"Very wise, my dear," Madame Olga was saying. "One man is better than no man at all. Tonight all will be clear to you."

Tonight, everything will be a mess, Marcia told herself. *Hilda will think I'm lower than low for showing up with Cliff at the Firefly. Cliff will think I'm his stooge—his pal. Alfonse wants me to look like an idiot with my hair done up. The smart thing for me is to stay clear of the Firefly.*

Hilda said, "How much do I owe you, Madame Olga?"

"One dollar, please."

Hilda tossed a five dollar bill on the table. "Thank you so much," she said. "Goodbye, Marcia."

"Good-bye," Marcia said. *I hope I never see you again.*

The door closed behind Hilda. Madame Olga sank down among the red cushions. Her dimpled white hands fondled the five dollar bill. "What fools we mortals be!" she murmured.

"Especially me!" retorted Marcia. "If you had only kept still about the Firefly!" She returned to the kitchen, banging the door after her.

Madame Olga looked faintly puzzled. "My daughter is displaying a little temperament," she said and reached for a cigarette.

By evening Marcia appeared unruffled and cheerful. She wore a full-skirted red formal that set off her dark eyes and her hair was arranged in a high cluster of curls. Cliff's camellias were on her shoulder, and her lips, shaped in a smile, were bright with lipstick.

Cliff arrived on the stroke of eight and sent her a sidelong glance of approval from under sun-bleached lashes. "Hi, Cinderella!" He looked past her to Alfonse who was innocently reading a newspaper. "What, no turban?"

"I gather, young man, you're making light of my profession."

"Not at all," Cliff grinned. "Every man to his own liking. I wanted to be a doctor, not an architect. Now I'm neither, thanks to Tojo."

"I wouldn't mind," Alfonse said, "if I wore a uniform as well as you do. Of course, when I was younger—"

Marcia, looking at Cliff, felt her heart twist. He did look like a million dollars. So strong and sure of himself. A man like that would stand by a girl, take care of her, be kind to her.

If I were Hilda—if I had his diamond on my hand—I wouldn't look at another man—not ever.

She hastily picked up her wrap. "Good-night, Papa."

Alfonse raised his brows, amusement glinting in his eyes. *What is he up to?* she thought as she turned away with Cliff.

"You're looking very beautiful," Cliff said as they drove down the street. "Is all this allure for me?"

Her heart pounded thickly. She had taken extra time with her appearance, hoping he would notice. She felt like shouting, "Yes! Yes! Everything I do is for you." Instead she raised her chin to a stubborn angle and said, "You paid for it, didn't you?"

"That's right," he said dryly. "I'd forgotten. Thank you for giving me my money's worth."

They drove on in silence. After a while Marcia said, "I— I don't want to go to the Firefly."

"What's the matter? Afraid to meet Hilda? I've let the cat out of the bag. I called her tonight and told her you were my secret romance."

What did he mean? Their going together wasn't a secret affair now. He had told Hilda—and so soon. Did he mean that...?

She drew a deep breath and said slowly, "Why did you do that?"

"I wanted to build you up for the big scene tonight. Remember you wanted to do right by me. You just told me I had invested money in you."

Pretty dumb, aren't you, Marcia. Kidding yourself along, telling yourself maybe Hilda didn't mean so much to him.

"Money again," Marcia said bitterly, "I hate it!"

"And all this time I thought you were a gold digger." Cliff sighed. "You never can tell about a woman."

He parked the car before the red neon sign of the Firefly. Sliding his arm around her, he pulled her close and lifted her small, pointed face to his. "Look out," he murmured, "I'm coming in on the beam."

She felt his lips warm and hard upon her mouth. Against her will she felt herself yield and respond. Her mind went spinning away like a golden top. The perfume of the rain-washed night was unbearably sweet. Desperately she summoned her pride and stopped the golden spinning in her head. Then her hands were pushing him away.

"That kiss didn't mean a thing!" she flung at him.

In the twilight of the spring evening his face looked flat and closed. He said casually, "Of course not. I was just practicing — in case I had to kiss you in public. Has to look convincing, you know."

"I hate you!" her mouth trembled. "I hate you!" She slammed the car door and ran up the steps to the Firefly.

He caught her at the entrance. "It's not polite to run out on a gentleman," he said.

"You're no gentleman," she answered shortly.

He took her arm and firmly assisted her to a table near the entrance of the room. She glared at him.

"Marcia — don't be mad at me. I know I had no right, but you…" he hesitated, "the way you looked…I had to kiss you."

"You hired me for a stooge," she said sharply.

"Let's forget that. Let's be free with each other — please — just for a little while. You're beautiful, Marcia. If I weren't engaged to Hilda — Marcia, have you ever been in love?"

She avoided his direct look. "No. You don't get to know people well when you're like us. We haven't any home. We just drift."

"You should have a home." His gray eyes became warm and intimate. "A Cape Cod cottage with roses twining the garden wall."

"Sometimes," she said, "I get sick of it — the endless moving, living in cheap places, telling fortunes. I think I can't stand..." she broke off, staring at him. "I don't know what's come over me. I shouldn't talk this way. I've had other things. I've met interesting people. I love my parents."

She picked up her fork and then paused, her eyes widening incredulously. At the door, only a few feet from their table, stood Madame Olga and Alfonse, resplendent in evening clothes that smelled faintly of moth balls.

Alfonse looked at Cliff and Marcia as though he didn't see them. He hailed a waiter and demanded to see the manager.

"Oh," Marcia said, "what is he up to?"

Cliff smiled and said nothing, watching Alfonse and Madame Olga, amusement glinting in his gray eyes. The manager was a plump Italian named Tuo. He trotted quickly to the door where the Williamses were waiting.

"Ah," groaned Alfonse in his best frustrated manner, "we have lost our chickadee. The beautiful girl — she has disappeared. We have been every place and we do not find her."

"This is sad," said Tuo. "What does she look like?"

Alfonse produced the autographed photograph of Sharitska. "There!" he cried. "There is my Sharitska. I am her manager, and Madame here is her companion. All over Europe we have been — until that man Hitler upsets the apple carts. And now we do not find her."

Marcia leaned across the table and whispered to Cliff, "Will you listen to that? Now you see what kind of father I have."

Tuo looked at the photograph of Sharitska. A slow smile illumined his round, fat face.

Madame Olga said wearily, ignoring the smile, "We shall have to call the police. Ah, such a pity! We wanted no one to know she is here. She is what you call 'incognito.'"

Tuo patted her dimpled hand. "Do not worry. Your chickadee is here with the young Sergeant McMichael. Such an honor it is to have the famous Sharitska in my club."

"Oh," Marcia muttered furiously, "the fool! Why didn't he keep still and let them go home?"

Cliff chuckled. "This is good!"

"Sharitska must leave at once," said Alfonse. "She must return to the hotel."

"Oh, please!" exclaimed Tuo. "Let her stay. She is just now eating her dinner. Come," he attempted to urge Alfonse and Olga to the other side of the room. "You will be my guests. Have you eaten?"

"How could we eat?" cried Madame Olga. "We were sick with worry."

"Then you shall eat now. What do you say?"

Alfonse hesitated. "Well…perhaps we could accept this gentleman's kind hospitality."

"I think it wise," Madame Olga agreed. "We will have less difficulty coaxing her back to the hotel if we let her stay a while."

Tuo promptly escorted them away from the vicinity of

Cliff's table, casting a sly and delighted glance over his shoulder at Marcia. Taking one of the waiters aside he said, "They are the manager and companion of the famous dancer, Sharitska. See? She is the one in red with Sergeant McMichael. They are my guests. Give them the very best."

Marcia had no appetite. She stared down at her plate feeling a sense of injustice and futility. Alfonse's little scheme wasn't funny at all, and it was going to be a hard task to face Hilda.

"What's the matter?" Cliff said.

"Oh, nothing." She looked up to see Alfonse approaching. Tuo had spread the news of Sharitska's presence, and the patrons of the Firefly watched with avid curiosity as Alfonse patted Marcia's hand and said, "You are to dance if they ask it."

Cliff stared at Marcia. "Another hidden talent?"

"I've taken lessons for years," she said indifferently.

"Your daughter amazes me," Cliff said to Alfonse. "I'm beginning to realize I don't know much about her."

"The mystery of woman," Alfonse said. "And where is the beautiful blond and Mr. Warren?"

"Here they come now."

Hilda was walking across the room, fragile and beautiful in blue lace. She was accompanied by a suave, worldly-looking man.

"Look, Alfonse!" Marcia exclaimed. "Look—it's...."

"Don't recognize him," Alfonse whispered quickly. "Leave this to me."

Hilda stopped beside the table. "Well," her voice had an edge of ice. "What a cozy little party. You're very clever, Miss Williams."

Alfonse tapped the dark man on the shoulder. "I must see you alone, at once. Let us go to the gambling room."

The sparkle dimmed in Mr. Warren's eyes. He stared at

Marcia and then at Alfonse. He opened his lips as though to speak and then closed them again. Alfonse touched his arm and together they started toward the gambling room.

"Well," exclaimed Hilda. "Who is that man? What does he mean treating Charlie that way?"

"That," said Marcia in a proud voice, "happens to be my father."

"I see," Hilda sneered. "Alfonse — crystal gazer deluxe."

"Wait a minute, Hilda," Cliff said quickly. "Sit down."

Hilda sat, her body tense with indignation. "And you —?" her cold eyes swept Marcia. "I thought you were nothing but a harmless little gal from a poor family. I confided in you. And all the time you were the one who was trying to get Cliff. You were the secret romance I kept hearing about. Double-crossing me to get his money!"

"Now, Hilda," Cliff began.

Marcia stood up, trembling. "I won't stay here and be insulted!" she said furiously. "I hate money! And I didn't know till last night that Cliff was engaged to you. I thought you were wearing Charlie Warren's ring. And I wouldn't have sent you to my mother if I had known you were going to snoop around and find out all about us. Get this straight, Miss Davis. *I don't want anything that belongs to you.* "

At that moment Alfonse walked up, looking very bland and pleased. In the lapel of his coat was a finely chipped Folsom arrowhead. He bent toward Hilda. "My dear young lady," he said. "Mr. Warren has been detained. Very urgent business. He can't come back tonight. He asked me to convey his apologies."

"Oh he did! And why didn't he take me home?"

"One doesn't always understand human behavior," Alfonse said, smiling. "Good evening. I must return to my wife."

A roll of drums came from the orchestra. Tuo, mounting the platform, held up a plump hand for silence. "We are honored," he said, "to have with us the beautiful and talented dancer, Sharitska, who is on her way to New York to complete her dancing tour."

A spotlight fell on Marcia who still stood beside Cliff's table, one hand clinging to Alfonse's arm. Loud applause swept the room.

"Dance!" someone cried. "Ask her to dance."

There was more applause and the rising of voices. Marcia looked at her father. "Dance, little one," he said softly.

She walked slowly across the room and consulted with Tuo. Could the orchestra play "Dark Eyes?" They could and immediately did. Marcia moved into the center of the floor, rhythm pulsing through every line of her slim, beautiful body. She gave herself over to the mood of the music, letting all the rebellious thoughts that possessed her find their expression in the intensity of her dancing. Her full red skirt folded and unfolded around her like flames in the wind. She was gay as a gypsy — wild and free — but dancing as though her very life depended upon it.

When she finished there was a moment of breathless silence. Then the people broke into thunderous applause. She nodded and smiled, her eyes frantically searching for Alfonse's table. Then she saw Cliff coming toward her. He took her hand and she saw little points of light dance in his gray eyes. "Marcia," he said gently, "come back to my table. Don't mind Hilda. Please. I want to talk to you."

"But after what I said — about not wanting anything that belonged to her...I, I really didn't mean that the way it sounded, Cliff. I was angry."

"I skipped it, Lovely." He was urging her back to the table where Hilda waited, her lips set in a stiff line and her eyes colder than before.

Marcia sat down trembling, conscious of her flushed cheeks and tumbled hair.

"So she's the type you prefer," Hilda said coldly, "a fake dancer in a vulgar red dress."

Marcia gasped in anger but Cliff put one hand over her shaking ones and said to Hilda, "She's not a fake. Anyone who can dance like that is no fake."

"You know she's a fake," Hilda cried. "What's more I'm going to show her up. I'm going to tell Tuo to stop this thing right now." She moved to get up, but Cliff was faster. His arm caught her, forced her back into her chair.

"Sit down," he said harshly, "and keep quiet."

"You —" Hilda's voice broke. "Wait until this makes the morning headlines. SOCIALITE APPEARS AT FIREFLY WITH FAKE DANCER."

"Keep still," Cliff said curtly. He turned to Marcia. "You're a strange family. Your father writes novels he doesn't sell. You dance, but not professionally. What's your mother's sideline?"

"She paints — terrible looking things — just for pleasure. What's wrong with that? Don't you do anything just for the fun of it?"

Cliff sighed. "I'm crazy about toy trains. Once I had a whole basement filled with them. My folks thought I had a fixation. They called a psychiatrist. Mother got rid of the trains."

"I should think so," Hilda said.

Marcia said, "How silly. If you like toy trains you should have them."

Cliff's eyes became dreamy. "A Cape Cod cottage," he mused, "and a beautiful basement complete with tunnels and switches."

"What did you say?" Hilda asked crossly.

The orchestra broke into what patrons classified as smooth boogie-woogie. Couples drifted onto the floor. Marcia watched them with brooding eyes. She felt a desperate longing to be home, away from the lights and the laughter, away from the cold eyes of Hilda Davis. She saw Alfonse and Madame Olga skirting the dancers. Tuo was trailing in their wake, his round face beaming.

"Come, my chickadee," Alfonse said, touching Marcia's hand. "We must go home."

Hilda turned a cold profile to the Williamses and selected a cigarette from her white leather case.

"Wait — Marcia —" Cliff said. "I'll...."

Marcia shook her head. She stood up. Her dark eyes met Cliff's gray ones and a long look passed between them.

Oh, Cliff, she was thinking, *this could have been so different. We had such fun together — until last night. Now there's no end except good-bye. I was only a stooge — but I might have been more — if you had let me.*

She lifted her shoulders and stood very straight and tall. "Thank you, Cliff," she said clearly. "It was fun. Thank you for everything."

She turned blindly away, sliding her hand into Madame Olga's. Tuo hastened to escort them to the door. "It has been a great honor," he beamed. "My patrons were delighted."

"Don't mention it," said Alfonse.

"Of course," continued Tuo, "I can never thank you."

"Think nothing of it," murmured Madame Olga.

Marcia sat between her parents in the taxi. Her lips were set in a stiff smile. "Alfonse," she said, "do you think it was right to mooch dinner from Tuo?"

"Certainly. If I put an ad in the paper don't I expect to pay for it? We gave him publicity. Why shouldn't he pay? He got off very cheaply, too — a little food for the free appearance of a great dancer. Mooching, indeed! Marcia, you surprise me."

"We won't be very happy if Hilda puts this in the papers tomorrow," Marcia said.

"What of it?" Alfonse shrugged. "Tomorrow we'll be on our way to a new destination. I can sell some of my inferior Yumas. I trust you noticed I acquired a perfect Folsom tonight?" His hand touched the arrowhead in his lapel.

"I wondered about that," Madame Olga said.

"I got Charlie Warren in the corner by the slot machines," Alfonse said, "and told him he had to take a back seat and let Cliff have his million dollar blond tonight. Charlie didn't like the idea at all and then I said to him, 'Charlie, remember that picture I got — the one with your autograph? You're standing before the freak show with a banana in one hand and a megaphone in the other.' 'So what?' he said, 'I've come up in the world since then.' And I said, 'I can always tell Miss Davis you were nothing but a cheap circus barker. She wouldn't like that, Charlie.' Then he got a little profane but I ignored it. I said to him, 'Remember those good old days in Chicago. You made a mistake giving me that auto-graphed photograph, Charlie.'"

Madame Olga laughed. "Alfonse, you're a devil."

"And then what?" Marcia asked.

"Well, I told him he had to let Mr. McMichael take Hilda home. Then he asked me what I'd take for the autographed photograph. I plucked this tie pin out of his tie. It's a beautiful Folsom! He assured me that tomorrow he'd start wooing Miss Davis all over again, but by that time Mr. McMichael will have had his chance."

He turned to Marcia. "My daughter is a little sad about the whole thing. Cheer up, my chickadee. We'll have a glass of sherry when we get home."

It was past two in the morning.

The Williamses were talking and having an occasional sip of sherry. Alfonse had taken off his shoes. Madame Olga was reclining among the red sofa cushions in a brilliant green kimono. Marcia was gloomily absorbed in telling her own fortune with a deck of cards.

"Why, it's worth five hundred dollars!" Alfonse exclaimed, holding the Folsom arrowhead up to the light. "Never have I spent a more profitable or delightful evening. And Charlie was quite willing to part with it."

"You're very clever, dear," Madame Olga said, "very clever."

The ringing of the doorbell made them instantly alert.

"At this hour!" Madame Olga looked apprehensive.

"I'll go." Alfonse padded to the door. "Well!" he exclaimed. "Well — come in, Mr. McMichael."

"Yes," murmured Madame Olga from the red cushions, "come in and have some sherry."

Marcia didn't trust herself to look up. She began to feel warm and unsteady inside. Shuffling the cards, she arranged them in three neat piles.

Cliff sauntered casually over to her and said, "Good morning, my little clairvoyant."

"Good morning," she said.

Alfonse watched them with shrewd dark eyes. He said to Cliff, "I trust your fiancée has seen the light?"

"She has." Cliff's eyes slanted sideways at Alfonse. "Mr. Warren was waiting on Hilda's doorstep. We had quite a talk — mostly about you, Alfonse. I thought you were after my money. It never occurred to me that you didn't want to part with your charming daughter."

Alfonse said proudly, "There are some things, Mr. McMichael, that one doesn't sell."

"Hilda and I parted friends," Cliff continued. "She loves

Charlie Warren — and I realized she had become nothing but a habit with me. Your daughter, Alfonse, is the one I've really loved — since I met her. I want to marry her — with your permission, I hope."

Silence fell over the room. Marcia kept sorting the cards with trembling fingers. Madame Olga sank deeper into the red cushions, a cat-with-the-cream expression on her pink and white face. Alfonse stared at his daughter. A sad, broken look lay like a shadow over his lean face. Then his mouth twisted and the old shrewdness came into his eyes. "Well, Mr. McMichael," he said dryly, "your money is not to be scoffed at. It might be convenient to have some ready cash in the family."

"That's what I thought," Cliff said. "You can come out to Wyoming and visit us. I'm instructing at an air base at Casper. Wonderful place to hunt arrowheads, you know."

"Wyoming, eh?" Alfonse yawned elaborately. He assisted his wife from the divan, and they moved toward the bedroom. "You know, dear, I'm going to start a new novel about the army. A tank will be the hero — an animated tank that thinks and talks. Isn't that unusual?"

"It's amazing, dear."

Cliff bent over Marcia who was still telling her own fortune. "I'm glad I didn't marry Hilda," he said. "She doesn't like trains."

"What a pity!" Marcia's dark eyes flashed up at him, brimming with laughter.

He pushed the card table aside, spilling the cards on the floor. He pulled her to her feet and into his arms. His mouth was deliberate on her smiling lips, the curve of her throat, and the pink lobes of her ears.

After a while he said, "Get your satchel, Lovely. I'm leaving for Wyoming come dawn — and I'm not going solo."

Her arms tightened about his neck, her dark head nestling on his shoulder. And Marcia knew that she hadn't really needed to be afraid of waking up. Her dreams had never been as beautiful as this.

CURRY'S SECOND GOLDEN Spur Award was presented to her by Western Writers of America in 1970 for "In the Silence." This was the second story based, in part, on Peg Curry's friendship with the late Hugh Duncan, father of Casper attorney Hugh M. Duncan.

The elder Duncan had come over from Scotland as a young boy to herd sheep for his uncle in the Big Horn Mountains. He got into ranching very young, having borrowed money from the Wyoming National Bank before he was of legal age. Once this was discovered, he then had to get a co-signer for his loan. For a while, he was a partner of the late P.C. Nicholaysen.

"There were so many stories, anecdotes...." said Attorney Duncan, interviewed in June 1991. His father told of floating down the Platte and of being hit by lightning several times while herding sheep. "He thought Peg was a marvelous lady," added Duncan. "Perhaps she reminded him of someone he knew, and maybe he reminded her of the Scottish people she knew in North Park (Colorado)."

"They'd have a few drinks. Dad would get tipsy. He and Peg would tell Scottish jokes and sing Scotch songs."

The families originally became acquainted when the younger Duncan and his mother, Blanche (Kassis) Duncan both took Peg's writing class, back when it was still held on the top floor of Natrona County High School.

"He raised his children by example," says Duncan about his late father. "He was never judgmental, was always kind and fair. Never lectured." He recalled his father's expressive hazel eyes which could dance with humor or brim with sadness.

"In the Silence" is many things: the coming-of-age story

of a young boy named Jimmy McDonald; Jimmy's relationship with his boss, the formidable Angus Duncan; a fine literary story, set against the old-time sheep business in Wyoming high country; a story containing many of Peggy Curry's sensitivities and sensibilities as a result of being raised in ranch country. It is the favorite story of both her husband and son. Throughout repeated readings, the story reveals new depths and retains its freshness.

In a somewhat different version, "In the Silence" was published in both *Boys' Life* (New Brunswick, New Jersey: Boy Scouts of America, 1969) and in the anthology *Networks* (Boston: Houghton Mifflin, 1979). The version included here was published in two Western Writers of America anthologies: *14 Spurs*, editor Will Henry (New York: Bantam, 1968) and *WWA Spurs: The Best of the West*, editor, S. Omar Barker (New York: Bantam, 1977).

IN THE SILENCE

D AYLIGHT WAS THERE at his eyes before it seemed he'd
been asleep. Then he saw the big foot by the tarp-cov-
ered bedroll, and the foot moved to prod him again.
"Are you sleepin' all day?" demanded Angus Duncan.

Jimmy McDonald sat up and blinked at the big red-haired
man who towered above him. Then he reached into the breast
pocket of his heavy wool shirt and his chapped fingers
brought out the silver brooch with its glinting purple jewel.
He'd worn the brooch on his kilt when he left the hills of
Scotland to come to Wyoming and learn the sheep business.

"Ah, that miserable glass and cheap silver," Angus Duncan muttered. "What kind of a never-grow-up are you when
you must carry a trinket in your pocket?"

Jimmy couldn't answer. There was no way to put into
words what he felt about the brooch. It meant home, the home
he'd left to be under the guidance of this distant cousin of his
father, the home he hadn't seen for two years.

*Aye, that was a green and wonderful land across the
ocean,* Jimmy thought, trying to stretch himself awake. *Not
mean country like this with its late, cold spring and its mountain always there, frowning down at you.*

Jimmy shivered. Already he feared the mountain that towered above the campground almost as much as he feared

Angus Duncan. Terrifying tales were told of those who lived too long alone on the mountains. "In the silence," the herders called it, and sometimes, they said, a man too long in the silence was daft for the rest of his lifetime.

"Get up and stir the sheep," Angus Duncan said now. "Lambs should be at their breakfast before we start them up the mountain. Then we'll not have the ewes hiding from us among the rocks and brush to feed their young."

Jimmy bent to pull on his boots. Finally he stood, tall for his fourteen years, and looked up at Angus Duncan. "And what's my wages for sitting the summer alone on the mountain with your sheep?"

Angus Duncan's frosty blue eyes looked down on him from under the heavy red eyebrows and the stern mouth moved at the corners in what might have been a smile. "Not content with grub and decent blankets anymore, eh? Well, I'll tell you—" Angus Duncan paused and looked at the mountain, its pines still black against the first morning light.

"Your summer's wages," Angus Duncan said at last, "will be the long-tailed lambs."

A terrible empty ache began in Jimmy's stomach. "But— they can die. The coyotes can kill them, and the wild range horses run over them, trampling them. I—I could work the whole summer and have nothing left to show for it."

Angus Duncan grunted. "Well said for a lad that's slow to grow up. You've spoken the truth, and the truth can be a hard thing to face. If you save the lambs, you'll beat the best herder's wages. If you lose them, you've got yourself to reckon with."

So Angus Duncan was laying out a hard lot for him, a mean job, and Jimmy recalled saying as much when he'd asked Angus Duncan to let him stay another month on the prairie with the other herders in their comfortable canvas-roofed wagons. "Let me stay with them," Jimmy had said. "Let me move to high country when they do."

Angus Duncan had laughed in his face. "Does a boy learn sheep business by sitting with old men under shelter? Why when I was ten years old, I trailed sheep to the Big Horn Mountains...."

Now, in the cold of this June morning, Jimmy went to where the sheep were bedded on the gentle slope that marked the beginning of the mountain. As he moved among them, they stirred like old gray stones coming suddenly to life and got up and stretched and nudged their sleeping lambs. These were the dock-tailed lambs, tails cut on the level prairie and with their legs already strong for the mountain trip.

He looked carefully for the swollen ewes, their bellies like gray barrels; the late lambs would run to sixty or seventy. *Aye, he thought, if I could keep only half I'd be a man of wealth.* But his lambs would be the late catches, born far from the familiar ground of the drop herd, prey to coyotes, early snowstorms that hit the mountain, and the salt-hungry horses that ran wild on the open range. Far from the world his lambs would be, brought to life near the sky, with no one to help him keep them from harm.

Jimmy's shoulders sagged as he moved toward the small fire with its smoke and fragrance of coffee. Angus Duncan silently handed him a tin plate, and they ate without speaking to each other, then loaded the packhorses and put saddles on the riding horses. On the packhorses were Jimmy's supplies for the summer — a tent, a small tipi, sacks of salt for the sheep, food and bedding.

It took five hours to get the sheep on the mountain, moving them slowly along the narrow paths between trees and rocks. But the dogs worked well. Jimmy and Angus walked, leading the horses, and it was hot before they nooned up in the high country. They rested while the sheep were quiet and in the afternoon moved them across the broad back of the mountain to where the snowdrifts still lay with their adjoining pools of water. Here the sheep would drink while there was water, and later use the springs that sometimes went dry by the end of summer.

"You'll set up your main tent here," Angus Duncan said, "and come back for food and to water the sheep. At night set up your tipi by the bed ground. I'll be back in a couple of weeks to move you on a bit. And one day, if you keep your wits about you, I'll let you be a camp mover instead of a herder."

He'll make me no camp mover, when my long-tailed lambs are dead, Jimmy thought bitterly. *I'll be at the herding till I'm an old man if all the wages I get are long-tailed lambs.* And in anger he said loudly, "Why do you come up here so soon — snow still on and nights like the middle of winter and not a soul to keep me company? I see no other sheep outfits up here."

"The early sheep get the best grass and plenty of water," Angus Duncan said. "You'll have company by July — and the finest lambs." Then Angus nodded to himself and rode away, leading the packhorses.

The silence of the mountain seemed to grow out of the grass and trees until it came to stand all around Jimmy. His heart beat loudly and sweat broke out on his body. He called to the sheepdogs, his voice sounding strange and hollow, then went into the tent where the small stove, left from last year's early camp, had been set up. He put his bacon in a white sack and hung it high in a tree, for the flies wouldn't go high in the wind or the thin air. He stacked his canned goods in the corner and put other groceries in a box with a strong catch to keep it shut. Here he had his flour, salt, sugar, baking powder, soda, and sourdough mix.

The silence kept coming into the tent while he worked. And suddenly he felt an overwhelming desire for candy. But Angus Duncan wasn't one to feed his herders anything sweet. Plain food, Angus said, kept a man lean and strong and did no harm to his teeth.

Forget about teeth, Jimmy thought, finding a can of condensed milk and punching holes in it with his pocket knife. Then he got a tin cup and filled it with snow from a drift near the tent. He poured canned milk over the snow and covered this with sugar. He ate greedily. *Maybe the silence won't bother so much with a full belly.*

Jimmy set up a small tipi near where the sheep were gathering to bed down for the night. "Don't bull the sheep about their bed ground," Angus had cautioned. "They know better than you where they'll sleep best." He set his .22 rifle in the corner of the tipi. It was a single-shot and Angus Duncan had said, "Enough gun for you, and see you don't ventilate a leg or foot with it. Nobody'll be around to bandage your bleeding."

No, Jimmy thought, feeling cold, *there is nobody around.*

Two of the late lambs were born just before twilight and no sooner had the mothers licked their faces clean and the yellow saddles of membrane started to dry on their backs than the coyotes began howling.

Jimmy hurried to build fires around the bed ground, heaping up broken tree limbs and sagebrush, swinging the ax until his arms ached. When darkness came, he lighted the fires that circled the sheep. The thin, eerie *yip-yapping* of the coyotes rang out from time to time. Jimmy got his gun and walked around the bed ground. Once he saw coyotes at the edge of the firelight, their eyes glowing red, and he rushed toward them, the gun ready. They slipped away into the darkness.

He slept little that night, curled half in and half out of the tipi, the rifle close beside him. And it wasn't until the sheep nooned up that he felt free to lie down among the sagebrush and sleep deeply, the sun pouring over him.

He wakened to the thunder of horses' hooves and sat up blinking. He knew before he saw them come racing out of the trees into the open plateau that these were wild range horses. Some had broken away from corrals and jumped fences and had run for years on open ranges. Now they wandered onto the mountain and were crazy in their need for salt, for there no salt sage grew.

While he screamed and groped for rocks to throw, they thundered past him, scattering the sheep. When they had gone, one of his new long-tailed lambs lay trampled and bloody and dead. He put out more salt for the sheep and vowed to shoot the range horses if they came back.

That night Jimmy again built fires to keep away the coyotes and from time to time paced around the bed ground. Five late lambs came during the night. The wind blew in from the north, spitting rain, but this he didn't fear as much as coyotes or the range horses. There was shelter for the new lambs under the big sagebrush, and Angus Duncan had told him that sheared ewes died from cold more easily than lambs. From the moment of breath, the lamb was at home in the chill, Angus said, but the sheared ewe was without the cover she'd grown used to and couldn't stand much cold.

When the sheep nooned again, Jimmy was in need of sleep, but now the great silence of the mountain plagued him more than weariness. He got on his saddle horse and rode quickly to the rim of the mountain where he could look down on the prairie and see the white-roofed sheepwagons of other herders.

It was almost like talking to another person to see the wagons. He reached into his shirt pocket and took out the silver brooch he'd worn on his kilt in that long-ago time when he'd left Scotland. He turned the brooch in his hand, as though the faraway herders could see it shining. The silence roared in his ears.

At last he rode back to the big tent near the melting snowdrift. He unsaddled the horse and put hobbles on him. Then he noticed the big footprints where the ground was moist near the water hole. *He was not alone in the silence.*

Jimmy ran to the tent, shouting, "Hey there!" But his voice seemed to bounce back at him from the canvas walls and he saw that the tent was empty. Disappointment filled him. It was surely a strange thing that a man would not stay and talk with him. In such a big, lonely country men didn't pass up the opportunity to talk to one another.

The silence of the mountain came pouring into the tent. He closed the tent flap as though to shut it out, but gigantic and real, the silence was there, all around him. *I must take hold of myself,* he thought. *I must look after the sheep.* And after a while the big silence ebbed out of the tent, much the way a tide draws back from the shore.

That night the coyotes were bad, circling the fringe of the lighted fires and making the sheep restless. Doggedly, Jimmy kept the fires going and walked around and around the ring of bedded sheep. Once he stopped and stared, for he was sure he had caught a glimpse of a man at the edge of the firelight. Then, it seemed, the man faded away. Queer little prickles ran up the back of Jimmy's neck. *Am I going daft?* he wondered.

At the end of ten days Jimmy was thin and hard, and his eyes, red from wind and sun, burned fiercely in his taut young face. Loneliness was in him, filling him like a bitter food he couldn't digest. Periodically the silence dropped over him in a smothering cloud and within it he'd stand, trembling and sweating. Once it was so terrifying he dropped to his knees and clutched the sagebrush to assure himself of his own reality.

There were now fourteen of the small long-tailed lambs. The bold, brassy blue sky mocked him, and out of it came the big eagles, plummeting down toward the new lambs. Sometimes he ran, shouting, to frighten them away. Sometimes he shot at them. Once, on the far side of the herd from where he stood, an eagle got a lamb, soared high with it, and dropped it. Returned and soared again and dropped it. By the time the eagle came in for the third catch, Jimmy was close enough to shoot at it. The eagle went away, but when Jimmy got to the lamb, the life had gone.

In these days that became more dream than reality, he ceased to hate Angus Duncan. He knew if Angus Duncan were to ride out of the aspen trees, now coming green in a quick mist, he'd run to the big man as though he were a lad again and running to his father.

On a late afternoon, when the wind was down and the shadows were long from the rocks and trees, a man came suddenly and stood by the big tent, a man with a gun in a bloody hand. There was something terrible and frightening about him; it breathed out of his dirty clothes, the blood on his hand, the mad light in his eyes.

He said evenly to Jimmy: "I've come to take the long-tailed lambs. The coyotes will get them anyhow."

Blinding anger came up in Jimmy. He tried to collect his wits, hold in check his rising terror. Then slowly he reached in his shirt pocket and brought out the silver brooch with the shiny purple stone that was the color of heather in bloom. He let the treasure lie in the palm of his hand where the sunlight struck it from the west.

"You'll kill me to get my lambs," Jimmy said quietly, turning the brooch to catch more sunlight so that it gleamed brighter than before.

"What's that in your fist?" the stranger asked.

"Silver and precious stone," Jimmy replied. "Worth more than all the band of sheep." He looked into the stranger's eyes and saw them glitter.

"If you steal this," Jimmy went on, "a curse will be on you. This can't be killed for or stolen. But it can be bargained for."

Now that he was making a story, he ceased to be afraid. It was like listening to his mother talk when the sea was rough and the fishing boats were in danger. Always his mother had told the children stories until the sea seemed a friend, and faith would come to them that their father would get home.

"I heard of a man who stole one of these jewels," Jimmy said, "killing a man to get it. Blindness struck him." And he turned the silver brooch until the sun glinted on the glass, making a light that fell full in the stranger's eyes.

"But," Jimmy went on, "it can be bargained for, and no harm done. I'll bargain with you—this for you, if you leave my long-tailed lambs." And he moved closer so the wild eyes could look more closely at the stone.

"I can take it—and the lambs." The stranger spat on the ground.

"Aye." Jimmy nodded. "That is so. And you'll have to kill me, for I'll fight. It's for you to choose whether there's a curse on you or not."

The stranger didn't speak.

Jimmy's hand tightened on the brooch. "I'll never be the same without it," he said, more to himself than to the stranger. "It is giving something inside me away."

Then the evil-smelling man moved close and held out the hand with the bloody fingers. "I'll take it—and leave your sheep."

When the brooch fell from his hand to the hand of the stranger, tears began to run down Jimmy's cheeks and the strength left his legs. He fell down to the ground and lay as one dead. When he awoke, it was dark, and he was cold and hungry. He jumped up, thinking only of the sheep, and ran to build fires and walk the bed ground. The dogs greeted him and licked his hands.

Two days later when Angus Duncan came riding up from the flat country, he looked sharply at Jimmy and said, "Have you forgotten to eat, boy? What's happened to you?" And the big man got off his horse and put his hand gently on Jimmy's shoulder.

Jimmy talked slowly and carefully, telling his story of the stranger. Afterward he waited for Angus Duncan to laugh at him or tease him. But Angus neither laughed nor spoke. He walked over to the dwindling water hole near the snowdrift that was now almost gone and looked at the ground. "There is no track of a man here," he said, "but, of course, the sheep have been in to drink and trampled the earth."

He came back to Jimmy and said, "I brought some sweets. Strange, how a man hungers for them on the mountain." And he took a sack of candy and put it in Jimmy's hand.

Once Jimmy would have stood there and stuffed the candy in his mouth and eaten until the sack was empty. But now he only held the sack and said casually, "I may have some tonight after my supper. Thank you."

"In the silence," Angus Duncan said, "a man learns to be strong. And the silence is not only on the mountain, Jimmy. Somewhere — before he dies — every man must meet it and struggle with it on his own terms. In the silence we must face only ourselves." Again Angus Duncan's hand touched the boy's shoulder. "I see now you have done that."

Jimmy's hand moved to his empty shirt pocket. *I could have lost the brooch, there at the edge of the mountain when I was looking to the prairie and the wagons of other herders,* he thought. *Still —*

"Well," he said, "you'll want to take a look at the sheep over there. I've lost only two lambs — one to the wild horses and another to the eagles."

He walked with Angus Duncan toward the sheep. The light of later afternoon had given new shapes to everything, making even the grass look thicker and stronger. The silence was still there. But Jimmy smiled to himself, letting it move beside him as an old and familiar friend.

*This book was printed on
55 pound Huron
acid-free, recycled paper.*